Bad Pucking Timing

A Steamy MM Hockey Romance

Michele Lenard

CMFR

Contents

Prologue   1

1. Niko   3

2. Xander   15

3. Niko   27

4. Xander   39

5. Niko   47

6. Xander   55

7. Niko   65

8. Xander   75

9. Niko   83

10. Xander   93

11. Niko   103

12. Xander   115

13. Niko   123

14. Xander   133

15. Niko   147

16. Xander   161

17. Niko   179

18. Xander	189
19. Niko	199
20. Xander	209
21. Niko	217
22. Xander	229
23. Niko	239
24. Xander	247
25. Niko	257
26. Xander	267
27. Niko	277
28. Xander	291
Epilogue -Niko	297
Also By Michele Lenard	303

Prologue

A s a kid you don't think about the sacrifices you'll have to make for your dreams. After all, dreams are supposed to be happy, so all you see is the finish line, not what you'll have to give up to get there.

I surrendered a carefree childhood to hours upon hours of grueling practices. Abandoned life with my family in favor of a boarding school that would hone my skills to perfection. But my biggest sacrifice, the one I couldn't predict I'd have to make as a little boy, is denying who I am.

To the world I'm the top rookie in this year's NHL draft. The most promising defender the league has seen in years. For years that's all I wanted to be, and now that I'm here...

I knew my career would intersect with my personal life at some point, I just didn't expect it to happen before I played my first pro game.

Chapter 1
Niko

"Maybe you should get laid. You know, to loosen the nerves." Anna bounces her eyebrows in a way that's nothing short of despicable, and thank *God* there's nothing in my mouth or it would've just become a choking hazard.

"Those are two words a guy should never hear coming from his sister's mouth." I pound my chest to get my breathing back in order.

"Don't be such a prude." Anna glances at the screen long enough to let me see her eye roll. "Have a little fun for a change."

"You know why I can't do that."

"No, I know why you *won't* do that, not why you *can't*."

"We've been through this."

Being gay might be more acceptable overall, but in the locker room it's still a bit of a gray area, which is why I've never told my teammates. That was a tough secret to keep living with three of them for the past few years at school, but I managed by finding a baseball player in the same boat as me. We kept our hookups to hotel rooms, which led to my teammates thinking I'm shy or discreet, not attracted to men.

I don't recommend that solution—the secrecy is a bitch to maintain—but I wasn't willing to sacrifice my shot at the NHL by coming out before making it here. Whether I'll stay in the closet my entire career or not I have no idea. It's too soon to make that call, which means it's too risky to do something that might take that decision out of my hands. I should get my bearings before thinking about getting laid. Too bad my sister planted the seed, and in the silence of this room, I won't be able to forget it.

"Hockey players hook up with people all the time. It doesn't make the evening news," she points out.

"It would if they were gay and deep in the closet. Like not just behind the door but cowering in the darkest corners of it."

"You're acting like you've got a film crew tracking your every move, but you're there on a trial basis. An extended tryout. As of this moment, you're a nobody. You could meet someone without finding your picture on TMZ tomorrow morning. Enjoy it while it lasts."

"Way to make me feel like a winner, Sis."

"You know what I mean. If you decide to hole up in your closet when the season starts, I'll respect that. Until then, the worst that can happen is someone claims to have hooked up with you with no proof."

I'm not sure that's the worst that could happen, although she may have a point about my current obscurity. I probably won't have a better window of opportunity to blow off steam for months, if not *years*.

"Just so I'm clear, your best advice to deal with my overactive nerves is to find a one-night stand?"

"Desperate times and all that." She transfers her food to a plate and pulls a fork from the drawer. *Are those eggs? Must be*. It's early morning for her halfway around the world. *Damn that looks good*.

"I'm not sold on your solution, but I do need to get some food. Maybe if I get out of this hotel I'll get out of my head, too."

"That's the spirit."

Signing off with a promise to let her know how it goes—within reason since she's my sister—I set off on foot to explore my neighborhood, which happens to be within walking distance of several blocks of restaurants and shops. There's a steak joint, a seafood place, a cozy looking pub, and a candy shoppe with a chocolate bar that beckons me to swing in after dinner. I'm not a sugar fiend, but I'm a sucker for dark chocolate. It's the one indulgence I allow myself during the season—on a daily basis—because it's not even that unhealthy.

Near the end of the second block there's a bar with a tiny rainbow sticker in the window. It's small enough that it's not the first thing you see, yet it's clearly visible. I'm tempted to head inside, until I get a whiff of the most heavenly barbeque I've smelled in years.

One of my teammates was from the south, and he considered himself a barbeque connoisseur. I visited his home once–over the Thanksgiving holiday I had no plans for since it's not something we celebrate in Sweden–and he made it a mission to educate me about what makes the good stuff.

Prior to that trip I thought all barbeque was the same, but he taught me about different spice rubs and sauces, and while I'm no expert, I understand now that it's not as simple as grabbing a bottle from the pantry and dousing meat in sauce. You have to prep everything just right, and it takes something like ten hours to cook it correctly in a smoker.

His family regarded the whole process as some sort of sacred ritual, and while that struck me as odd–who willingly gets up at four in the morning to spend the day cooking–there's no denying the end result was phenomenal.

It's been a while, but the aroma wafting from this restaurant makes me think it could be the real deal. I help myself to a seat at the empty bar, wondering why a place that smells so good isn't packed shoulder-to-shoulder, and order the brisket.

The first bite is like being teleported back to my teammates house. An explosion of sweet and spicy mixing together, tender meat that falls off the bone, it's easily the best meal I've had in months.

"This is incredible," I tell the bartender when he asks how it tastes. "Why isn't this place packed?"

"We just opened last week. I don't think many people realize we're here yet."

I make a mental note to come back here frequently, if my trial goes well and I make the team, and get momentarily lost in the combination of savory barbeque and the basketball game on the TV behind the bar.

Midway through my meal a guy takes a seat one stool over. It occurs to me that he's close enough to talk with but far enough that we don't have to say anything at all, and I'm not sure what to make of that since there's at least a dozen other seats along the bar he could've chosen.

Did he choose this seat because sitting close to another person makes him feel like isn't dining alone? Does it just have a good view of the TV behind the bar? Is he trying to hint that he's open to conversation without sitting so close as to force it, or is there no ulterior motive behind his seat selection at all?

Normally I wouldn't think twice about where someone chooses to sit, but the silky smooth baritone that wafts over me as he places his order for ribs sends literal chills along my spine, like fingertips ghosting sensually over my skin. It makes me want to talk to him so I can hear more of it, and look at him without trying to hide the fact I'm looking at him, just to see if his features are as sexy as his voice.

Unfortunately, I've never picked anyone up or been picked up, so I don't have the first clue where to start. Hell, I don't even know for sure he plays for my team since this is just an average barbeque joint and not a gay hangout. I'm that ignorant of how these things work since the ballplayer and I found each other on an app–no awkward flirting required.

Several years' worth of hiding this part of me has left me woefully out of practice, which means I shouldn't make any bold moves. Or any moves at all, considering I know nothing about this stranger and I need to be discreet. Still, his proximity–and his profile–fascinates me, and I find myself risking a covert glance in his direction, purely for curiosity.

Fair skin. Dark hair. Lean build, though I wouldn't call him skinny. Slim seems like a better fit. He's intriguing in a starving artist sort of way. Or rockstar, given his t-shirt and worn converse shoes. The realization makes my pulse spike since I find that look sexy in a brooding, mysterious way, and couple that with how his Adam's apple bobs as he licks sauce off his fingers...

My perusal is cut short when he lifts his head, and I flick my gaze to the TV as if I hadn't just been staring. The home basketball team is in the playoffs, and for a moment I get sidetracked because...sports. But after a few minutes I feel like I'm being watched, and I let my eyes drift to the side to see if I'm right.

The man is looking down, focused on the beer in front of him, though the stray lock of hair swaying over his forehead makes me think he just abruptly turned his head. A pulse of energy ripples through me, sparked by the notion that he was checking me out, and I have to force myself not to grin like a moron as I surreptitiously mimic him.

It's hard to know for sure without turning my head, but I get the impression he has an angular jaw, and he definitely has high cheekbones, which gives him sort of a timeless attractiveness.

Timeless attractiveness? Is that even a thing?

I sneak another peak, and yeah, I'm pretty sure this guy would be considered good looking across the span of time. There's just something classic and refined about his features, which even the too long hair that curls slightly at the ends can't hide.

I've never really taken the time to analyze whether I have a type, but if I do, I'm pretty sure he'd be it. The contrast between his fair skin and dark hair draws me in like a moth to flame. And while tall, dark and handsome might be cliché, there's a reason that combination has universal appeal.

Turning back to the game before I'm caught staring, I make a conscious effort not to look in his direction. It works for a few minutes, until the hair on my arms starts to tingle, and I'm certain his gaze is on me.

Should I?

No, it's not worth it.

But he's definitely looking at me.

Talking doesn't have to mean anything, right?

No, bad idea.

He's still looking. Subtly, but I see it.

Fuck it.

"I can't remember the last time I watched such a boring game." I give myself an imaginary pat on the back for coming up with such a great opener.

"They're not all this boring?" he replies before taking a sip of his drink.

Hmm, not a resounding invitation, but I'm a personable guy. I can work with it. "Admittedly I don't watch many, but I feel like the ones I've seen had more action. Especially during the playoffs."

He lifts his head to face me, a curious line appearing between his brows, which only draws my attention to his eyes—so brown they're nearly black. They're the most soulful pair of eyes I've ever seen up close, and it's a fight not to get lost in their depths as I try to imagine what he's thinking.

"It's the playoffs?" he asks.

I'm too distracted by my own heartbeat to give a polite response, so my athlete brain takes over. "Seriously? No offense but we're in Denver and Denver's playing. How do you not know it's the playoffs?"

Nice recovery, genius. Guys love when you insult them.

"I'm not much of a basketball fan." He quirks a thick brow, though whether in amusement or admonishment I can't tell.

"You and the rest of the city, I guess. This place is surprisingly empty for a game night." I sip my water, not sure what to say next.

Yeah, he's officially the hottest guy I've ever seen, and it's making me trip over my words like a bumbling idiot.

"This place isn't really known for its sports coverage." He tips his head toward the TV behind the bar, which now that I think about it is the only one in here.

"Okay, fair. Still playoffs are playoffs. And it's Denver. I feel like it's required to pay attention if the team representing your city makes it to the final rounds."

The corner of his lip twitches like he's fighting a smile. *Damn that's sexy.* "I've lived here all my life and I don't feel that obligation."

Ouch. That actually hurts my athlete's heart a little.

"Not a sports fan?"

"Not really."

"How is that possible? I mean, Denver has every major sport there is, so odds are there's something for everyone, right?"

Something like sadness or regret seems to cloud his eyes briefly before he gives a small shake of his head. "I guess I'm not much of a spectator."

"What would make you watch?" *He literally just said he's not much of a spectator and I follow up with 'what would make you watch?' Could I be any worse at this?*

That little crease appears between his brows again. "I don't understand the question."

"Pretend you could build your own team. Who would you want to watch?" *I guess I'm doubling down.*

"I don't know any basketball players."

"I never said it had to be basketball players. You can put any five people on a basketball team. Any at all. Who would you pick?" I lick my lips, wondering if this is the world's worst icebreaker. I think it might be, until I realize he's looking at my mouth. I'm pretty sure he's not interested in the actual words coming out of it so much as the fact that it's moving, which has a wave of heat rushing to my face and...other places.

"How would picking different people make the game more interesting?" His gaze flicks to mine just briefly before traveling back to my mouth, down my neck, over my torso, shooting a spark of electricity up my spine.

I lick my lips again. "Haven't you ever heard of fantasy teams?"

His eyes narrow slightly, and I nearly roll mine before I remember it'd be a bad idea to further insult the guy I'm trying to chat up. *So he doesn't know fantasy sports, no biggie. I can teach him.* "Okay, I'll go first. Obi Wan Kenobi. The Ewan McGregor version."

The corner of his mouth ticks upward a notch. "That's not a real person."

"I never said it had to be."

The dark stranger sips his beer pensively and sets the mug on the bar. "Alright, why him?"

"Duh, he's a Jedi. Whatever shot he takes he can use the force to make it go in." *My science nerd is showing. Great. First sports, then sci-fi. Could I be any less suave?*

I'm waiting for the inevitable excuse to end the conversation when a pair of bottomless brown eyes meet mine, and I swear they seem to sparkle a little bit as he speaks. "Mister Fantastic."

Now it's my turn to frown. "Who is that?"

"He's in the Fantastic Four."

Fantastic Four? A comic book fan... Suddenly, my Star Wars references don't seem so nerdy. I breathe a sigh of relief knowing I'm not the only superhero fan in this conversation.

"The stretchy guy?"

"Yup," he says, taking another sip of beer.

"Because he could dunk from anywhere on the court." I nod absently as I guess his reasoning. "Nice. Now you're getting it."

"Then I'd take The Hulk, since he could block any shot." He lifts his brows, a signal that it's my turn, I think.

"I'm going with Invisible Woman. The Hulk would never see her coming."

"These are coed teams?"

I lift my shoulder. "Sure, why not."

"Okay then, Jessica Rabbit."

I wipe a hand over my mouth to disguise my snort. "In what way would she contribute to a basketball team?"

"Guys would be too busy drooling over her to play the game."

My heart plummets to my stomach. Full on drops out of my chest. "Not this guy," I mutter under my breath, thinking I misread the coy looks he's been giving me.

"You aren't on the team, though. Are you?" His chocolatey gaze holds mine.

"If I was?" My breath catches in my throat unsure of how to read him.

A knowing smirk ghosts over his lips as he leans toward me. "Ryan Reynolds."

"Ha," I bark out a laugh. "If you want to distract me with a guy, you'd have better luck choosing one I could actually score with." *Should I have said that out loud? Oh well, too late now.*

"Isn't this a fantasy game?" Those dark eyes seem to gleam with an unspoken challenge.

"Yeah."

"Then why can't you score with fantasy Ryan?"

I say a little prayer that my sister hasn't steered me wrong before answering. "He's not really my type."

"Not your type?" The man arches a thick brow. "Even straight guys have a crush on Ryan Reynolds. He's literally everyone's type."

"Not mine. I like dark and mysterious." My gaze travels from his mop of nearly black hair to the dark eyes framed by thick lashes, resting there in charged silence. It's not until I hear the bell by the front door that I snap out of it. "I guess that means I should put fantasy Ryan on my team to distract you."

"That'd be ineffective." His Adam's apple bobs as he swallows thickly.

"After that little rant are you saying he's not your type either?"

"Oh, he's definitely my type." He leans forward, speaking in barely more than a whisper. "But your dimples are sexier."

I can't stop the broad smile from stretching across my face as my stomach does a somersault. "Dimples are your weakness?"

"One of them."

"Care to share the others?"

His gaze travels over me, cataloging. "Tall. Like six feet or more."

"Check." *Oh my God, did I say that out loud?*

I swear a wave of heat passes over his face. "Blue eyes."

"Check."

Crooking a finger at me so I close the distance between us, he whispers a final weakness. "A long, thick dick."

I clear my throat. "Would I sound like a jerk if I said check?"

"Would you be telling the truth?"

"I mean, we did already establish that I'm tall..." I duck my head to rub the back of my neck. *Is this really happening?*

"So, you're saying you're proportionate." His lip curves up in a slow grin.

I look at him from under my lashes as I shrug.

"Care to let me be the judge?"

Chapter 2
Xander

I wasn't kidding about the dimples. They can make even the most roguishly handsome man seem cute, and for some reason that contradiction ramps up the sex appeal for me. So much so that I'm following this jock home.

As a general rule, I don't do jocks or gym rats, and this guy is big enough I'm certain that's what he is. But like he implied at the restaurant, he's proportionate, his width a reasonable ratio to his height, and he isn't so musclebound he can't rest his arms comfortably at his side. Yet, he could probably manhandle me if he wanted to, an image that makes me chub up a bit.

The walk to his place is brisk, though I don't miss the longing glance he gives the candy shoppe as we hurry past, which almost brings a smile to my lips. It's probably the third or fourth time he's gotten me to, and that's a little unsettling since it's a bit of a foreign expression for me. I don't think I'm an asshole, but I'm not one of those people who can find joy in any situation. Yet all it takes is a happy grin from the gentle giant and my lips start to pull at the corner.

Once we're inside his hotel room, I barely have a second to take in the cookie-cutter decor before he's got me pressed against the wall, caged between his arms, his full lips pressed to the spot where my neck meets my earlobe.

No small talk, thank fuck.

"Kissing or no kissing?" He licks along my neck, and while I'd usually say no, the fact that he asked tempts me to say yes.

"Not my favorite but I'm into it if you are." I tilt my head to give him better access to my collarbone, threading my fingers in his short, silky hair. "Top or bottom?"

He chuckles softly. "We probably should've established that first. I prefer top, but I'm not opposed to bottoming." He rocks his hips forward, giving me a preview of what's to come.

"Same. Well, opposite, but same."

He stops sucking on my neck and pulls back just enough to see my face. "Fuck, you're gorgeous." Then suddenly his mouth is on mine, his tongue swiping hungrily into my mouth. Despite the urgency of the kiss, and the way his barely-there stubble chafes at my skin, his lips are soft. Smooth. Giving everything they take as they brush against mine. And I don't hate it.

There's a reason I don't kiss much. It makes me feel vulnerable, and I hate not being in control. That may sound strange coming from a guy who prefers to bottom, but I've never felt powerless during sex. The opposite really, since I know *my body* is what's bringing my partner pleasure. Besides, condoms offer a barrier between me and the other person, so there's a level of detachment I find comfortable.

That doesn't exist with kissing. Sharing each other's air is about as intimate as you can get, unless you add staring into each other's eyes to the mix, although that's not usually an issue with random hookups. But kissing? I don't know why I said I'd be okay with it. Maybe because he gave me the opportunity to make the decision. Or because of the damn dimples. Either way, with his lips on mine, his tongue licking seductively into my mouth, the only thought I'm capable of forming is that this is a fucking incredible kiss.

A low moan rumbles from my throat before I can stop it, his echoing response making me go full on hard. I assume he feels that when he cups my ass and hauls me against him, guiding my legs around his waist.

Damn that's hot.

I'm not a small man. I'm not as big as this guy, but I'm hovering around six feet, and I'm not scrawny, just lean. Most men can't effortlessly pick me up, and it's not typically something I look for in a hookup. But I have been picked up before, and I can't deny there's a certain thrill that comes from knowing another person has the strength to do it. The fact that this guy can has me hornier than I've been in a long time.

Depositing me by the foot of his bed, Ewan, as I've nicknamed him, breaks our kiss to clasp the hem of my shirt and tug it over my head. I mirror him, reaching for the button on his pants once his top is out of the way. We rush to kick off our shoes and shed our bottoms, pausing only when there's nothing left to take off, and the evidence of our chemistry is glaringly obvious.

I've got a friend who could lecture you on the merits of what makes a nice dick, and on a subconscious level I probably agree with him, though I've never felt the need to dissect my partners. And I don't share my exploits, ever. But the tight skin wrapped around the cock pointing at me right now, the smooth crown dripping just a bit at the tip... I confess to being turned on by the mere sight of it.

"Damn." Ewan's raspy voice sends a warm shiver over my naked skin as his eyes travel my body. "I wasn't expecting you to be so cut. Or for us to be the same size." He wraps a fist around his heavy cock, a casual movement that emphasizes his biceps, and the solid muscle of his pecs to a clearly defined Adonis belt. *Jocks really do have the best bodies.*

"I'm only a few inches shorter than you." I remind him that height doesn't always go hand-in-hand with dick size.

"And about forty pounds lighter, I'm guessing. But your abs are ripped." He lets go of himself to trace a finger along the ridges of muscle lining my stomach, causing my skin to pebble along the path. "This is so fucking sexy. How'd you get a body like this?"

Objectively, I know I'm attractive. And that I have a decent physique. But no one—literally no one—has called my body sexy before. It's...nice.

"I grew up in skate parks. Mostly skating but a little BMX. I still ride sometimes."

"Those might just be my new favorite sports." His finger slides lower, along the 'V' by my hip, pausing when it brushes against the tuft of hair at the base of my cock. My breath catches in my throat as I fight to hold still, waiting for him to move. Then he takes me in his fist and gives a long, firm tug.

Holy Hell! I shoot my hand out and grip his arm to steady myself as sparks of electricity ripple through me. "Just like that, Ewan."

"Who the fuck is Ewan?" His hand stills, blue eyes glaring at me so intensely I'm sure they've pierced my skin.

"Um, you are. Fantasy team, remember?"

His expression softens, a resigned smile ghosting over his lips as he catches on. "I guess that makes you Reed." He takes a step closer, taking both our cocks in one of his large hands. Once again, my knees nearly buckle.

Between the heat of his palm, the pressure of his rigid length next to mine, even his words, I'm on sensory overload. And not just physical senses, but mental ones, if that's a thing. I mean, it can't be emotional—that doesn't apply to one-night-stands—yet his vocal admiration of my body has my mind reeling with...confidence? Pride? Some unnamed thing that makes the physical touch *more*. And the way he stepped into the fantasy names... Don't even get me started on how that makes my heartbeat accelerate.

"Reed?" I arch my brow.

"That's Mr. Fantastic's real name, right?" He gives our cocks a squeeze and pulls his hips back, dragging his smooth tip along the sensitive skin of my shaft. "And while you're every bit as fantastic as I hoped, I'm not screaming that when I come."

This jock really knows his superheroes. Why do I find that so fascinating?

"But you'll scream Reed?" I suck in a breath as he presses his cockhead against mine and lets it linger there, like they're kissing.

"Unless you want me to use your real name?" He nips my jaw, soothing the bite with his tongue.

"No." I shake my head firmly, not because I have a rule against it, but because this guy is already making me have *feelings* I don't usually experience. Like amusement, and intrigue, and a touch of vulnerability. Besides, fantasy names are hot.

"Good." His thumb swipes over my slit before he gives my chest a little shove. "Sit. I want to taste you."

Doing as he asks, I fall to the bed and spread my legs wide so he can kneel between them. I don't usually allow this type of perusal, but after his earlier admiration, I'm happy to have his hooded blue eyes move over my body as if he's mesmerized by it. It makes my skin pebble, and my cock swell.

Using both hands, Ewan runs his warm palms down my pecs, over the ridges of my stomach, along my thighs, leaving a trail of sparks in his wake. Back and forth, he maps my contours, inching toward but never actually touching my sac. It's both hedonistic and sensual, making me feel slightly dirty yet...treasured? I'm sort of basking in the attention when suddenly, without warning, he leans forward and runs his nose along the underside of my dick.

"Fuck you smell good. What kind of soap is that?" He nuzzles my balls, inhaling deeply, and I swear that makes my cock stand even taller.

"Rosemary mint," I rasp, gripping the comforter as Ewan licks a line from root to tip, closing his eyes with a contented moan when he wraps his lips around the swollen head and starts gently sucking, a look of euphoria on his boyishly handsome face.

My eyelids flutter as I try to contain the urge to moan. *Holy fuck!* I've been sucked off dozens of times before, but never by someone who seemed this blissed out by my dick. It's kind of mesmerizing, watching him lick and kiss and suck my crown. His fingers gently massage my shaft, pulling on my balls, and savoring my most sensitive places. Once again, he drags a satisfied little groan from my throat, smiling around my cock when he hears it.

"God, those dimples." I reach out to run my fingers through his hair. "It's so fucking sexy to see them framing my dick."

Ewan flicks his eyes to mine with a wicked little grin that somehow magnifies those little hollows before taking me all the way to the back of his throat.

"Holy fucking..." I can't even find words to finish that sentence. The warm, wet heat of his mouth. The slide of his tongue. The suction. This is the best head I've ever gotten, and he's barely touched me.

Eyes closed, like he's in some sort of erotic trance, Ewan laps at me, relishing me with his tongue. Though he's only touching my dick, prickles of excitement radiate from my crown to my fingers and toes. It's a full body high that has me yearning to combust even as I want to stave it off. To make it last.

Torn between holding out and giving in, I'm about to tip over the edge when he releases me, and cool air rushes over my damp skin. I whine from the sudden absence of friction, until he sucks a nut into his mouth, and I sigh heavily.

Dick straining toward the sky, I pant as he licks around my sac, sucking my swollen balls. I think I hear him moan, maybe say something about soap again, but spoken against my junk the words are too muffled to make out. And frankly, I'm too high on pleasure to care.

Ewan's mouth is a dream. Hot. Wet. Alternating between hard and fast, soft and sweet, he brings me to the brink again before abandoning my sac and swallowing my length, using the leftover moisture to soften my puckered hole with his fingertip.

My back arches involuntarily, pushing my cock further down his throat. He makes a little choking noise but doesn't stop, working me like a man tasting his first meal—or cherishing his last.

Did I seriously just romanticize a blowjob? Wow, his mouth really is heaven.

Head cloudy, body vibrating, it takes me a second to register the wet heat is gone. Then I hear the muffled slide of a drawer and turn my head to the side.

"Still good to bottom?" He holds up the condom and lube he pulled from the nightstand. But I'm too focused on the thick dick pointed at me to answer. Shooting my arm out, I take it in my fist and squeeze, loving the way it makes him groan.

Holding him firmly, I admire the vein that runs along the underside of his shaft. The neatly trimmed thatch of hair that covers his hefty balls. Framed by thick thighs and chiseled abs, it's a mouthwatering sight.

"Gonna hold my dick all night Reed, or you want me to put it in you?"

I stroke his length lazily, loving the feel of smooth skin sliding over steel as I think out loud. "I like the way it looks in my hand." I like the way it looks period, but something about the wide girth in my average-sized hand does things to me.

"Me too. But I'm kinda anxious to watch it sliding in and out of your ass."

There's a feral, desperate tone to his words that has my cock twitching with desire, so with a final squeeze I let him go and roll to my stomach.

"Uh, uh." He rolls me back and resumes the spot between my legs. "I want to watch these sexy abs flex while I'm inside you."

Somewhere in the back of my mind a voice says no, but for the life of me I can't think of why. Then I hear the cap of the lube open, the squelch of the gel oozing out before he rubs it over my hole. By the time his finger breaches the ring of muscle, the only word in my vocabulary is yes.

Slowly, methodically, Ewan pumps his finger in and out. My cock sways back and forth, lust drunk, as he fingers me, curling the digit slightly to tickle my prostate. The contact makes my hips shoot upward as tiny tremors ripple through me, and has precum seeping from my slit. Ewan grins and winks at me—fucking *winks*—as he adds another finger. And my eyes roll back in my head.

What is happening to me?

I'm not usually such a complacent lover. I'm more of a power bottom, just as active and aggressive as the guy dicking me down, and vocal to boot. Yet this man has worked my body to a comatose state, and the only thing I'm capable of right now is letting him have his way with me.

I don't hate that idea.

The tear of the foil packet lulls me back to the present just in time to watch Ewan roll the latex over his thick length. I lick my lips, eager for more, and he gives me another glimpse of those sexy dimples.

"If you're this sexy now, I can't wait to see what you look like when you come." He leans over me and places a chaste kiss on my lips as his tip nudges my hole. Then he pushes forward.

I groan long and loud as he enters me, causing him to pause about halfway. "Too much?"

"Not enough," I exhale heavily. "More."

Eyes closed, Ewan pushes forward steadily until his pelvis rests against me, the corded muscles in his neck straining as he holds himself still. Coiled tight, like he's ready to spring into action when I give the word, I've never felt so powerful. So desired. I'm suddenly desperate for him to move.

"I'm good," I rasp.

"I need a second," he grits, jaw locked tight, and I swear I detect the faint hint of an accent. Or maybe he's just that close to the edge. Either way, that comment makes my lust unbearable, and I clench my muscles around him, needing the friction of his thrusts like I need air.

"Oh fuck." He squeezes his eyes even tighter. "I'm not sure I can hold back."

"Don't."

Ewan's eyes snap open, that searing blue gaze draining the air from my lungs. I have just a split second to remember why I avoid this position before he starts to move.

Though he pulls his hips back slowly, he snaps them forward hard and fast, causing us both to groan. Hooking his arms under my legs for leverage, he starts to pump in earnest, the momentum sending us up the mattress until my head reaches the headboard. Gripping it in his strong hand to keep us somewhat steady, he pounds into me, grunting the most deliciously dirty words.

"Look at that heavy cock bobbing against your abs as I pound into you. Fuck that's a beautiful sight. Tell me when you're close. I want to hold it in my hand when you shoot your load. I want to feel it pulsing while your cum drips down my fingers."

"Jesus you're filthy."

"Too much?" He pants between thrusts.

"Nah, it's hot..." My words falter as his tip rubs against my prostate, and my vision goes momentarily dark, except for the tiny pinpricks of light that burst at random behind my closed eyelids. "That's... Oh God, right there."

I'm no stranger to having my prostate milked, but something about what Ewan's doing... Maybe it's the angle. Maybe it's the rhythm. Whatever it is, it has my body careening out of control, unable to do anything but receive the pleasure he's building in the deepest recesses of my core.

If I thought I was on sensory overload before, this is otherworldly. My entire body hums with a level of ecstasy that until this moment I was unaware existed. My limbs, though so heavy they're basically useless, tremble under the onslaught of pleasure being driven into me with each thrust. And my eyes—eyes that I'd intended to shut when he wouldn't let me focus them on the mattress—can't look away from the face hovering above mine, whose gaze appears riveted by the sight of my swollen cock twitching with the need for release.

I don't know why that image is so intoxicating, but his fascination with my body has my fingers gripping the sheets, and my balls ready to blow.

"Shit you just got tight." The tendons in Ewan's neck strain as he plows into me.

"Oh fuck. Oh yes. I'm close. Hold my dick."

I'm not sure if I demand that because he asked me to or because I want it. Either way, he releases my leg and wraps his fist around my cock, giving it a firm jerk. Then once more and I detonate.

Ass clenching around his cock, my toes curl and cramp while fireworks explode behind my eyelids. Cum spurts from my tip, coating my neck, my chest, and dribbling down his fingers as he pumps me dry in rhythm with his own erratic thrusts. Then he rams me one final time and holds still while his cock pulses deep inside me, a look of astonished bliss on his face.

Holy.

Fucking.

Shit.

Chapter 3
Niko

My hand is clamped so tight on the headboard my knuckles have turned white, and my triceps are starting to shake from the effort of holding my weight off Reed. Still, I can't bring myself to move.

What the hell just happened?

It's not like it's been a while. When I got the invitation to this trial practice a few weeks ago, the baseball player I had an arrangement with gave me a sendoff, so the whole drought thing doesn't apply. And yeah, I was wound pretty tight earlier, but this isn't the first time I've used sex to blow off a little steam, and it's never left me this boneless. Or breathless. Or...*gobsmacked.*

Mustering the last of my energy, I fist my shrinking cock to hold the condom on as I pull out, then flop to my back on the bed. "I think I saw stars."

"You sound surprised." Call me crazy, but the forced calm in Reed's voice makes me think he's blown away too.

"I am. I didn't know sex with strangers could be so intense."

"You've never had sex with a stranger before?"

"No." I sneak a glance in his direction, relieved to find he's staring at the ceiling and not me, because I'm pretty sure the look of awe on my face would send him running. "You have?"

"I prefer it. So, you're a relationship guy?"

Shit, this is wading into personal territory, and I'm supposed to be avoiding that. Even though Reed seems pretty cool, and I'm more than a little curious about him, that doesn't mean our encounter can't come back to haunt me later if he ever learns my real identity. Best to keep that to myself.

"I'm more of a friends with benefits guy." I pull the condom off and tie it shut, hoping that statement is vague enough to answer without telling him too much as I let it drop to the floor.

He clicks his tongue. "You're not out."

"No."

I feel his head turn, but keep my gaze focused straight above me so I don't have to see his reaction. Guys will tell you all day long that it's fine to be in the closet and okay to come out on your own terms—and maybe they really mean it—but I'm always afraid I'll see a little disappointment in their eyes, so I try not to look.

"Pretty bold to pick me up."

What the...? I didn't take Reed for a funny guy, but maybe a killer orgasm loosened him up.

"You picked me up." I prop myself on my arm to face him.

"I didn't start the conversation."

"You were looking at me. And you asked to see my dick."

"I asked to be the judge of whether your dick met my standards instead of taking your word for it. *After* you asked what my weakness are."

Closing my eyes, I scrub a hand down my face. *Maybe I did pick him up?* "Well, did it?"

"Did it what?"

"Meet your standards?"

He wipes his neck, smearing a drop of cum into his skin. "You really need to ask that?" His chocolatey gaze holds mine for a beat before he turns his head back to the ceiling. *Damn that's hot.*

Flopping back to the bed with a satisfied grin, I take a moment to just enjoy my post sex haze. Unfortunately, this being my first one-night stand, I have no idea how to do that. "What comes next?"

"Sorry?"

"First stranger encounter, remember?" I twist my head to face him. "What comes next?"

"Depends. What's your recovery period?"

"My what?" I blink to hear him better.

"Well, if you're done for the night then I take off. If you've got another round in you, I stay."

"What've you got?" I follow his eyes as they drift down his body, coming to rest on his half-hard cock. I swear the damn thing twitches under the weight of our stare. "Are you...?"

"Yeah."

"Already?"

"This is a little fast, even for me." His brow wrinkles slightly, like that confuses him, and while I'd like to explore that statement further, it's not my priority right now.

"Well, whatever it is, it's rubbing off on me." I nod my head toward my own growing erection.

"Is it?" He props himself on one arm and drags the tip of his fore-finger over my length, causing it to stretch even more. "I was hoping I'd get my own turn."

"To top?"

"To taste, to top. Whatever you're up for." His shoulder lifts slightly before dropping so he can reach my balls.

Cupping them in his hand, he rolls them slowly around his palm. Something between a sigh and a moan rumbles from my throat as he massages me, and I let myself melt into the bed a little while he explores. With gentle pressure he squeezes, pulls and plumps my sac, lulling me into this weird state where I'm both horny and content. An aroused calm, if there is such a thing.

The attention soon has my cock at full mast, pointing straight at the ceiling. Every once in a while, he'll push my balls up against the base, teasing his fingers around it. Then he'll tug them away from my body just firm enough to hint at a little pain before rolling them around his palm. It's fucking heaven, and while my cock aches for more friction, I'm not in a huge rush for him to stop what he's doing.

Of course, that's when his hand stills, and I feel wet heat surround my crown. "Mmm," he mumbles.

"Mmm?" I look up to see he's crawled between my legs, my cock-head trapped between his swollen, pink lips. "I don't taste like cum?" I feel my face heat as I recall that we never cleaned up.

"A little." He swirls his tongue around my tip. "But I like it. And there's something else too. Outdoorsy. Like fresh air."

"Irish Spring," I groan as he takes me fully in his mouth, and my brain short circuits a little as I watch my length sink down his throat.

I'm still a tad sensitive from earlier, which he must sense because he doesn't hollow his cheeks and pull with any force. Instead, he slides his mouth back and forth over my shaft with measured strokes, slicking me with enough saliva that he can add his hand to the mix without chafing my skin.

One hand on my balls, the other loosely fisting my cock, he bobs rhythmically, the squelching sound of slick skin inside a wet mouth echoing around us. It's so primal. So *dirty*. I fucking love it.

My fingers clench at the bedspread as I try to hold my hips still, but the wet heat of his mouth feels so good it's impossible not to chase it.

That's it. *Fuck, just like that*," I rasp as I thread my fingers through his silky hair, though whether it's to hold him still or move him over my length I'm not sure. All I know is after the best orgasm of my life, I'm already hovering on the verge of another, which physically speaking shouldn't be possible. At least, it's never been possible until now. Not gonna complain about that though.

For whatever reason, my body really responds to this guy. I don't understand it—hell I can barely reconcile the fact that someone as gorgeous as Reed came home with me in the first place. Not that I'm unattractive, but I'm a closeted twenty-year-old who awkwardly picked him up—his words—over dinner at the bar. Now he's lapping at my dick like it's his favorite candy. The universe works in mysterious ways I guess, and I'm all for it. I'm fucking loving it, actually.

The harder I grow the harder he sucks, as if he can sense my earlier sensitivity is no longer an issue. The suction has me damn near delirious with pleasure, and my back arches off the bed as I get ready to go. Then he pulls off my dick with an audible pop, and I whimper—*whimper*—at the loss.

Reaching over to snatch the lube near the foot of the bed, he gives me the same slow grin he did at the bar. "Did you think I was gonna let you come that quickly?"

"Well, you got me hard again pretty quickly, so yeah."

Peeking at me from under his thick lashes, eyes so dark with lust they're nearly black, he shakes his head as he squirts the gel in his hand. "Trust me, you'll like this better if I take my time."

Though he rubs the liquid in his fingers, it's still cold when it meets my hole, and I clench down tight.

"Relax." His voice has a velvety, soothing quality that for some reason calms my racing heart. Or maybe it's the other hand drifting softly over my thighs, my abs, my dick. "Focus on the friction between my hand and these big muscles. Do you feel hot where I touch you? Does it make your cock ache for more?"

My skin does sort of tingle under his hand, and I feel my muscles loosen a bit as he caresses them. Then he wraps his fist around my junk, squeezing it lightly, and the rest of my body seems to go pliant as a surge of electricity pools in my dick.

I exhale heavily, realizing as I do there's a fullness in my ass that wasn't there before. He's worked a finger in, and is pumping it in and out. There's no urgency to the movement, no agenda like working me open as fast as he can, just the slow, sensual caress of his finger exploring my body, teasing me to the precipice.

Hooded eyes focused on the view I'm giving him, Reed licks his lips as he curls the digit, nudging my prostate. Once again, I clench, mouth falling open with a soundless moan as shockwaves ripple through me. A preview of the finish to come.

"Fuck, that's impressive. I can't wait to feel you grip my cock with this tight ass." He leans forward to lick the precum seeping from my slit as he squeezes the base, adding another finger while I'm distracted by what he's doing to my dick.

Unfortunately, my body is determined not to make this easy, fighting the pressure invading it. Reed takes his fist off my junk and flicks it with his finger. Hard.

"What the hell?" I bark instinctively, realizing only after my outburst that the pain has faded to a curious pleasure. "Fuck," I rasp as he does it again.

"That's better." I feel two fingers scissoring inside my hole, stretching me wider. It's mildly uncomfortable. Mostly it's just an unusual sensation, not because it hurts. It actually feels pleasant once my body starts to adjust, the fullness intriguing instead of strange. I'm starting to sink into a blissful headspace when out of nowhere another shockwave hits my body.

My abs contract as my breath gets caught in my lungs, and my dick gives a near violent twitch. *Damn, Reed is a fucking master at finding that sweet spot.* Having got a taste of that bliss my body wants more, and my hips start to rock on their own accord, trying to pull him deeper.

"You ready for me?"

"Fuck yes," I pant, hips swiveling as my ass clenches around him.

He pulls his fingers out and gives me a quick but firm slap on the ass. "On your knees."

The steel rod between my legs makes it awkward to change position, but I manage to work myself to all fours as he covers himself with a condom I suspect he pulled from my nightstand. *Why does the idea of him using my protection turn me on so much?*

There's no time to dwell on that before I feel the cool slide of the lube between my cheeks, his cock nudging at my entrance. Gritting my teeth, I push back as he rocks forward, pausing after his crown breaches my hole. He's big, and I'm tight, so I'm hoping the pause is just as much because it feels so good as it is that he doesn't want to hurt me.

"Holy fuck, Ewan."

I smile to myself as I push back a little further, taking him another few inches.

"You're gonna make me re-think my position on jocks," he mumbles.

"What?" I turn my head over my shoulder, hoping his expression will make sense of what I think I heard. One look at him and my confusion evaporates.

His eyes are squeezed shut, square jaw locked tight. The tendons in his neck strain beneath the skin as his head tips back, chest rising rhythmically as he seems to grasp for control. But it's those abs, coiled tight with the effort of holding back, that undo me. It's the sexiest thing I've ever seen, and it damn near sends me over before he even starts to move.

I did that. He's struggling not to lose it because of me.

My ass clenches, coaxing a long, low groan from his throat that I match because, *damn*. I've bottomed before, but it never appealed to me the way it does right now. I'm not sure if that's because Reed got me so needy with his fingers, or he just seems to *fit*. Regardless, the sensation of being filled has never wound me up this much.

Taking a final, shuddering breath, Reed brings his head forward and meets my gaze, those chocolate eyes glazed with desire. "Still with me?"

It's official. I like being his bottom because it blows his mind.

"Yeah," I rasp, uttering a groan of my own as he reaches around to fondle my balls, which sends so much blood down south it makes me lightheaded.

"Your ass is fucking heaven. I'm not sure I can hold back."

I steal his comment from earlier. "Don't."

His nostrils flare slightly as his pupils blow, damn near drowning out his beautiful brown irises. Then he braces his hands on my hips and starts to thrust.

The first few pumps are tentative, testing my limits. When he doesn't find any—I'm all in on bottoming—he starts to move in earnest, slapping his pelvis against my ass as he rams his body into mine. The smack of skin-on-skin echoes throughout the room, the filthy sound of fucking making me harder than I thought possible.

The bed creaks as we come together, our desperation testing its limits as well as mine. I drop my head to the mattress, my arms too exhausted to bear my weight any longer, giving Reed total control of my body.

"Fuck. I can feel that perfect dick of yours swinging back and forth. It's hitting my thigh," he grits as he thrusts.

"Hold onto it."

"No. I like it." He picks up the pace, making me hyper aware of each time my cock connects with his thigh. It's so sensitive I swear I can feel the hairs tickle it just before our skin collides, shooting a bolt of electricity down my shaft.

Devious fucker. Now I need his hand.

"More," I grunt. "Jerk me."

"Not yet."

I open my mouth to protest, but nothing comes out as his cock rubs over my prostate, and I bear down so hard my vision goes dark as a quiver of straight up nirvana ripples through me. *Fucking hell that's intense.*

"There you go." Reed's voice slides silkily over my skin as he drives into me, brushing against my prostate with each pass. "That's the spot, isn't it? Each time I hit it, it feels like you're gonna strangle my cock."

The moan that rumbles up from my chest doesn't sound human, but fuck if I care. My entire body is coiled tight, ready to blast off. I could probably get there from his pounding alone, but my dick fucking *aches* for attention, the skin so taught I'm betting even a feather light touch would do it, and I want it so bad I'm willing to beg. "Touch me. *Please.*"

"Not yet."

Taking matters into my own hands, I reach between my legs, but he smacks my hand away. "Touch it again and I'll stop. I told you I like feeling your dick slap against me..."

"I'm so close, please I need more." I'm babbling, unable to stop myself or disguise the desperation any longer. "Fuck, Reed... "

"I like hearing you beg." He lets go of my hip long enough to give me a stinging slap on the ass, which has precum oozing from my slit. Then, mercifully, he takes me in his fist, and I swear I almost cry with relief.

The dual sensation of being filled and stroked simultaneously is pure heaven. The onslaught of carnality so mind-blowing it pushes me to the edge almost instantly. I hover there for just a second–a glorious, euphoric second–where it feels like every nerve in my body is somehow drawn to my core. I can't stop it. My body has taken on a mind of its own, demanding the orgasm he's been trying to stave off. Currents of pleasure shoot throughout my limbs, my ass gripping at Reed's dick while my own twitches in his hand. I nearly come apart at the seams as my release drenches the sheets beneath me.

Sparks, fireworks, seeing stars—whatever cliché reaction you can think of—it all happens at once. My body convulses like I've been possessed and the most intense orgasm of my life batters through me. I'm fucking gone. Baptized by bliss. Enlightened.

"Holy... Oh God. Oh Jesus. I..." Reed's voice fades to a guttural moan as he unloads, collapsing on top of my back as he spasms deep inside me, and fuck if that sensation isn't as fulfilling as my own release, which seems to go on and on with him still buried in my ass.

As the spasms finally wane, I sink fully to the bed, his weight a pleas-ant blanket in the midst of my near comatose state. It's so comforting, I think I actually doze off for a few minutes, until the sudden absence of heat and pressure jolts me back to the present.

"Uh, want a shower?" I roll to a seated position as he bends to pick up his clothes, the condom seemingly already disposed of. *When did that happen?*

He pauses before tugging his pants on. "I don't think I've got another round in me."

"I didn't mean... You don't have to race out. You can clean up if you want to."

"Thanks, but I'm good to do that at home." He pulls his shirt over his head and reaches for his shoes, making me painfully aware that I'm still naked.

Rolling off the bed I walk to my dresser and pick out a pair of sweats. Reed glances at me briefly when they settle on my hips, then finishes lacing his chucks and stands up.

"I'll walk you out." I gesture to the bedroom door, letting him walk through it as I follow, wondering how to make this any less awkward.

As we reach the front door Reed faces me, and we stare at each other blankly as if neither of us can find the words.

"Uh, what next?" I blurt, choosing to break the awkward silence before it can swallow me whole. Scrubbing my hand over the back of my neck, I peek up at him and wait for an answer.

His brows seem to pull together slightly before they relax. "Sorry. I forgot you're new to this. Usually, I just say goodbye and leave."

"Say goodbye how? A wave? A handshake? A kiss?"

His eyes go round. "Honestly, no one's ever walked me to the door before, so... A handshake?"

I shift my head back and forth as I turn the idea over in my mind. "Seems kinda...*lame.* All things considered."

"What do you do with your *friends*?"

A sheepish smile tugs at the corner of my lip as I answer. "Toss their clothes at them and say, 'see ya next time.'"

"I don't really do next times."

"Yeah, I shouldn't either." I don't miss how that makes him bite at the inside of his cheek, almost like he was hoping for a different answer, but he doesn't dwell on it.

"So, handshake?" He holds his arm out.

Fisting the front of his shirt I yank him to me, the force causing our chests to smack together. Reed sucks in an astonished breath as his mouth drops open.

"If we only get one night, I'm gonna end it properly." I dip my head and softly press my lips to his, savoring the way they seem to fit so perfectly against mine. Then I release his shirt and take a step back. "See you around."

For a second I think he might gift me with one of those smiles he so rarely seems to offer. Instead, he gives me a little nod and lets himself out the door.

"Welcome to Denver," I mutter to myself as I turn the lock and head to the shower.

Chapter 4
Xander

The fresh air doesn't make it any easier to breathe.

Retracing my steps to the restaurant where we met, which happens to be the same direction as my apartment, all I can think about is how much I wish I was still lying naked in bed with Ewan. And not because I want to go another round.

I've never been tempted to linger with a random hookup before, but buried inside him, his warm skin flush against mine as we lay motionless, I had no desire to move. In fact, I think I wanted to...cuddle? That's why I had to get out.

The man is sexy as sin, which in and of itself is reason not to overstay my welcome. But underneath all that sex appeal is a decent guy. Someone I think I could like. And the idea of liking someone who's not out terrifies me.

I did that once before. With a jock of all people. And while enough time has passed that I'm capable of admitting things didn't implode *because* he was a jock, I'm also keenly aware that it was a contributing factor to him not wanting to come out. That's why I made it a rule not to get involved with another one. Usually that means no hookups, much less dating, but... those dimples.

Why that particular feature is such a weakness for me I'm not sure. All I know is I'm damn near helpless to resist them, especially on guys who have a very masculine physique. And possess the ability to overpower me, if I want them to.

It's too bad Ewan ticked all my fantasy boxes, because in addition to having possibly the best sex I've ever experienced, I had fun just talking with him. His innocence is sort of endearing, his manners refreshing.

As a bit of a moody guy who's prone to assume people will disappoint you, he was a spark of light I wasn't expecting, and I'd be lying if I said I didn't want more of that. Yet I've been around enough to know that was a one-off. The minute he's around people who don't know his secret, he'll be a different guy, and he'd disappoint me just like my last jock did.

The one rule I can't break is the closeted one. I don't mind fooling around for a night with a guy who isn't out, but that's where it has to end. The memory of being hurt is still too fresh, even after all these years, and I can't put myself through that again. That means no more Ewan.

No more Ewan? What the hell am I thinking? The guy's living in an extended stay hotel. Yeah, that could mean he just moved here, in which case I guess bumping into him again is a possibility. But it's just as likely he's here for a work project or something, and he'll go back home in a matter of days or weeks. There's absolutely no reason to worry about seeing him again, much less him being the kind of guy I could actually fall for.

Why do I hate the sound of that?

Feeling a slight vibration in my pocket, I pull my phone and glance at the screen. *Shit!*

"My bad," I answer. "Something came up."

"What could possibly be more important than watching a shitty band with a killer logo?" I can barely make out Tripp's voice over the background music.

Tripp and I both work at a visual production company that specializes in film and TV, but he loves music and has a side gig doing videos and graphic design for local bands. His current project is for a country group, a genre neither of us particularly like, which is why I was supposed to suffer through the evening with him.

"You do realize if you try to drum up business at a country concert you might get more country clients, right?"

"That's not the point." His voice comes through loud and clear. He must've gone outside. "I've been calling you every half hour for two hours, and now you answer sounding perfectly normal and... Wait. Why do you sound normal?"

"As opposed to?"

"You."

"What's that supposed to mean?" My brows pull together.

"Most of the time your voice is bland. Bored. Right now, you sound kinda...peppy. It's freaking me out." When I don't say anything else he gasps. "Who is he?"

"Who is who?"

"The guy you met tonight. I assume that's the reason you bailed on me."

"Why would you assume that?" Tripp might be my best friend, but I'm not a sharer, so I like to think I'm not that easy to read. That fact that he so effortlessly guessed where I was is a little unsettling.

"What other reason would you have for ditching me? He must've been epic."

"I could've been in a car accident. Or robbed. There are a million reasons besides a guy for me to ditch you."

"And if it was any of those things, you'd have called to tell me you couldn't make it."

Dammit, he's actually right.

"You do know I haven't said there was a man." My pride won't let me concede that easily.

"Silence is golden and all that shit."

"I don't think that means what you think it does."

"Maybe not, but that doesn't change the fact that something's up with you, and I bet that something is eight inches or more."

"Jesus," I mutter, wondering for the millionth time *why* Tripp is my best friend. I may not have much social grace, but at least I don't deliberately shock people with my nonexistent filter. I just don't sugarcoat things.

"Is that his name, or what you screamed when you came?"

I pinch the bridge of my nose between my fingers. "For the love of God, would you drop it?"

"Not until you admit you stood me up for another guy."

"Stood you up? What are we–dating now?"

"You wish. I'm the closest thing to a boyfriend you've had in years."

"That's the sad truth," I mutter.

"Not my fault you're afraid of commitment." I've never told him that, but after years of watching me limit myself to casual flings I'm not surprised that's the conclusion he came to. Fine by me. I prefer that to the truth–that I'm afraid of another broken heart. Perpetually unavailable, a lone wolf, even emotionally damaged. I'll take any label that doesn't include the word scared.

"What can I say, I like my *me* time." I blow out a tired breath. *Huh, he's right. My normal voice does sound bored.*

"Not tonight you didn't. And I'd pat you on the back except I'm pissed your dick decided to make friends when I needed you to be my wingman."

"Are you telling me you tried to pick up a cowboy? Damn, that I am sorry to have missed."

"Not a sex wingman, a work wingman. Two business partners together are legit. One is like an ambulance chaser hunting for scraps. Creepy." I can picture him shuddering on the other end of the line.

"I'm not your work partner though. Not for the music thing."

"They don't have to know that. I'll just look more important if I have a lacky standing next to me."

"In that case, I'm not sorry I stood you up."

"You will be when I come up with a way for you to make it up to me. He better have been worth it."

He was.

"Still nothing?" He grunts when I don't reply. "Damn, either he sucked big time or he rocked your world."

For a second I consider confiding in Tripp. It's not like I've never admitted to hooking up before, so there's no big secret here. But I've never gotten so wrapped up in a guy that I forgot my previously scheduled commitments, and I'm having trouble accepting that myself, much less saying it out loud. Plus, for reasons I can't explain, I want to keep this just for me.

Despite his constantly running mouth, Tripp is a nice guy, and I actually like him. But if I open up to him and he betrays my confidence, even by accident, I'm not sure I can forgive that. It's better not to say anything.

"You know I'll just make up my own story if you don't tell me," he taunts.

"Wouldn't be the first time."

Once, years ago, I disappeared from a concert a group of us went to and never told Tripp where I went, though we both know a guy was the reason for my disappearance. He was...not famous exactly, but recognizable. Part of a band that had a pretty decent local following. I didn't want to get caught up in any speculation about the two of us, so I kept quiet.

Tripp made up a story to fill in the blanks, but he didn't just invent a bunch of fake details, he put it to video. The resulting stick figure sexcapade was pretty funny, even if it was at my expense. And truthfully, his made-up version rivaled the actual event. If he wants to do it again, I'm fine with it, though this time around I'm fairly certain his pretend version won't surpass the reality.

That thought nearly brings a smile to my lips, though it never fully forms. The sting that flares up in my chest stops it cold. *That's odd.* I haven't felt anything like that since...

Oh, I get it. I cave to the charms of *one* jock and my mind starts playing tricks on me, confusing ghosts from my past with the present. It has nothing to do with Ewan, it's just a memory I reawakened.

"The first time was a warmup. This one will be a masterpiece." Tripp saves me from my own mind.

"Can't wait to see it." I hold my ground.

Monday morning, the whole office has a video in their email. This time instead of stick figures Tripp uses cartoon mice, but really buff versions who try to outdo each other with their physical prowess in the gym before going at it so hard the bed breaks.

They power through, neck muscles so corded in the throes of release that their eyes nearly pop out of their sockets. Then the mouse who's supposed to be me fizzles like a popped balloon when he blows his load, shriveling down to a scrawny version that's an oddly accurate representation of my true physique.

It's over the top ridiculous and gets a good laugh from our co-workers, who rib me good-naturedly about having a great weekend. And just as I predicted, this time the made-up version pales in comparison to the real event.

I give myself a few seconds to mourn the fact that incredible night is over, never to be repeated again, then take a bow and get to work.

Chapter 5
Niko

"Say that again," I tell my agent, Jim.

"Which part? That the Colorado Bulldogs took you with their first pick, or that I negotiated two hundred K *over* the minimum salary?"

"I... I... *Shit*. When we didn't hear anything after that week of practice, I thought for sure they were gonna pass on me."

"Coach Nydek likes to keep things close to the vest until he's ready to make a move. Speaking of which, you have three days to get your ass to Denver. They have a team condo you can stay in to start, and I'll put you in touch with a realtor to get something more permanent. Will you be flying, or should I rent you a car?"

"I don't have a license, so...yeah. Flying it is."

"You don't have a license?" Jim doesn't sound shocked very often, but I manage to put that tone in his voice. "Don't you have dual citizenship?"

"I do. That doesn't mean I have a license."

"How did you get around campus?"

"Walked. Bummed rides with roommates. Took the bus here and there." Public transit on campus didn't measure up to Sweden, but it was pretty efficient. And since I didn't have a car, I didn't see any reason to learn how to drive.

"But, you moved to the US in high school," he stutters, like that makes all the sense in the world. To him maybe it does since most people here learn to drive as teenagers.

"Yeah, but I was in boarding school. When would I have had time to learn how to drive?"

"I guess I'll be telling the realtor to look for places within walking distance of the arena," Jim mutters to himself. "Do I have to arrange to have anything shipped to you, or will you check everything you need on the plane?"

Glancing around my bedroom I note a few pictures of family and friends I'll need to take, but all the furniture here came with the house, so it'll stay here when I leave. Otherwise, all I have is clothes and gear. "Maybe a box or two. Nothing much."

"Okay, check your email for flight details. Great job, kid." Jim disconnects, leaving me a little shell shocked.

I'm going to the NHL. Holy shit! I'm going to the NHL!

This was the dream, of course, but I never let myself get attached to it. I tuned out the chatter from my teammates, took everything my coaches said with a grain of salt. I even instructed my family to say *if* I make it, not *when*. And I got an associate's degree in business as a backup plan. Not that I could succeed in business—I barely retained the information past the tests I needed to take because hockey was always the goal—but I have a piece of paper that says I can. Theoretically.

I hoped I wouldn't need to use it, and with that phone call it seems like I won't. I won't have to sit behind a desk looking at spreadsheets or whatever the hell it is businesspeople do. I'll get to be on the ice. Every day.

This is what my family sacrificed for. This is why I finished high school in the US and started college here while they stayed in Sweden.

They thought about coming with me. For my mom it would've been like coming home since she's from upstate New York, but she loved Sweden just as much as dad did. The people. The outdoors. The... well the food I think she tolerated. I have to say that's one thing about this country that did not disappoint. But hockey players in North America make much better money than they do in Sweden, and when my parents realized I might be able to go all the way, they figured the best opportunity for me to get scouted was to be in the US.

I wasn't sold on that plan at first. Lots of Swedish guys make it to the NHL, so I figured my chances were just as good there as here. Would I still be a first-round pick if I'd stayed there? Who knows. And in the end, I guess it doesn't matter. I made it! *I fucking made it!*

Wiping my eye to prevent the dampness from becoming a tear, I call my folks with the good news. Then my sister, who forces me to scream with her, which brings my roommates barreling into my room to see what the commotion is. Ten hours later, still half drunk from my impromptu celebration, I pack up my shit and catch a ride to the airport.

As the plane takes off, my mind drifts to a certain pair of chocolatey brown eyes. The same ones I see every night when I close mine despite the fact it makes no logical sense for the memory of one night to linger so long. *I wonder if I'll ever see them again?*

***

"Good to have you here, son." Coach Nydek shakes my hand two days later as I enter the arena. For a brief moment I have a sense of déjà vu, just as I did the first time I saw him when we met during my practice in the spring. But I shake it off without putting too much thought into it. I'm probably just feeling a little starstruck, which I'll have to get over pretty quickly.

"I appreciate the opportunity, sir."

"It's Coach or Coach Ny. None of this sir crap."

"Yes, si... Yeah. Okay." I can't keep the grin off my face no matter how much I try to tell myself to play it cool. *It's the friggin NHL!*

Coach takes me around the locker room, giving me a moment to say hi to some of the guys I met during my practice week a few months ago. Even though it's not the first time I've shaken their hands, it's the first time I've done it as their teammate, and that distinction has me smiling so hard my jaw actually hurts.

We end the introductions with the equipment manager, Gabe, a leaner, lankier version of Captain America. "This guy is gonna show you your locker and get you squared away with all the gear you need," Coach points to him. "Get unpacked and meet in the team room in thirty. We'll have an orientation before a warm-up skate."

I turn to Gabe and shake his hand, following the finger he points around the room to highlight where to find clean gear and discard the old, get tape for the sticks, and have adjustments made to skates and helmets. Seems like he runs a tight ship, and I respect that. When he's done giving me the highlights, he crooks a finger and has me follow him to a locker that already bears my name.

"Surreal, huh?" Another of the new guys, Justus, elbows me. Looks like we're neighbors.

"I mean, it's not my first locker room, but it feels like it is." I glance around at the veterans, who are laughing and taunting each other as they put away their gear.

"They spelled my name right." He jerks his head toward the gold nameplate on the door. "That's never happened on the first day."

"That's what a six-figure salary gets you."

"I guess. The salary is even more surreal than the nameplate."

I put my skates in the locker with a little chuckle. "Yeah, I'm still trying to wrap my brain around that part."

"I'm still trying to wrap my brain around being in the same locker room as Luca Daniels. Guy's a legend." His hazel eyes take on an almost dreamy quality as he glances at the man I assume is his idol. If I was a forward, I'd feel the same. Luca's scored more postseason goals than anyone in the league. *Ever*.

"Just don't get so starstruck you freeze to the ice." I bump his shoulder with mine.

"I probably won't see much ice time." Justus gives me a rueful smile. "I'll be lucky to make the third line."

"Third lines still get lots of action." I'm not just saying that to make him feel better. This game moves so fast, and the long season means it's unlikely we'll get to the end without an injury here and there. Plenty of opportunity for the next guy up to step in and make a difference.

Justus nods—he knows the deal, he's just feeling overwhelmed—and I get it. That's how I felt when I came here for practice. In a lot of ways, I'm fortunate to have had that opportunity. This is still a dream come true that's hard to fathom, but at least I got some of the 'I don't belong' jitters out of the way a few months ago. Right now, my hangup is believing I'll be making enough money to take care of my family in a sport I'm passionate about.

After we get our lockers situated, we head into the team room to go over some of the basics, introduction to all the staff, the practice schedule, and speeches from coaches and captains. We also get a copy of the playbook to study. Then, after what seems like hours, we finally hit the ice.

The cool blast of air in the rink makes me come alive after sitting still, my tight muscles loosening as the blades of my skates hit the slick surface. A lifetime of muscle memory floods my body, carrying me around the rink on instinct rather than conscious thought.

Nothing feels quite as exhilarating as gliding over the ice. Sure, you put a lot of effort into it and move like a bolt of lightning, but you can also just coast with ease. With the right angle you can even feel weightless when you turn, just for a second, when you're leaning so far you should fall but your speed whips you around before you succumb to the pull of gravity. And moving backwards... There's just something about skating backwards that makes me feel like a little kid no matter how old I get.

Today is just a warmup, so no drills or sprints. We just coast around with the puck, shaking the dust off. From time to time a guy will launch end-to-end, mimicking a fast break, to take a shot on the empty goal. Even now, with no opposing team on the ice, my adrenaline spikes and my heartbeat goes into overdrive watching it. It makes my mouth water for the first game, when it'll be real.

Once the skate is over, we all shower then head to Coach Nydek's house for a pre-season barbeque, something that seems to be tradition.

I catch a ride with Justus, who I learn was called up from the minors. That's pretty impressive considering most guys who make it to this level come as soon as they turn eighteen, skipping the minors and college altogether. I only did the college thing because I wasn't old enough to enter the draft when I finished high school, and at twenty I'm considered old for a rookie. Justus is twenty-two, practically ancient. It explains why he had the deer in the headlights look in the locker room.

"What were the minors like?" I ask him as we pull into a gated neighborhood in a part of town called Cherry Creek, though don't see any cherry trees that would justify the name.

"We had fewer games for one. Not gonna lie, playing double the games feels a little intimidating."

"Double? For me it'll be triple." My stomach drops a little as those words sink in. It's not like I was unaware of the increased workload coming my way, I just hadn't allowed myself to think about it until now.

"The AHL is a little slower too. Or so I'm told."

All hockey games move quickly, but the pros read the game better and faster, meaning even tiny mistakes can be catastrophic.

"Yeah, I practiced with these guys a few months ago, and it was intense. I got the hang of it the second day but the first my head was bouncing all over the place trying to keep up."

"Great," he mutters as we pull into a circular drive sitting in front of a massive brick house that would rival the size of the dorms at my old boarding school.

"Hey, that's why third lines get a lot of action though. No one can keep up with such a fast pace for longer than a few minutes."

"I know that, but after watching Luca on the ice today, it's hard to put myself in the same zip code, much less the same uniform."

I shoot him a wry smirk. "Maybe don't compare yourself to the greatest player in the league on your first day."

"Yeah, good point." He grins back.

We follow a few of the veterans through to the backyard where a bunch of tables and chairs have been set up on a massive patio and around a rectangular pool. There's several coolers with drinks of all kinds, and a grill that's so big it looks more like three combined instead of just one. I guess if you feed guys our size on the regular, you need it though.

Coach introduces us to his wife and says to make ourselves at home. Taking the beer Justus hands me, we sit with some of the guys by the pool and shoot the shit about what people did over break and how we think we'll stack up against other teams this season. The goalie, Noah Garrett, drills me on how I'd play different scenarios. I already know what he expects of the guys defending him since we worked together a few months ago, but I'm more than happy to have him spell it out for me. After all, the better we work together the better our chances of success, and if I know how he's likely to move in goal, I can better protect him.

After stuffing ourselves with grilled chicken—coach swears it's better for us than actual burgers—the guys start jumping in the pool to cool off. Justus and I don't have suits, but everyone says it's fine if we swim in our shorts. So, we strip down to our boxers and join in on the water volleyball.

Midway through the first game, right after I make an epic serve that has the other team scrambling, coach barks at me and Justus to get out. I'm wondering if the new guys just got hazed and our swim attire is *not* okay, until I see the man standing next to coach, and the reason for my earlier déjà vu becomes frighteningly clear.

Chapter 6
Xander

"Your dad will kill you for bringing me here. You know that, right?" Tripp says as I push through the front door.

"As long as you don't hit on anyone he won't care." My dad has no issues with me or anyone else being gay, but he's super protective of his players. Even I'm not allowed to get too close.

"Don't hit on the gorgeous athletes that star in all my fantasies?" His eyes gleam mischievously under a head of bleached blond hair that's just long enough in front to contrast his dark irises. "It's like you don't know me at all."

A few years ago, when I brought Tripp to the annual barbeque my dad hosts at the start of each season, he sort of lost his shit when he got a glimpse of the man candy known as the Colorado Bulldogs. I don't blame the guy—jocks may be relegated to my *break glass in case of emergency* list—but they're tempting as hell. It's why I hate coming to this event, and why I brought him as backup.

Big, sexy athletes have been a constant presence in my life given my dad's occupation, so it's no wonder I gravitate toward them on a physical level. But never—not once—has the physical attraction been worth the emotional fallout. Best case, my infatuation wasn't returned because the objects of my crushes were straight. Worst case, well, that's why I try to avoid jocks altogether.

Unfortunately, I'll never be able to escape them completely, which is why I have Tripp in tow. Keeping him off my dad's radar will prevent me from getting too close to anyone I shouldn't, particularly since I'm still pining over the jock I did break the glass for this past spring. No one has piqued my interest since, which has me feeling out of sorts. Not a great state of mind when you're heading into the equivalent of a live thirst trap.

As far as I know, all the guys on the team are straight, so theoretically I shouldn't need backup. But I also know better than to believe a guy is straight just because he tells his teammates he is. I've been the secret gay boyfriend before, a scenario I don't want to repeat, and Tripp is here to make sure I don't. His brash mouth makes him a horrible choice to play the voice of reason, but he's sort of my only option.

"I know you too well. Why do you think I don't bring you to the games?"

"Because you hate them and don't love me enough to suffer through them so I can get close to a hot hockey god."

As usual, he's right, though my father and I have an unspoken agreement that I won't badmouth the sport he loves, so I neither confirm nor deny.

"These guys are straight, Tripp, so you can look but don't touch. Or proposition or flirt or initiate any contact whatsoever."

"What happens if I do?"

"My dad really will kill you." I lead him to the back patio and wave at my dad when I spot him chatting with Luca, his star player, and my mom.

My parents excuse themselves and come give me a hug. "Xander," Mom scolds as she turns my arm over in her hand to inspect the red marks on my elbow and forearms. "Still not wearing elbow pads I see."

I roll my eyes, another thing she admonishes me for. "Don't give me that look."

"It's too hot for those, but I did have a helmet on." That's one body part I don't fuck with. Scrapes and bruises don't bother me, but I like the way my brain functions right now, thank you.

As mom fusses Dad holds his hand out to Tripp, though his eyes narrow slightly.

"Do I need to remind you to be on your best behavior?" he asks Tripp.

"In my defense the guy really did have a bee on his chest. But yes," he rushes. "I will behave."

"Good," my dad harumphs. "Come meet the rookies."

We follow him toward the pool as he yells for a few guys to get their asses out of the water. I'm not really paying attention as two people make their way to us—half the guys don't make it beyond the first season, so I don't attempt to remember names—but as I hold my hand out like I'm supposed to when I'm introduced to the rookies, something familiar flashes before my eyes. *Dimples.*

Being sort of a moody guy, I'm not prone to showing emotion. But fuck if I can keep away the astonished look as I come face-to-face with the guy who's been running through my mind for damn near two months.

I'm vaguely aware of my dad's voice next to me, something about the player from Sweden he was talking about, though I only hear one word clearly. *Niko.*

Clutching a towel around his waist that does nothing to hide his sculpted abs, or the water droplets trickling over them, Niko clasps my hand in his. Visions of our night together flash through my mind, like a movie trailer of memories. Smooth, hard skin. Raspy whispers and moans of pleasure. *Dimples.*

Niko squeezes his fingers around mine, but what looks like a handshake feels like a caress when his thumb slides over the back of my hand.

What does a man do when he runs into a former lover he's not supposed to know but he can't stop thinking about?

I don't get to come up with a solution before my dad gets that tone only parents seem to have when they're bracing for something they don't want to hear. "You didn't mention you met one of my players, Xander."

"We didn't actually meet." I find my voice the same time I find the strength to pull my hand away. "We just happened to sit next to each other at the bar while having dinner."

Mirroring my stoic expression Niko elaborates. "Yeah, I tried to distract myself from thinking about practicing with the team by talking basketball." He runs a hand through his dripping wet hair.

Don't follow that hand. Don't watch where the water droplets fall. Shit! Blink. Look away.

"Basketball?" My dad's voice provides the jolt I need to turn from Niko. "Since when do you know anything about basketball?"

"I don't, which is why it was a pretty short conversation. He probably only remembers it because I didn't realize it was the playoffs." I do my best to come off as bored, though my heart's going so fast I think I'm on the verge of breaking a sweat.

Tripp, sensing my distress, jumps in with his hand extended. "Hi. I'm Xander's best friend, Tripp." He pumps Niko's hand then turns to the other guy. *James maybe?* "I'm sorry I didn't catch your name."

"Justus." The man returns the handshake.

"Like the Justice League? Sweet."

"Uh, no. Just us. Justus." The man enunciates.

"Ignore him," I sigh, shaking my head at Tripp. "He makes cartoons for a living so his primary point of reference is anything animated."

"You have the same job I do." Tripp slaps my chest with the back of his hand.

"Yes, but I also know most people don't name their kids after superheroes." I allow myself to glance briefly at Niko, wondering if he's thinking about some of our fantasy basketball picks. Those damn dimples tell me he is.

"Superheroes have some of the best names. Peter Parker, Clark Kent." Tripp lifts a finger with each name he recites.

"Reed Richards." Niko's voice teases goosebumps to the surface of my skin, and though I feel his baby blues watching me, I don't let myself look. I can't.

"Ooh, good one," Tripp agrees. "That's an enviable skill. Being able to stretch any part of your body. Imagine how..."

My dad clears his throat.

"Many goals you could stop with that ability," Tripp redirects as if that's what he was going to say all along.

Giving in, my eyes find Niko's, which are full of laughter as he presumably finishes Tripp's sentence in his mind. I have to bite my cheek to keep from smiling, especially with my dad standing between us.

Even if it was pure coincidence, he wouldn't approve of me hooking up with his player. That's a line I've been forbidden to cross for as long as he's been a coach. My whole life really. That didn't stop me from crossing it with other athletes, but I learned my lesson there. Or rather, I learned to limit my discretions to one night instead of becoming someone's dirty little secret.

I drag my eyes away from Niko's before my dad can get suspicious. Even if he didn't have the rule against getting close to his players, I know for a fact Niko's still the closet, and I won't out him. Nor will I give him the impression a repeat is on the table.

"We're going to grab some food." I tug on Tripp's arm, signaling the need for us to exit. "Nice to officially meet you." I nod at Niko, then Justus, before steering us toward the grill.

"You're forgiven," Tripp says once we're a safe distance away.

"For what?"

"Standing me up at that concert. You're forgiven."

"I have no idea what you're talking about." I hand him a plate as I start to fill my own.

"Deny all you want, but I saw the way you clammed up. That's your mystery guy."

"I clammed up because I had trouble placing where I saw him before. I didn't want to be rude and admit I didn't remember." I stack pickles on my sandwich, avoiding Tripp's prying eyes.

"Oh, but you did remember. You even remembered the basketball game was part of the playoffs, which would be insignificant to you unless something momentous happened at the same time."

Damn his totally logical logic.

"Okay, maybe I thought he was incredibly hot, and I was sort of speechless because I never thought I'd see him again, and suddenly there he was. But I didn't hook up with him because he's straight."

"How do you know?"

"He didn't make a move on me." I'm not that guy—really I'm not—but I get noticed, and Tripp knows it. He's the one who brought it to my attention, so he'll buy that excuse.

"Hmm," he gives me the side eye as he *finally* starts to put food on his plate.

After we've eaten Tripp helps me play host, chatting with the players as we sip beers by the edge of the pool. With my back to the water,

I can't see Niko, so I can almost pretend he isn't here. And since I have to keep my lust-struck friend in line, I actually manage to put the man out of my mind for the better part of an hour. Up until I head into the house to use the bathroom, and walk right into his beautiful chest when I'm done.

He steadies me with a hand to my forearm but makes no move to back away, his pecs brushing against mine with each heavy breath.

"Did you follow me?" I swing my head left to right to see if anyone else is around.

"If I did?" A slow smile stretches across his face, calling my gaze to the sexy hollows in his cheeks. *No! Focus.*

I lock my jaw to mask the thrill that gives me. "I'd tell you for a guy who's not out you're taking a big risk, and for what? A little pleasure?"

"A lot of pleasure if I remember right. And maybe I think you're worth the risk."

"Maybe I think you aren't," I counter.

His mouth falls to a flat line. "Because I'm not out?"

"Because you play for my father. Do you have any idea what the fallout would be if he knew about us? How could you forget to mention you're a hockey player?"

"Like you told me what you do for a living? Hell, you wouldn't even tell me your name. I like it by the way. Is it short for Alexander?"

"Yes," I grunt. "And Niko is short for Nikolas I assume? A Swedish name?"

He nods, the barest curve of his lip offering just a hint of those sexy dimples. I shake my head to clear it.

"You barely have an accent."

"I've lived here since I was fifteen. It's faded over the years."

"Hmm. Well, ignoring the fact my dad is your coach, eighteen is too young for me." I'm not sure why I focus on his age when his being in the closet is the bigger issue, but I'm really not trying to pick on him for choosing to hide his sexuality. As much as I don't want to be part of that, I do understand it.

"Eighteen?" His brows pull together. "What makes you think I'm eighteen?"

"You just got drafted. Eighteen is the standard age for that. Hell, you probably only finished high school a month ago."

"I finished high school two years ago."

"Why are you just now getting drafted then?"

"I wasn't old enough to enter the draft when I graduated so I went to college for a year. Sat out a good portion of it with a groin injury that lingered so I stuck around for another season to up my chances of getting scouted." His thumb ghosts over my forearm, making me hyper aware that he's got me pinned between his body and the door. Too close, yet I don't push him away.

"So, you're what... Twenty? Not much better than eighteen."

"If you're that concerned about my age, you'd have already told me to fuck off."

"I'm trying to be polite."

"I don't think you do polite. I think you tell it like it is, so what is it?"

How this guy knows that about me after one night I have no idea, but since he wants honesty, I'll give it to him.

"I don't do jocks."

"You did me."

"Once."

He presses his body against mine, leaning forward just long enough to growl in my ear. "You're saying once was enough?"

"Friends with benefits is *your* preference, remember? I'm more of a one and done guy."

My eyes drift to his mouth when he pulls a plump lip between his teeth, then asks coyly. "How many one and done's have you had since me?"

"What happened to the gentle giant who picked me up at the bar?" I arch a brow, dodging his question with one of my own. "The one who had to work up the courage to talk to me."

Niko doesn't miss a beat. "That guy can be bold when he sees something he wants. How many?"

A warm shiver travels up my spine. Though shy Niko was ruggedly cute, commanding Niko is *hot*. It takes me back to that first night, when he was so lost to his lust that he picked me up and carried me to bed. I've replayed that so many times in my head, imagining I could relive it. And while I want that again, there are too many obstacles here. Too many ways people—beyond just the two of us—can get hurt.

"One night doesn't give you the right to ask that question," I say softly.

Niko goes rigid with a sharp inhale. Then the chest pressed against mine deflates as he steps away, putting at least a foot between us. "You're right."

Dammit, I shouldn't miss the feel of him this much.

"Getting drafted at twenty instead of eighteen is a big deal, Niko. You don't want to screw that up by getting caught with the coach's son. And I don't want to be your secret." I put my hand on his firm pec, both to ease him into what I'm saying and to feel him one last time. "Go back to your teammates. Celebrate your accomplishment with them and get ready for your season instead of chasing what you can't have."

Though his head is already bowed, he nods slightly. Then he pushes past me into the bathroom, leaving a tiny pinprick of pain where his skin made contact with mine. I give myself a minute to wish things were different, that my past wasn't still impacting my future. Then I remember everything I've learned from my past and lock my feelings down, heading off to find a drink before a pair of wounded blue eyes make me lose my resolve.

Chapter 7
Niko

I rear back, grabbing the doorframe to steel myself against the shock of nearly running Tripp over on my way out of the bathroom.

"Jesus." My hand flies to my heart.

Arms crossed in front of his chest, he studies me with a critical gaze, clucking his tongue when his eyes reach my face. "None," he says.

"What?"

"The answer to your question. None."

"I don't..." *Xander hasn't been with anyone since me?*

Tripp's dark brows disappear beneath his yellow hair, silencing me with a look that suggests I should know exactly what he's talking about. Then he spins away, leaving me alone in the hall.

Hours later, those words still echo in my mind. Hours later, my heartbeat still won't return to normal.

That could mean nothing—not all guys feel the need to hook up every weekend—but since his friend made it a point to tell me, I have to believe it means something. What that something is I have no idea considering he shot me down, but that one little word fills me with hope. Hope that somehow, our one night meant as much to Xander as it did to me.

Am I thinking rationally? Probably not. Definitely not. If I was being rational, I'd do exactly what Xander said and focus on hockey. But believing I'd get to the NHL wasn't exactly rational, so I'm not sure there's any reason to start thinking that way now. Especially since the man has been on my mind long before running into him today.

I went to that restaurant every night for the rest of my stay over the spring, and two nights ago when I got back to town, hoping I'd run into Reed—Xander—again. And not because I wanted to get laid, although I wouldn't have objected. It was more that I felt like myself around him.

He didn't tease me for bringing up jedi's and superheroes and morphing those things together with a goofy fantasy team conversation. Or for being a novice in the one-night-stand department. And he didn't seem put off by my admiration of his body or wanting to fuck him face-to-face.

More often than not, I hold something back when I'm with other people. My sexuality when I'm with my teammates. My desire to explore and appreciate instead of just fuck when I'm with a man. My nerdy side from just about everyone. None of that crossed my mind with Xander. I was just *me*.

I knew it was unlikely I'd ever see him again, yet that didn't stop me from trying to force fate by returning to the scene of our first encounter. Then to see him at Coach's house, and learn that he's Coach's son... It was like destiny called and said *just kidding*.

My chest physically ached to have Xander so close and so far. To know that he was within reach yet totally untouchable because I'm not out. Even if I were, given the way Coach jumped to conclusions about us knowing each other, it's clear he wouldn't approve of the history we share. My sense is that's more of a conflict-of-interest thing than a gay thing since Coach didn't seem to have an issue with gay guys in his house, but over the years I've learned not to assume anything. I think that's why I followed Xander to the bathroom.

During our night together he made no secret about the fact that he prefers casual hookups to any type of arrangement, but he also said he prefers not to kiss and still locked his lips to mine. Besides, just because he *did* feel that way doesn't mean he still *does*. Hell, I wasn't interested in more until I couldn't put the night out of my head, so you never know when things can change.

It may have been just one night, but between that and the cookout today, I've seen enough to know that I can trust Xander. That he can be a safe place for me to be...me. Yeah, him being the coach's kid complicates things, and it's still a bad idea for me to come out now when my career is just getting started. But Xander made an impression on me, and if Tripp is right, I may have made an impression on him. Isn't that reason enough to see if we can find common ground?

That question plagues me for the rest of the evening, robbing me of a good night's sleep. Thank goodness practice starts with weightlifting instead of wind sprints, which will give me a chance to wake up.

Admittedly, being sleep deprived isn't great for hoisting metal plates around, but at least it doesn't make me too short of breath. And being the first day in the gym, we're all given a little slack. Mostly.

Rookies are paired with veterans so we get to build a rapport with more senior members of the team. As a defender I'm paired with our goalie, one of the best in the league, who doesn't give me as much slack as I'd like.

"Two hundred pounds?" Noah balks at me as I rack the bar. "You should be squatting at least two hundred percent of your body weight."

"You want me to bust a groin on day one?" I wipe the back of my neck with a towel.

"I want you to be able to get your ass back to the goal faster than anyone else." He adds ninety pounds to the bar and jams out eight reps before turning it back over to me, shaking his head when I take off the extra weight.

"What?"

"You've gotta be at least five years younger than me. No way I should be lifting more."

"You won't be for long." I rest the bar on my shoulder blades and get ready to squat. "But I'm smart enough not to take your bait and hurt myself coming off a two-month break."

"Two months? You've got bigger balls than I gave you credit for."

"What do you know about my balls?" I count in my mind as I start my reps.

"I know you've gotta have big ones if you slack off that long and think you can come in here and keep up."

"Bigger than yours it would seem." This right here is why I don't tell people about my sexuality. Stupid locker room banter takes on a whole new meaning if guys think you're talking about *their* balls specifically.

"Careful, rookie. You're playing with the big boys now."

Eight. Nine. Ten. I rack the bar and cup my junk with a wicked grin. "Never had any complaints."

"Jesus, tell me there aren't two of you," he mutters with a not-so-subtle eye roll.

"Two of whom?" I add the plates back on so Noah can do another set of reps.

"Two cocky bastards."

I glance around the weight room, counting bodies. "There's like fifteen of us in here."

"So?"

"So, aren't all hockey players cocky bastards?" I'm not trying to be a smart ass, but in truth, you don't make it to this level unless you've got a shit ton of self-confidence.

Noah chuckles darkly. "Fair."

"Why did you think I'm one of two?" *Did I blow my secret already? How?*

"You're openly proud of your dick. Showing it off, like Luca."

"Okay, first, I was just messing around, not trying to show off or anything. And second—isn't everyone proud of their dick? Why is Luca different?" I try to keep my voice level, though internally I'm freaking out. I mean, if I'm not the only gay guy here that'd be a relief, and if the other one is Luca, a hockey god, that's even better. But there hasn't been so much as a whisper of Luca being gay, and it's unlikely he could be out *only* in the locker room, so I don't want to get my hopes up.

"Luca's got a thing for being watched. On *and* off the ice."

"Still not following."

Noah steps to the bar for his set, grinning wryly. "He's got a strict pregame ritual he adheres to."

Now it's starting to come together. Tons of athletes are superstitious, but hockey players take it to the next level, or so I'm told. Luca's superstition must involve jerking off, but that's not unusual.

"Lots of guys need to blow their load before a game."

"True, but he's at his best when he's got an audience."

"Oh." Understanding dawns. "*Ohhh.* Yeah, that's not my... I mean that's cool if it's your thing but... What kind of audience?"

"He's not gay if that's what you're asking."

"It wasn't." For all of two seconds I thought I might not be alone, which was a nice fantasy, but Luca's sexuality wasn't the point of my question. "It's just... Who...?"

"You're familiar with puck bunnies, right?"

"Duh." *Duh, what are you, ten?*

Noah finishes his set and racks the bar before slapping me on the back. "No shortage of them. But Luca isn't shy either, so if you're his roommate either steer clear until he's finished or be prepared to settle in for the show."

Obviously, watching a guy fuck is not a problem for me, even if it's with a woman. Or women. Watching a teammate is a line I've never crossed though, and even if Luca isn't shy that doesn't mean he'd be okay with a gay guy as his audience. I need to make sure we don't end up as roommates.

"Speaking of bunnies." Noah removes the extra plates so I can take my turn. "Coach is pretty strict about them. He's not an idiot, but he's not gonna openly condone it either. Fastest way to get benched is to get caught with your pants down, so if you chase the bunnies be discreet about it."

"Don't worry about me. I don't plan to fuck up my career over pussy." Truer words have never been spoken.

Noah gives me a subtle up-nod, seemingly satisfied I mean that. "I saw Coach introducing you to his family at the barbeque. Was that the boyfriend his kid was with?"

The change of subject catches me off guard, and I falter a little as I try to get my shoulders set under the bar. "Tripp? He was introduced to me as the best friend. Why?"

"He kept looking at me. Seemed a little weird since I thought they were boyfriends, but if they aren't together it's..." His eyes dart briefly around the room before locking on the weight bar as if to say *you're up*. "Well, I guess it's not disrespectful to Xander."

On the surface it seems like Noah's just showing concern for Coach's kid, but I don't know him well enough to assume that's his intent, so mention of Xander and the word *boyfriend* in the same sentence has me on edge. "You have a thing for Coach's kid?"

I regret the question as soon as it's out of my mouth, but my jealous side reared up before I could stop it.

Noah's brows draw together. "Fuck no. I like my starting position. But Xander hasn't brought anyone to the cookout in the three years I've been here, so I was curious. Especially since his friend seemed...distracted by the players." He runs a hand through his hair with another quick glance around the room. "Free weights next?"

Racking the bar, which conveniently camouflages my sigh of relief, I grin at Noah. "I'm pretty sure his friend's goal was to get as close to the players as he could. And if I'm reading him right, Xander seemed more amused about playing babysitter than jealous."

"You talked to him quite a bit then?" He starts wiping down the machine for the next group.

I have the eerie sense that I need to watch what I say, and keep my comments strictly limited to what Coach already knows. "Not really. But when I came here for that practice week, I ended up sitting next to him when I grabbed dinner one night, so the cookout wasn't the first time we met. Or, it was the first time we met, but not the first time I talked to him. Why?" I remove the last of the plates from the bar to avoid looking at Noah and giving anything away.

"No reason. I see Coach's wife around but not Xander so much, and when I have seen him, he's usually alone. I mean, if I had access to a suite at the arena, I'd be there every game. With a whole crew of people. If I wasn't playing, obviously."

"I didn't get the impression Xander's much of a sports guy," I say lamely, though now I have to wonder if that's all it is.

Seeing as how the dark and mysterious vibe is what first drew me to Xander, I was more focused on how my body reacted to that than what made him that way. Now that I'm seeing him through Noah's perspective, I realize it might not be just a look. Xander isn't exactly an open book, and people don't get that way for no reason, right? I wonder what happened to turn him into the brooding guy he is today.

"Makes sense." Noah's comment jolts me back to the conversation. "His friend didn't strike me as a sports guy."

"What makes you say that?"

"The Queen t-shirt he was wearing."

"You remember what he was wearing?" I don't remember what boxers I have on, much less what people were wearing yesterday. Well, unless you count Xander, who I know was wearing black jeans, chucks, and a vintage short-sleeve button down with a Budweiser logo that looked like a trucker's uniform. The top two buttons of that shirt were open, giving just a slight glimpse of his lean, smooth pecs. *So hot!*

"I said Queen, right? One of the greatest bands ever."

"Aren't you a little young to be a Queen fan? I know they have a song that's popular at sporting events, but I think they're categorized as classic rock, and that's the type of music that's even older than my parents. Yours too probably." Insulting a guy's music taste, or age, probably isn't the best move, but daydreaming about Coach's kid in front of a teammate has to be worse.

"Good music is timeless. Plus, that movie about the band was pretty epic."

"Okay, so if you're an athlete and a Queen fan, how come Tripp can't be, too?"

"Never said he couldn't be, just that it wasn't likely." He moves to the free weights and grabs one in each hand to start doing lunges. "You a music fan?"

Yes, please change the subject away from Xander and his friend before I say something I shouldn't.

"I mean, I like music. I've never been much of a concert guy though." I grab a set of weights and start lunging.

"Why not?"

Switching the weights in my hand for a heavier pair I lift a casual shoulder. "No reason. Just never had the opportunity I guess."

"There's a decent local band playing this weekend. We should get some guys together and go while we've got a little free time."

"You've got an extra ticket?"

"Who needs tickets? Perks of being a Colorado Bulldog." He nudges me with an elbow.

"Sure, why not." Maybe some good music and a night out with my teammates will help get a certain brown-eyed guy out of my head.

Chapter 8
Xander

"You seriously don't plan to use any of this footage?" I ask when Tripp says it's okay if the lighting isn't ideal since he's not going to keep what he records.

I'm not complaining—I get to see a lot of free shows by tagging along with Tripp for his musical side gig—I just don't get why you'd record something without perfect lighting.

"The band wants an animated version of a live concert so I'm going to record some clips of them playing that I'll use to recreate their avatars."

"That might actually be hot." Animation has progressed so much, sometimes it almost looks real, and when you take an already attractive guy and make his jaw a little more pronounced, his torso a little more sculpted, the end result is usually pretty spectacular. If you give that guy a guitar and have his muscles flex as he plays, or his hair flop over his eye as he's concentrating on the chords...damn.

Some people think it's a travesty to use characters instead of real people for images and videos because it sets an unreal standard. But the artist in me appreciates that a cartoon can be made to look sexy. I might have even doodled such an image of Niko, though in his case I can't claim the animated version surpasses reality.

"That's the idea," Tripp says as he angles the lens where he wants it. "Hey, can you grab us some drinks before the show starts. I want to touch base with the band real quick to make sure the set list is still the same."

"Why does that matter?"

"Some of the songs they like to get up near the front of the stage and interact with the audience. I want to be on the floor for those to capture the right angle."

"Alright. You want your usual?"

"Of course."

Weaving my way out of our box seats—perks of being with the band—I head to the bar in the VIP lounge. There's still a line, but it's minimal compared to the general admission crowd, so it only takes a few minutes to get close enough to order a few Beam and Cokes.

As I wait for the drinks, I watch the crowd. There's a mix of ages and styles, and I make a little game of trying to guess peoples' ages and professions based on their drinks. It's not as easy as it sounds. Growing up, I remember the men drinking amber liquid, whiskey or scotch, while the women had white wine. Now it's bougie to drink things like Old Fashioneds. As I'm trying to place a preppy-looking woman with a craft beer I get a whiff of crisp, clean air that absolutely shouldn't be present in a concert hall.

It's sort of like...

Spinning to my left, a pair of searing blue eyes meet mine, and my stomach does a little flip as I register the heat in them.

"I thought I recognized that ass." Niko's deep voice rumbles, just loud enough for only me to hear.

Do not make him think you're happy to see him. "You're stalking me?"

"I tried that, unsuccessfully by the way, but fortunately you keep saving me the trouble."

I drop a bill on the counter as my drinks are delivered, keeping my eyes on the bartender instead of the temptation next to me. "What do you mean you tried?"

He rests an elbow on the bar and hits me with those sexy dimples. "I may have popped by that barbeque restaurant one or two or ten times just to see if you were there."

"No wonder you suck at stalking. If the target knows where you'll look for them, they'll avoid it."

"You didn't know where I was looking until just now."

"And now I know where I shouldn't eat again. You're not hoping I'll buy you a drink, are you? I know better than to contribute to the delinquency of a minor."

"No need." He flashes those dimples to the clearly smitten bartender as she sets a beer in front of him and takes his cash. I arch an eyebrow in his direction, and as the bass from the opening band's final song reverberates through the room, he leans close enough to whisper in my ear. "I haven't been carded in years."

Damn that's a sexy voice.

"I guess it pays to be a famous hockey player, huh?"

He rubs the bridge of his nose with his finger. "In this case, I think it's more to do with being six-four and two-hundred twenty pounds."

My brow wrinkles as I try to connect the dots.

"I've been this tall since I was fifteen. It made me pretty popular and earned me a frequent customer discount at the liquor store since I was always in charge of buying drinks for house parties."

I allow myself to give him a subtle once over, though I keep my lips pressed together so he doesn't know I appreciate the view. "I didn't peg you as the rebellious type."

Niko accepts his change from the bartender and pockets it with a casual shrug. "In Sweden we can drink at eighteen, so... Who's the other drink for?" He nods his head toward the two sitting on the bar in front of me.

"Tripp."

"Cool. I'm here with some of the guys. We'll join you."

"I didn't invite you to."

"That's why I invited myself."

Keeping my expression blank, I try another angle. "Didn't we talk about how you need to focus on hockey?"

"I *am* here with my teammates. And now I'm talking to another friend."

"Is that what you want us to be?"

"No." A single word has never made my chest feel so hollow, and despite my best effort not to, I swallow thickly. Then, under the guise of trying to be heard over the music, he leans close enough to growl in my ear. "I want more."

His fresh mountain scent floods my nostrils as he pulls away and sips his beer with a satisfied grin.

"Think what you'd be risking." I grab a couple cocktail napkins just to give my hands something to do.

"Right now, the only thing I'm risking is getting shot down."

"The guy I went home with a few months ago knows better than to believe that. It's why he's still in the closet."

"That guy also kept his sexuality a secret from his roommates for several years, so he knows how to navigate...*friendships*."

"I'm exposure you don't need. And you're a headache I don't want." Both are true, though the longer I'm in his presence the harder that is to remember.

"Yesterday, I might've believed that."

"And today?" I sip my drink, feigning boredom.

His cobalt blue eyes hold mine. "Today I ran into you. Again."

"So?"

"So, I figure there's no point in fighting the inevitable." Glancing over my shoulder, he places a bright smile on his face. "Justus, look who I ran into. Xander invited us to join him."

Dammit, there's no way to make my exit now.

Justus holds his hand out. "Hey, nice to see you again, man."

I clasp it while Niko signals to their remaining teammates, who seem to nod in agreement with his unspoken suggestion. Then he faces me with a smug grin. "Lead the way."

Drinks in hand I head toward our seats, half hoping I lose the guys in the throng of people. Even though I'm not pushing six-and-a-half feet, my six-one frame is too big to fade into the crowd, and they flank me as I make it back to our seats. Tripp's eyes double in size before they land on one of the guys to my left–Noah, the goalie, I'm assuming since a Thor lookalike is just his type–and a sly grin spreads across his face.

"You really brought the drinks." He takes a glass from my hand, letting his gaze wander slowly over each of the guys before finding the one who caught his sight earlier. "Who do we have here?"

"Justus, Luca, and Noah." Niko points to them each in turn. "Guys, this is Tripp." He nods toward my friend. "You probably saw him at Coach's cookout."

"Yeah, I remember," Noah seems to speak for all of them, who merely nod.

"Well, don't just stand there. Grab some seats." Tripp pulls out the chair next to him with an arched brow toward Noah. The big man takes a seat and asks about the camera he's holding while the rest of the group pulls up chairs. Soon, I'm surrounded by obscenely large men, packed so close we're all brushing arms and legs in an effort to squeeze around one tiny table.

I feel nothing where I'm pressed against Tripp's leg, just the vague pressure of another limb next to mine. Being pressed against Niko's is another story.

There's a hum of energy that crackles up the length of my thigh as if every atom of my being is vibrating, excited by his nearness. The slightest shift causes them to riot, so I sit as still as possible to minimize the friction between us. Somehow, the stillness only magnifies the intensity of the connection.

"You coming to the first game?" Luca asks me, predictably. None of these guys ever talk to me about anything besides hockey, and while part of me knows my aloof attitude contributes to that, part of me resents that they assume I'm interested. Only Niko has ever talked to me about something besides the game, and only because he didn't know my father. Still, I answer like I was raised to.

"I'm not sure which games I'll make this season."

"The one against L.A. should be good. Jersey, too. Hey that reminds me," he faces Justus, "didn't their new coach used to work with your AHL team?"

The two of them start talking game strategy, leaving me with the option of joining Tripp's conversation with Noah about the camera, or talking to Niko. Great.

"So, you come here often?" Niko's leg nudges mine under the table.

"That's your best line?"

"Nah, I'm being serious. I'm new here. I don't know where to go or what to do. Is this the spot to hang out?"

"If you like music it's not bad."

"What if I like a guy who likes music?" With his head angled slightly toward mine, I'm the only one who can see the bashful smile on his lips.

"Tripp does come here a lot," I retort, earning a subtle eye roll.

"What's he doing?" Niko tilts his chin to where Tripp seems to be giving Noah a lesson on the camera. Knowing Tripp, he's drooling internally over his proximity to the big guy, but outwardly he's his normal, confident self. Even though that can be a lot to handle, and probably involves more *accidental* contact than necessary, Noah doesn't seem put off by it. He actually seems pretty fascinated by the lesson he's getting.

"He's making a music video. We're here so he can get footage of the band."

"I thought that stuff happened in a studio, or a soundstage. Is that the right word?"

"It depends what kind of video you want. These guys want something that looks like a live concert, so here we are."

"This is what you do for a living? Make videos?"

"Music is Tripp's thing, but yeah. I make videos."

"What kind?"

"Whatever people pay me for."

Niko's brows draw together when he realizes I'm not going to elaborate, but before he can say anything the lights dim and the band comes on stage. The volume of the music makes it all but impossible to talk. Fine by me. We can't become friends—much less *more* than friends—if he doesn't know anything personal about me. Or, more than he already does.

Feigning an intense interest in the band, I keep my eyes glued to the stage while the guys to my left spout hockey nonsense and the guys to my right talk music. Apparently, Noah has a similar passion for it, and when Tripp gets up to go film his close-ups, he takes his new friend with him.

For a brief moment I feel a pang of jealousy that they can just...be. Two people with a common interest, two friends hanging out—Tripp may have a massive crush on the big guy that I assume Noah isn't oblivious to, but since they both know it won't go anywhere it seems to be a non-issue.

I don't have that luxury with Niko. Even though it was only one night, it's still a past, which makes any future association a risk. Not to mention Niko's actually gay, so being friends with an openly gay guy is a bigger gamble for him than the rest of his teammates, who have a track record of hooking up with women to downplay any potential rumors.

Being close to me, even under the guise of being friends, is a bad idea. Not just for his career, but for my sanity. I need another drink.

Chapter 9
Niko

He's adorably tipsy.

I know that's my fault. Every time I breathe he tenses. I thought a few drinks would ease his nerves a bit. However, it's obvious Xander's focusing on the small straw in his glass to avoid talking to me. He's smiling far too hard, a permanent glow on his cheeks, and keeps sending sultry glances my way.

As much as I like him looking at me, it won't be long before someone else notices it. On the surface that doesn't matter—two guys can be friends, even if one of them is gay—without raising too much attention. But I'm in this weird place where I want more without having to come out, and he's professed that he doesn't want anything committed, which means one or both of us needs to get out of here before something happens we can't take back.

As Tripp and Noah make their way back to the table during intermission, I tug Tripp aside. "Is he..." I tilt my head toward Xander.

Tripp follows my gaze, his eyes growing wide when they land on Xander, who's got an uncharacteristically content look on his face. "Overindulging is my thing, not his. What did you give him?" He accuses me.

"Nothing." I hold up my hands like I'm innocent.

"He's not scowling."

"That's why I'm asking."

Glancing at his watch, Tripp curses. "Fuck. I guess I can make do with the footage I already have."

"Would he want that?" I ask.

"What choice do I have?"

"I can get him home."

Tripp studies me with a mix of skepticism and...mischief. *Fuck*.

"Do you need me to tell you where he lives?" I pull up the maps app on my phone and thrust it out to him, which earns me a cocked brow. He chews on his lip a second, which under different circumstances I might find kind of hot since he's got this near ethereal beauty that he downplays with grungy clothes. But like I told Xander, dark and brooding is my weakness. "So you haven't been to his place. Interesting."

"Can you just..." I trail off, spinning my finger in the air to tell him to hurry the fuck up.

"Jesus. I'm going. No wonder why he likes you. You're bossy as hell." Tripp snatches the phone and begins typing at lightning speed. "I'm trusting you. Let me down, you'll have me to answer to. Got it?" Satisfied with my nod, he gives my phone back and I have to fight the smile pulling at my lips. "I put my number in there. Call me if you have any issues."

Tripp tells Xander the plan, who predictably protests that he's not that drunk. They argue back-and-forth until Tripp gets a triumphant smirk on his face and Xander sends me a wary glance. I get it, but he brought this on himself, and no way am I going to pass up this opportunity. I'm not going to take advantage of the guy, but I'm not above seizing every second we can be alone together.

Saying goodbye to the group, which earns me the title of brown-noser—whatever the fuck that means—I help Xander to his feet and guide him to the exit. He doesn't stumble as we make our way to the door. Even slightly drunk, he has this stoic grace about him when he moves, though his eyes appear a little glassy, and he has trouble fishing his keys out of his pockets. That might be the skinny jeans that make it hard not to ogle his ass.

"Here." He dangles them in front of me when we get outside. "You have to drive."

"I can't."

"How are you my DD if you're drunk too?"

"I don't know what a DD is, and I'm not drunk. I can't drive because I don't have a license."

"Designated driver," he huffs as I search for an Uber. "Don't you have those in Sweden?"

"Why would you need one when we have a kick ass public transit system?" *Dammit, I closed the map app and now I don't know where to take him.*

"You don't live in Sweden, and public transit sucks here. You need a car. And don't tell me you can't afford one. I know the starting salary for the NHL." I fight the urge to chuckle when I see his trademark scowl return.

"I'm not gonna buy something I don't know how to use."

"They have...classes and stuff."

"Like I have time for that. Uber works just fine." *Mostly. When you know where you're going.* "Where do you live?"

"I'm not telling you that. You tried to stalk me at the restaurant, no way I'm giving you my address."

Shit, he's got a decent memory for a drunk guy. I could call Tripp, but I'm actually a little surprised Xander hasn't called his own Uber and ditched me. Fuck it, I'll take him to my place.

"Sure, Uber's great if you want a record of where and when you visit your *friends.*"

My eyes snap to his, looking for signs that will clarify his meaning. Either he wants to be my *friend*, or he's criticizing me. His signature scowl says one thing but the unwavering gaze that does a slow perusal of my body says another.

"You going to teach me to drive, *Alexander*?" I show him the dimples he seems to love as his name rolls off my tongue.I swear the man shivers.

"Do you want me to, *Nikolas*?"

Oh shit.

His gaze falls to my mouth as I lick my lips, but before I can respond a car pulls up to the curb. Checking my phone, I confirm it's the Uber and open the door so he can get in.

Xander slides to the far side, but the car is compact and we're both pretty tall, so no matter how close to the window he gets our legs still touch, just like they did at the bar. Only now they rub against each other with each turn, which makes him hold his breath throughout the ride. *Yeah, I feel it, too.*

Fifteen minutes later we're at my team-owned condo, and Xander is wearing his customary scowl. *I guess the alcohol's wearing off.*

"What are we doing here? I thought you were taking me home," he protests even as he follows me up the front walk.

"That was the plan until I accidentally closed the maps app, and since you won't give me your address, here we are. That is, unless you'd like to tell me where to go? I suppose I could call Tripp and get the address again."

"No... I..." A growl rubles in his throat as I watch a roller coaster of emotions race across his face. Finally, he settles into the glare that's starting to become more of a turn-on by the second. "You've graduated from a stalker to a kidnapper. I just want you to know that."

"You're saying hero wrong." I unlock the door and hold it open for him to enter, though my large frame means he can't do that without brushing his arm against my chest. It's slightly—okay, fully devious—but I'm hoping it brings playful Xander back.

"How are you the hero when this is all your fault?" He flops onto the couch.

"What's my fault?" I take a seat at the other end.

"This." He sweeps his arm around the room. "Me being here. Me drinking too much."

"I didn't pour those drinks down your throat. If I was going to force you to swallow something, I can promise it wouldn't have been alcohol."

He scoffs. "You said you wanted to be more than friends."

"I do."

"You realize that being your *friend* doesn't translate into me being your dirty little secret, right? I'm out and proud of who I am. I won't shove myself back into a closet because you can't say the same."

My mouth opens in protest although no words come out.

"Typical," Xander mutters as his head falls to the back of the couch.

"What's that supposed to mean?" A cool shiver races through my body as my adrenaline starts to spike.

"It means you're exactly who I thought you were. We had a good night a few months back, we should leave it at that."

"How, when we keep seeing each other everywhere? Doesn't that imply there's more here?"

"You're a *sign guy* now?" He rolls his head to the side so I can see his brows draw together.

"Maybe." I clamp my jaw shut.

"Well, I am too, and all signs in the universe are pointing to you being the egotistical jock who wants to fuck me when it's convenient and pretend I don't exist when it isn't."

My fists are flexed so tight my fingers ache, and the bullshit thing about that is I can't lash out at him for pissing me off because it's true.

"Fuck!" I grip my hair and give it a firm tug, hoping the pain will relieve some of my anger. All it does is make me hate myself a little. "That's not what I want, but you're not wrong either. What am I supposed to do?"

"Make a choice," he sighs heavily.

"How? The pull I feel toward you is just as strong as the one I feel toward my career."

For the first time all night he seems to soften. "You barely know me."

"Yeah, but I know *me*. I've never felt so comfortable around another person, and not just in bed. I didn't hold anything back with you. Not my nerdy comic fan side or my love of sports. Not my desires. I have no idea why since you're moody as fuck but for some reason I feel like myself around you. I don't know how to ignore that."

Xander's brown eyes appear bottomless on an average day, but right now the quiet calm in their depths seems almost agonizing. "I get it. But we have to."

"You get it? What do you get?"

Closing his eyes, he drags a hand over his face. "You think I don't feel the same way? I forgot how to smile years ago, and when I'm with you it's all I want to do. You're so fucking *happy* it's contagious, and usually people who act like rays of sunshine piss me off. Yet, look at you. I can't stay angry when you look at me like that."

"So, what's the problem then? If we like being around each other, why should we stay away?"

He lifts his head so he can look me in the face. "I don't want to be your secret. "

"I don't want you to be. Not forever. Look," I exhale, hoping my comments don't scare him off. "I haven't made any public declarations about my sexuality because I didn't have a reason to. It doesn't mean that won't change. I just don't want to announce it and have my teammates look at me differently until I have something—someone—real, and committed, to do that for."

That's way more than I meant to confess, but I feel pretty proud of myself for doing it. I mean, I've never had to confess my feelings, much less had any feelings to confess, and I think I nailed it. Until I see Xander slowly shaking his head.

"I've heard that before."

"What?" A sharp pain ripples through my chest like a lightning bolt.

"When I was seventeen, I hooked up with a football player. I was out, he wasn't. I understood why. I grew up surrounded by sports and I knew being gay in the locker room isn't widely accepted. I didn't care that he wasn't out, or that we had to sneak around. I was happy to do it because I thought I loved him, and he said one day we wouldn't have to hide. I told him I'd wait forever. Then he left for college, on a football scholarship of course, and ghosted me. Never answered a single call or text."

"I'm sorry. I can't imagine—"

"You're right. You can't," he interrupts me. "You've never experienced it. If you had, you wouldn't be asking me to go through it again. I spent months waiting for him to respond, only to wonder what was wrong with me, or what I could've done to make him pull away. You'd think the unexplained silence would be deafening, but it's not. It's a throbbing, relentless echo that tears up over and over again. All it does is remind you how worthless you are..."

His gaze turns away from me, locking to where his fingers wring together. "Someone who was supposed to have been in love with me washed their hands of my existence, because they couldn't overcome the scrutiny and culture of the sports industry. So, forgive me for not falling for the 'I'll come out one day' line again. If it was a different world, maybe I'd be open to it, but having grown up in it as a gay man... I know how hard it is. I'm not blaming you, either. I just don't want to go through it again."

The force of his words is like a slap across the face, a searing pain that recedes to a dull ache, but doesn't go away. Only this pain lingers in my chest, throbbing in time with the beat of my heart as I realize my words added to the misery he must feel in his.

No wonder he's trying so hard to push me away.

And until I come out, that's what he'll be. Out of reach. I understand that now.

Unfortunately, I don't know how to change that. Not yet. Would I come out while still in the NHL for the right guy? Yeah, I think I would. Could Xander be that guy? The part of me that isn't afraid to dream big says yes. The part of me that's on the cusp of achieving his lifelong goal says it's too soon to tell. And given how much the memory clearly hurts him, I'm not sure Xander will wait around while I work through this.

"That's the thing that made you forget how to smile." I piece everything together.

"One of them." He picks at a thread on this shirt, signaling the topic is closed. Too bad for him I've been taught never to give up.

"What are the others?"

"Not your concern."

I venture a guess anyway. "I'm not like your football player."

"How are you different?"

"That's not something I can just tell you. You have to see it for yourself, if you'll give me the chance." I'm making this up as I go, and I get that on the surface my situation doesn't set me apart from the guy who hurt him. But even though the circumstances are similar, I'd handle them differently. Regardless of what happens between us, I'd never ghost someone. I just have to figure out how to prove that, if he'll let me.

"I hope you aren't planning to whip your dick out because that would make you exactly like him."

I bite back a wry smile. "Okay, I see how I walked into that one, but I promise that's not what I meant."

"Then what did you mean? How can you show me you're different if you can't be seen with me?"

"I have no problem being seen with you. I'm still working through the whole 'will dating you tank my career since your dad is my coach' thing, but I'm not going to pretend we aren't friends."

The corner of his lip seems to lift, making me think I've won him over. Then the grim look returns to his face. "We can't be friends when you want more."

"We both do, don't even pretend otherwise, but it's also very clear that neither of us is ready to be more yet. Fair?"

He holds my gaze for a bit before giving me a curt nod. "Fair."

"So, let's try the friend thing first."

"How?"

"Well, for starters, you need a place to sleep for the night, so let's get some rest. We'll figure it out from there." I hold my hand out to help him stand.

He stares at it without moving. "Ever slept in the same bed as someone? Actually slept. No sex."

"No. That doesn't mean I can't do it though."

"I can just take the couch."

"Neither of us is gonna fit on that thing." I dismiss it with a wave of my hand and head toward the bedroom, assuming he'll follow, and taking a relieved breath when I hear his footsteps behind me. "The bed is plenty big, and I'll even sleep in my shorts if it makes you feel better. Want some water or an aspirin?"

"I'm not that drunk."

"Okay." I stop at my dresser and pull out an extra pair of sweats. "Want these?"

His shoulders droop as he sighs, whether from exhaustion or defeat I'm not sure. "It's too hot for those."

"Yeah, it is sorta warm in here." I turn on the ceiling fan, stopping cold when I turn back around and find Xander stripping down to his boxers. *The body on that man is... Damn.*

He pauses with his pants halfway down his legs. "You said you could do this."

"I can." I swallow when I make out the bulge in his shorts. "I just might need a minute in the bathroom first."

"You and me both," he mumbles as my own shirt comes off.

This is gonna be a long night.

Chapter 10
Xander

A low moan pierces my consciousness, though not enough to wake me completely. Instead, it lulls me to that place in between sleeping and waking, where your body and mind aren't fully in sync. That's fine by me since the firm pressure rubbing against my cock feels divine, and I want to feel it a little longer.

I rock my hips to feel it again, loving the way the friction makes my balls tingle. Back and forth, long and slow, this is heaven right here. This ass, rubbing all over my... Wait. What ass?

Cracking an eye open, I realize I'm snug against a naked back, one leg draped over...someone else's. And that someone else is jerking off.

"What the hell?" I pull back and glare at the man whose ass I suspect I'd been dreaming about.

"I swear it's not what it looks like." His hand stills on his length.

"You expect me to believe that? Your dick is in your hand."

"Only because you've been rubbing yours against me for the last twenty minutes and I couldn't take it anymore."

"There's an easy fix for that. Get out of bed."

"I tried. You threw your arm around my neck and started griding all slow and sensual, and fuck that was hot, so I figured I'd just let you do it. About ten minutes in I couldn't hold back anymore, so..." His hand flexes around his cock.

"We're supposed to be platonic friends." I groan.

"Yeah, well, tell that to your dick. How do you expect me not to react when *that's* rubbing on me." He jerks his head toward my lap.

Up until he pointed it out, I'd managed to ignore the fact that my cock is painfully hard. Now, it's all I can think about.

Gripping it over my shorts I grit, "Bathroom. You first."

"Not gonna make it." Niko starts stroking again, brushing a bead of precum off the tip with his thumb.

"Let go of your cock and get out of bed."

"Can't. Feels too good." He flicks his wrist as he moves from root to tip, not even trying to be discreet, and my body starts to tremble with the desire to feel what he's feeling.

"Jesus." I struggle against the covers, trying to extricate myself from their grip. But I'm hopelessly tangled, and the rhythmic motion of Niko's arm bringing him to the brink is impossible to tune out. "Fuck it."

Fisting my own cock, I set a pace to match his, and even though it's my familiar hand doing the work, it somehow feels like he's holding me. Moving with me. Coaxing my pleasure to the surface.

I've never jerked off in front of another guy. A playful little tug to show off or build anticipation...sure. But actively trying to make myself come while someone else watches, the two of us mirroring each other's movements as we both strain for the finish? Nope. And right now, I'm wondering why.

Yeah, we're supposed to be just friends. And yeah, this is breaking a major rule I have about guys who are still in the closet. Yet all this pent up desire, being on the cusp of release alongside a guy who isn't even touching me... I sort of don't give a shit about my rules.

The sound of his fist hitting his pelvis and the groans rumbling from his throat have me teetering on the edge, visions of our night together coupled with the show he's putting on now flashing through my mind like my own private porno. And when he goes rigid with a guttural moan I follow, the two of us panting heavily as we coat our chests in cum.

That was... Holy shit that was...

"Maybe we say the friend thing starts right now instead of last night." He wipes his chest with a t-shirt before passing it to me.

"Deal."

"So, friend, do you drink coffee?"

"What?" I hand the shirt back, trying not to notice the powerful stride as he crosses the room to drop it in the hamper.

"Coffee, Alexander. Do you want some?"

A warm shiver courses through my body as he speaks my name. I rarely hear it in full, Xander became the norm so my father and I didn't both answer to Alex, and until just now, I didn't realize I like it.

"Yeah. Sure."

Niko pulls on a pair of gray sweats—we'll have to talk about how that's *not* friendly attire—and heads off, leaving me to get dressed in private. Predictably, the quiet has me overthinking.

Though the situation is eerily similar, there are definite differences between Niko and my ex. Rather than dismissing my concerns or trying to distract me from them with sex, Niko basically asked for the chance to prove himself. I'm not sure what that will look like since he still isn't ready to come out, but being seen with me, an openly gay man, is a start. Even if that's just in a friendly capacity.

It's not enough, yet it's more than I was expecting, so from that perspective things are already different.

Then there's that confession. The one about feeling like himself around me and only me. Though I wanted to believe that was true with my ex, he never explicitly said that. Niko did, and he didn't try to use it as a way to sway me. He admitted to not understanding what that meant or why it was happening, and I can respect the honesty in that statement.

Too bad none of that means he won't pick the easy road in the end.

If anyone can understand his predicament, it's me. Part of the reason I backed away from team sports is because I knew that "team" was supposed to extend beyond the field, and that wouldn't apply to me. Not even my famous father would be able to make kids accept me for me, and the idea of living a lie sounded exhausting. But I was never going to go pro. Not even with my dad's expertise to guide me. Coming out was an easy choice.

Niko's at the start of what could be a brilliant career, but he's still a rookie, and rookies have to prove themselves. Not only will he have to work harder than he's ever done before, he'll have to behave like a saint off the ice, or at least appear that way.

It's not unheard of for young guys to come into the league and go overboard with the partying and the spending, living the lifestyle they think they've earned. Unless your talent makes that headache worth it, most teams don't have time for such bullshit. So, guys who want a career instead of a season should try to avoid getting on the coach's radar for the wrong reasons. An "unconventional" sex life is a quick way to end up on the wrong list.

I should have told him that. I should have put a stop to this whole charade before we actually try being friends, because I can't help feeling it will end in disaster. The damn happy idiot makes it hard not to have hope though. Hope in the league, hope in his teammates, hope in him.

Guess I have a new friend.

I find him in the kitchen, pouring two steaming mugs of coffee. In nothing but his sexy sweatpants, damn him.

"I hope you aren't a milk or sugar guy, cause I don't have any of that." He pushes a mug toward me.

"Black is fine." I bring the cup to my lips and take a small sip, doing my best to choke it down without actually choking.

"Too strong?" His dimples frame the mug as he takes his own sip.

"Now I know why you're so fast on the ice. Jesus, that's like rocket fuel."

"You know how fast I skate?"

Shit. Busted. "I may have googled your stats after the barbeque at my folks."

"Because you wanted to see more of me?"

"Because I wanted to know if you really got drafted after two years in college or you were just trying to make me think you were older than eighteen." Although I did verify that fact, I was primarily interested in what the pundits were saying about his potential. If he wasn't projected to be a standout maybe he'd have a short career, in which case... It doesn't matter. He's projected to have a great career. "So, nuclear coffee is your secret?"

Niko chews on his lip, giving me the impression he wants to stay on the topic of my cyberstalking. When he sets his mug on the counter, I know he's talked himself out of it.

"It's strong but it's also smooth, and it has more flavor than the shit they sell here. Take another sip."

I do as he asks, letting the liquid roll over my tongue. Once you get past the initial surge of flavor, it settles into something almost sweet. Like chocolate. There might even be a hint of fruit. It's not at all bitter like I'm used to, though that first taste is so overwhelmingly strong it's hard to find the flavor in it.

"Okay, I see what you're saying. Where'd it come from, if not here?"

"Sweden. My parents send me some every month. Sleeping at my house comes with extra perks." He winks at me.

"So far, this friendship consists of you jerking off in front of me and bribing me to sleep over, and we've only been friends for," I check my watch, "twenty minutes. Am I going to have to constantly remind you friends don't fuck?"

"I've never been friends with someone I wanted to fuck, so...probably."

Dammit why does he have to be so cute?

"What's your address?" I change the subject, pulling my phone from my pocket to open my contacts. "I need to get an Uber back to my car."

"Uh, uh. No address until I get your phone number." He smiles triumphantly around a mouthful of coffee.

"Didn't Tripp already give you my information?"

Niko rubs the bridge of his nose. "Your address, which I lost while I was trying to copy it in the Uber app, so no."

"Typical jock." I can't stop the corner of my lip from ticking up as I shake my head.

"Don't avoid the subject," he barks. "Phone number, or you're walking. And stop pretending you don't like jocks."

"I don't."

"You like me."

"I tolerate you." I drink my coffee to disguise what I'm pretty sure is a grin.

"You *tolerate* hockey. You like me. That smile you're trying to hide says so." He crosses his arms in front of his broad chest with a proud smirk.

I look at him from under hooded eyes. "Still not fucking you, Nikolas." *Flirting yes, fucking no.*

"*Yet...* Alexander." His blue eyes seem to promise there's a distinction.

Jesus he's going to give me a semi.

"Address." I tap the screen of my cell.

"Phone number."

"Address first."

"Same time." He slides his phone toward me and picks mine up, arching a sly brow as he waits for me to meet his challenge.

"Fine." We each tap at the screens, entering the information, and the moment my phone is back in my hand it starts to vibrate.

"Just checking." He flashes me those coy dimples.

My eyes travel to the back of my head as I pull up my Uber app and request a ride.

"So, when's our first lesson?" His perfectly timed question makes me gag on the coffee again.

"What lesson?"

"Driving. You're gonna help me get my license."

"I... Why would I do that?"

"So there's no record of where or when I visit my *friends*." He puts the last word in air quotes, making it impossible not to notice how the muscles—everywhere—ripple with that simple gesture.

Am I that big of an idiot? Did I really offer to teach him to drive?

"Don't tell me you're backing out?"

"I... No?"

"Is that a question?" His eyes lift in amusement.

"No. It's just, I don't know the first thing about teaching someone to drive."

"You drive. Just show me what you do."

"I don't even know what I do." My brows pull together as I try to picture how I drive. "It's second nature at this point."

"Then it shouldn't be that hard to teach."

"I'm pretty sure that's not how it works." The phone says my ride is two minutes out, so I take a last sip of coffee and start making my way to the front door.

"I'm pretty sure you're right and I need to learn to drive. Please." He holds his hands together like he's in prayer.

"Fine," I sigh, trying not to crack a grin when he pumps his fist. "How about tomorrow around four? I'll pick you up."

"Deal."

I reach for the door handle, but the big oaf is standing right in the way of where it needs to swing open. "What?" The scowl on my face is real.

"How do friends say goodbye?"

"What?" I repeat.

"Handshakes still seem lame, all things considered, and kisses are..." He scans my face quickly. "Out. Definitely out. So..."

I was ready to just walk out the door, but a sexy jock who's adorkably nervous about saying goodbye—I can linger til he makes up his mind.

"Ass slaps are for jocks, and you don't like those, except for me." He runs a hand through his hair, mussing it even more than it was from the pillow. "Chest bumps are gay. Not you and me gay just...gay. Fist bumps, then?"

"Sure, fist bumps." My phone dings, and I give it a quick glance. "Ride's here."

"Fuck it." He grabs the front of my shirt in his fist and yanks me to him, wrapping his arms around my neck when our chests collide. He only holds me for a second, but it's long enough to feel the tension leave his body. Then he pulls away and touches his knuckles to mine. "See you tomorrow."

Safely out of sight on my way to the car, I give in to the urge to let my lips lift at the corners. *I'm so fucked.*

Chapter 11
Niko

"You're doing what?" Anna asks when I video call her first thing the next morning.

"I'm learning to drive."

"That's so American." She wrinkles her nose.

"Well, I have lived here for six years so it makes sense."

"I guess. I still can't imagine not being able to take the train everywhere."

"I'm kind of looking forward to the freedom of it. I'll be able to go anywhere I want whenever I want. Door to door."

"Don't you do that already? With Uber?"

"Yeah, but then someone else is in the car and you have to talk to them, and sometimes that's fine but sometimes you don't feel like talking." Up until yesterday I never really gave that much thought, but sharing an Uber with Xander, who I couldn't talk to the way I wanted because we weren't alone, I realized how much privacy having my own car would afford. Plus, the whole 'no record of my whereabouts' thing is hard to ignore.

"Hmm. So, who's teaching you to drive?"

"A friend."

"A friend who makes you blush." The dimples that are a mirror image of mine fill the screen. "Tell me more."

Stupid video calls.

"Seriously... He really is just a friend." I swear my pause is brief, but sisters have some sort of mind-reading ability that hears what you don't say even better than what you do. Especially twin sisters who are three minutes older and act like your mother.

I'll never admit it, but I kind of like how she's always fussing over me. It makes me feel close to her despite the distance. Plus, she really is a voice of reason, and even though I don't always take her advice, I know it's given with my best interests in mind.

"You want him to be more, don't you?"

I don't know why I thought I could keep her in the dark until I had more to say.

"Yes, but that's not an option right now. We're doing the friend thing."

"Niko." She shakes her head with a heavy sigh. "How long are you going to do this to yourself?"

"Do what?"

"Deny who you are. You have someone you're interested in but you're not going to pursue it because you're hiding part of you."

"That's not the only reason." I regret saying that even as I hear the words coming out—no chance she'll overlook it—but I'm feeling defensive.

Anna and I have always been close, and she's my biggest supporter, even when it came to me moving to the states for hockey when neither of us wanted to be separated. I think that's why I want her approval so bad, like her being proud of me will make up for leaving. Too bad my mouth gets in front of my head sometimes when I'm trying to prove I'm not a total idiot.

"Is this friend in hiding too?"

"No."

"In that case this sounds like a *you* thing."

"It's more like a me *and* him thing."

Her eyes narrow to little slits as she draws my name out. "Niiiko. Who is he?"

"Remember how you told me to get laid during my trip here a few months ago?"

"I do."

"Well, I took your advice." I paste a smile on my face like she should be happy I followed her orders.

"And?"

"And I hooked up with a super hot guy who likes superheroes and dimples." I point to my face as evidence, as if that'll get me off the hook. "He's sort of a moody smartass but you know I like that, and—"

"Who is he?"

I scrub a hand through my hair. "Okay, remember this whole thing was your idea, and I had no way of knowing—"

"Who is he?"

"Coach Nydek's son."

Catching Anna off guard is a feat, but it's hard to enjoy watching her jaw drop knowing a tongue-lashing will follow. I may hold my own against literal giants on the ice, but I'm no match for my tiny wisp of a sister. She's the only thing I'm truly afraid of.

"Nikolas Karl Scott Sven." She invokes the grandfathers I was named after. "What the hell have you done?"

"You cut me off so maybe you didn't hear the part about me not knowing who he was, but I didn't know who he was."

"You didn't get his name?"

"I don't think that's how one-night stands work."

"Well, if you had, maybe you'd have realized who he was."

She glares at me when I snort. "Even if I had got his name, it's not like it would've made a difference. We didn't talk about our dads."

"How did you find out who he is?"

"He was at the team barbeque last week."

"Oh my God." Now it's her turn to blush. "Did your coach realize—"

"We told him we ran into each other during my first trip out here. As far as he knows we're just two guys who happened to sit next to each other at a bar."

Anna rubs her temples with her fingertips. "So, you screwed a hot guy and now you kind of like him but you're in the closet and he's related to the man who can make or break your entire career?"

"You're forgetting the part where I took your advice," I add helpfully. It only makes her glare harder.

"I'm remembering the part about this guy teaching you to drive. Why would you pick him for that of all people? You've already slept together, and you like him, do you honestly think you can be friends?"

"My ultimate goal is a friends with benefits thing."

She doesn't laugh at my joke. "You do arrangements, Niko. Not friends with benefits. If you're wanting to see this guy beyond just a casual hookup you already like him."

"I said that, didn't I?" Sometimes I wish I didn't tell her *everything*.

"No, actually. I said it and you reluctantly agreed with me. Normally, I'd be excited for you but this... This could be really bad. Falling for your coach's son could tank your career."

"Who said anything about falling?" It's terrifying that she went there, mainly because just yesterday I thought it myself. That's not where I'm at, but I freely admitted I was open to coming out for the right person, and that's not something I thought I'd consider at this point in my career.

Now it's her turn to snort. "You think you can casually hook up with the coach's son and it won't bite you in the ass? No, you either keep your distance or do right by him. Anything less and you're risking your spot on the team more than you already are."

She's right. I know she is. To get to this point, I left my home, giving up years of birthdays and holidays with my family. I've damaged bones, muscles and tendons—hopefully, not permanently—sacrificed sleep, foods I love, and most normal teenage experiences. And as Anna never fails to point out, I've hidden the core of who I am. All for a shot to get to the place I'm at right now.

It'd be the epitome of stupid to throw all that away to be *friends* with someone I just met. And yet, the only line I'm not willing to cross right now is the one keeping me in the closet. Getting to know Xander better, exploring whether there might be more than chemistry between us, those things don't feel like they should be lines.

And if doing the friend thing does lead us to that final destination of something serious, well, I guess I'll have a decision to make. Until then, is it really so wrong to want to see more of a guy that makes me feel like *me*?

"Niko," Anna calls me out for drifting off. "You're not saying I'm right."

"I mean, you're not wrong..." I rub the back of my neck.

"Don't give me a but. There is no but."

"What if there is though?"

"In what universe is there a but?"

"The one where the guy on the expansion team hooks up with his coach's daughter and they pretend to be engaged then get engaged for real." I regurgitate the plot of a book she made me read. "He kept his spot on the team."

Anna throws her hands in the air with a dramatic eye roll. "That was a romance novel, you idiot. Not a biography."

No wonder I couldn't recall the name of the team.

"Seriously, Niko, it's not worth it. Find someone else to teach you to drive and leave the coach's kid alone."

"Okay, yeah. I'll call him to cancel."

***

I totally didn't cancel.

I did think about it, during our morning skate, and again in the weight room, and again during our mid-afternoon scrimmage. And each time I thought about it I felt this hollow void growing in my chest.

That's a new one for me. I mean, I felt sort of empty like that when I left home for the first time. Okay every time. And I felt it when I left my high school teammates and again when I left my college teammates, but I've never felt it when I wasn't making a big life change.

It makes sense to me that I'd feel something like sadness or nostalgia each time I close one chapter of my life to start another. Only that's not what's happening here. I don't know what *is* happening. I only know the idea of not seeing Xander today doesn't sit well with me. So, instead of canceling, I'm halfway out the door by the time he pulls up to the curb.

"What are you doing?" He rolls down the window as I approach his side of the car.

I point to where he's sitting. "I'm trying to get in the car, but you have to move first."

"You get in on the other side."

"There's no steering wheel over there."

"Exactly."

I scratch the bridge of my nose, flashing those dimples he seems to love. "Maybe I'm misunderstanding this whole thing, but I thought you needed that to—you know—*drive*."

"You can't just drive on public streets without a license. Besides, there are too many obstacles on the street. We're going to a remote parking lot where you can't do any damage to my car. Until then, I drive."

It's sort of amusing to see a guy who looks like he doesn't give a shit about rules telling me how to obey them, but instead of teasing him about it like I want to, I walk to the passenger side and get in.

"What kind of car is this anyway?" I buckle myself in and try to make sense of all the images on the dash.

"You don't even have your license and you're already getting pretentious about cars."

"Does pretentious mean doing my homework to make sure I'm picking a good one?" I know it doesn't, but I feel like fucking with him.

He glances sideways before turning his stoic gaze back to the road. "Range Rover."

"Is that good, or...?"

"Depending on who you ask, they're safe, reliable and fun to drive."

"Why do you drive it?"

"It's what my dad bought me when I graduated college."

"And? Is it safe, reliable and fun?"

"How about some music?" He pushes a button on the dash.

I push it a second time, turning it off. "How about we don't start over every time we see each other."

"What does that mean?" He pulls into a big empty lot.

"It means we were having a good time yesterday, so there's no reason for the cold shoulder, Alexander." Using his name makes him shiver, just like it did after the concert, so it's now my secret weapon.

"This isn't the cold shoulder. This is me, dark and brooding. Isn't that your thing?"

"If I was trying to fuck you, yes. But I'm trying to be friends with you."

I lurch forward in the seat as the car comes to an unexpected stop. He puts it in park, and twists to face me. "I didn't think there was a difference with you."

"You asked for the difference, I'm trying to honor that." *Okay that made sense in my head but hearing it out loud it seems off.* "Is that what's happening here? You want me to want you so you're playing the role you know I like?"

"No." He presses his lips together.

"Then what, because dark and brooding I like but you're creeping into asshole territory and I don't know why. Did I do something?"

"No."

"Did I do something, Alexander?"

His dark eyes seem to turn almost black as his lips twitch, his gaze locked on mine. Finally, he looks away and lets his head fall to the headrest, running a hand through his already mussed hair.

"I don't really do...friends."

"What? Why?"

"Friends know things about each other. Things I don't share with people."

I have a sneaking suspicion this might go back to the boyfriend who ghosted him, but the man is sharing right now so instead of bringing that up I stick to the topic at hand. "What about Tripp?"

"Even he's... And I've never fucked him. You might already know me better than he does, and I'm... I don't know how to do this."

"Fuck, is that all?" That earns me another glare, so I rush to continue. "Look, I'm weirded out by this too. I've had teammates, and in some ways they're like brothers, but that's never been like... this. I've never been this honest about who I am with anyone, and that scares the shit out of me. But it's more the newness of it than *you* that scares me. I actually feel pretty comfortable about you, all things considered."

"What the fuck does that mean, all things considered?"

I mirror him, resting my head against the back of the seat, and proceed to stare out the front window. "If I had to make a list of people I should avoid sleeping with or being friends with, knowing I'm attracted to them, my coach's kid would be at the top of it. Even if I were openly gay the two of us are a massive conflict of interest for my career."

"Then why the hell are we doing this?"

"Because now that I know what it's like to be myself with someone besides my sister, I don't want to give that up."

Xander doesn't say anything, but his head does seem to nod slightly as he closes his eyes. I think that means he agrees, or at the very least he's done arguing, but I'm afraid to break the silence before he does in case I'm wrong.

Finally, he turns to me with a somewhat relaxed expression. "Sister?"

"Yeah, my twin. Anna."

That relaxed expression turns wary. "There's two of you?"

"Don't worry, she's not as charming as me."

"Are you close?"

I nod my head, smiling as I think of her. "She's three minutes older but likes to act like my mother. Fortunately, she's easy to ignore since she's in Sweden."

"Why would you ignore her if you're close?"

"She thinks I'm being an idiot right now, hanging out with you." I risk a glance in his direction in time to catch his eyes getting darker.

"Lovely," he mutters.

"Don't worry. It was also her idea for me to go out the first night I met you, so if you think about it, she set all this in motion."

Xander doesn't finish rolling his eyes before catching sight of the dimples I'm deliberately sporting, and I mentally pump my fist when I see his lip fighting a smile.

"What do you know about driving?"

I guess we're back to being friends. Cool.

"I know you push the pedals to go and stop and turn the wheel to point the tires where you want to go."

Xander takes a deep breath, like he's gearing up for battle or something, and gives me a rundown of how the car works. Then we switch seats so I can have a go.

"Remember," he says as I shift the car to drive. "You don't have to stomp on the pedals. In fact, just lifting your foot off the brake will have you moving forward. Try that to get a feel for it."

I take my foot off the brake and the car starts inching forward. Then Xander lurches forward as I press it down again.

"No stomping," he reiterates. I do it again, this time gently pressing the brake, and his body doesn't jolt when we come to a stop.

We do that for several laps around the parking lot before he lets me push the gas. The first time I do, he grabs the dash, and shouts at me not to stomp the pedals.

"Sorry, I couldn't help myself." I grin as I brake, then start over, pressing the gas gently like I'm supposed to.

"When do you turn twenty-one?" Xander asks me as we circle the lot.

"Are you asking when you can legally buy me a drink?"

"No, I'm trying to figure out if you need a learners permit before you can drive on the road."

"And?"

"You can either wait or get a permit."

"I don't think I like either of those options."

He gestures for me to stop so we can switch places, and when I'm back in the passenger seat he starts heading back to my place. "You can take the permit test online, and there are videos you can watch to prepare. If you don't want to wait, I'd do that."

"Will you help me study?"

"I'll drive you to the DMV to get your permit."

"Do I have to wait until then to see you?"

His bottom lip curls under as he chews on it, and coupled with his trademark frown, that does things to me. Let's hope he has trouble resisting our chemistry too, otherwise this *friends* thing is gonna be a lot harder than I first thought.

"Yes," he concludes.

That's disappointing, but I can't say I don't get it. He's being cautious, and the smart thing to do is to follow his lead. "Okay then. I guess I've got some studying to do."

Chapter 12
Xander

The vibration next to my leg startles me before I realize it's just my phone. I hesitate before pulling it from my pocket—I rarely get texts, and never during the middle of a workday—and have to fight the urge to chuckle when I see who it's from.

Niko: Did you know it takes a small car going fifty-five two hundred feet to stop? Two hundred feet! That's the size of a hockey rink.

Xander: Seems excessive.

Niko: IKR! And there's a procedure for how cars are supposed to get around each other if the road isn't wide enough. Why on earth would a two-way road not be wide enough for two cars to pass?

Xander: Mountains are only so wide.

Niko: You mean if I'm driving downhill and I come to a car driving up I have to back up ON THE SIDE OF A MOUNTAIN?

Xander: That's the rule.

Niko: Why doesn't this country have trains again?

Xander: Trains have to share the tracks.

Niko: Yes, but they're scheduled so no two are on the same track at once. None of this backing up bullshit required.

Xander: With great freedom comes great skill at driving backward.

Niko: That's a lame attempt to quote Uncle Ben.

I love that he got my Spiderman reference.

Xander: Still true though.

Niko: I suppose. Still good to drive me to the test?

Xander: When?

Niko: Tomorrow.

Xander: Already? You only started the training five days ago.

Niko: I was motivated to finish quickly.

Xander: What time?

Niko: Three.

Xander: I'll be there.

"Oh. My. God." Tripp props his ass on the corner of my desk. "Hell has frozen over."

"What?"

"You're smiling. I mean, it'd be sort of a grimace on anyone else, but for you it's a smile. Does your face hurt? Using new muscles sometimes has that effect."

"In that case I should be asking whether your jaw is tired." I don't usually stoop to Tripp's level of shameless goading, but the other day he overshared about the biggest cock he'd ever blown, and I need to deflect.

He rolls his eyes. "I deserve more credit than that."

"My mistake. I forgot you have a superhuman ability to deep throat."

"Damn straight." He grins at me. "So, what's got you smiling?"

"What's got you using my desk as a chair?"

Tripp shakes his head with a heavy sigh—a typical gesture when I refuse to open up—and hands me a thumb drive. "I finished the music video and wanted your opinion.

Plugging the drive into my computer, I open the file and hit play. Spotlights sweep across a dark stage, teasing silhouettes of the musicians, before the lights flash on, illuminating them completely. The lead singer, who also plays the guitar, starts a solo riff that goes into

their most popular song. Deft fingers move over the strings in a mesmerizing blur, though it's the muscle detail in his arms and torso that
really draw my eye, and not just because I happen to like guys.

I'm looking at a manufactured image, but that's hard to tell since
Tripp's done such a good job of defining each muscle and highlighting
how they react as the avatar plays. Even the throat muscles expand and
contract seamlessly as he sings, showcasing the angles and planes of a
body in motion.

If it weren't for the fact that the avatar is over-enhanced, by design,
you'd question whether you were looking at a real person. Only the
fact that it's too perfect gives it away, but at the same time it's so perfect
it's hard to believe it isn't real.

"I can't take my eyes off it," I admit.

"You think the band will like it?"

"I'd question their taste if they don't."

Tripp visibly relaxes, making me wonder for a second why I've never
been able to bring myself to confide in him the way he does me. Yeah,
lots of his confessions I don't need to hear, but he also seems to value
my opinion in a way that I've never reciprocated. Why does he even
bother with me? And why do I give Niko, who I barely know, more
access to my thoughts than the guy who's supposed to be my best
friend?

Is it a sex thing? I've been with Niko so there's already a connection
between us that I've never had with Tripp? Or did I convince myself
it was okay to open up with Niko because I believed I'd never see him
again, therefore he couldn't hurt me? I suppose either could be true,
although thinking about how I interact with each of them has me
feeling like an ass for the way I've treated Tripp. I didn't even give
him a chance not to hurt me—I operated under the assumption he
eventually would.

It's on the tip of my tongue—literally—to tell him why I was smiling. To confess what's been going on, maybe even get his opinion on it since the whole friends versus lovers mixed with my dad's presence has me spiraling. For the first time since I've known Tripp I *want* to talk to him, and I can't. Niko's secret won't allow it.

By the time I pick him up for his driving test the next day, I've been stewing about my predicament for way too long, and I'm on edge over it.

"Hey, thanks for picking me up." Niko gives me one of his smiles that's part sincere, part flirty, and all dimples.

"Hmm." I nod my head and pull into the road.

"Jesus," he groans. "Can we ever pick up where we left off, or do I have to start from scratch every time?"

When I don't answer he tries again. "What did I do now?"

"Nothing. Absolutely nothing."

"It's something or you wouldn't be even more moody than usual. What happened?"

"Why did something have to happen?"

"If I didn't do anything then something happened."

Caught between the urge to concede he's right and the need to rant about the position I'm in, I go with rant. "I've been out for years, but because you aren't it's like I'm still in the closet."

"What?" He couldn't sound more shocked if he tried. "Are you seriously implying that hanging out with me is like taking a step backward?"

"Yes."

He runs a hand through the hair that's starting to get a bit longish on top, mouth opening several times before he gets any words out. "I can't come up with any explanation for why you should feel that way."

"I fucking smiled the other day and Tripp saw it, and he wanted to know why. I started to tell him, but I couldn't go through with it because it would mean telling him your secret."

Niko's brow furrows as his blue eyes get smaller. "I thought you didn't do the sharing with friends thing?"

"I decided I want to try."

"Okay. Well, do you trust Tripp?"

"Why?" My gaze finds his just briefly before I turn away, the lack of anger in it too confusing to contemplate.

"I trust you, so if you trust Tripp I do too."

"Just like that?" Another quick glance doesn't reveal a smirk, or a wink, or anything else to suggest he's teasing.

"Well, yeah. I mean, if he betrays you—and in effect, me—I'll have to kick his ass. But I have my sister to talk to, and I know how sane that keeps me, even if she thinks I'm acting like an idiot. If Tripp can be that person for you, I'm okay with it. I really will kick his ass if he makes me regret this though, fair warning."

This time he does end his sentence with a wink, and while that tells me he won't actually beat anyone up, the fact he mentioned it twice tells me his biggest fear is having the choice about what to say and when taken away from him. Both Tripp and I can relate, so that won't be an issue. What's still an issue is the fact we're going through this friend charade when we both want more.

I don't know why I struggle so hard with telling the man no. It's not like he's the first gorgeous guy to share my bed, and it's not like me to let a few mind-blowing orgasms cloud my judgment. Okay, to be fair he gave me the best orgasms I've ever had, but still. I know a few seconds of pleasure isn't worth the lingering heartache that comes with falling for someone who can't or won't reciprocate the way you deserve.

Plus, just stating that we're friends doesn't mean that's where things will stay, and I'm not referring only to the sex thing. If I didn't genuinely like the guy, maybe we could fool around and leave it at that, but like Niko admitted the other day, I feel...content around him in a way I haven't felt with anyone in a long time. I'm not sure I could keep my feelings out of it if this were to get physical again.

Talking to Tripp might help me sort through all these thoughts. Then again, it's Tripp. The man lives to push people's buttons and be as lewd as he can. There's a chance that when I tell him my predicament, he'll say I should drop the whole friend thing and just fuck. Zero contact outside the bedroom and nothing but orgasms in it. And he'd probably ask for a picture of Niko's dick.

Still, he might be better than no one, so at least now I've got that option if I need to vent. Chances are, my inability to say no to Niko will mean I have to use it soon.

"Tripp wouldn't deliberately out anyone, but if I say anything, I'll be sure to reiterate that the stakes are higher in this particular situation."

Niko gives me a brief nod, then shakes his head back and forth with a resigned smile. "He's gonna have a field day with the whole me playing for your dad thing, isn't he?"

"What makes you say that?" It's true. I'm just curious what brought him to that conclusion.

"The team cookout. I got the sense Tripp likes to get as close as he can to pissing your dad off without tipping him over the edge."

"He's crossed the line before, which is why that was his first cookout in three years." I pull into the DMV and guide us into a parking spot.

"Why?"

Turning the car off, I face Niko with a noncommittal shrug. "My dad doesn't object to gay people, but he's not overly comfortable with

Tripp's level of shameless, and he's protective of his players. He doesn't want them to be subject to Tripp's antics if that's outside their comfort zone."

"You make it sound like the guy would strut around naked at the—" Niko catches my wary look and stops mid-sentence. "No shit. He really did that?"

"He didn't take it quite that far, but he had the guys flexing their legs to see if he could wrap his hands all the way around their thighs. When he grabbed one guy's chest under the guise of swatting off a bug my dad lost it."

Niko's dimples are on full display as he tries not to laugh. "It shouldn't be funny, but damn if I can keep a straight face thinking about it."

"You better get in there." I tilt my head toward the DMV. "They aren't exactly known for their flexibility if you miss your appointment."

A crease forms between his brows. "You're not coming?"

"Too many people."

"You were at a concert a few weeks ago. Don't tell me you're afraid of crowds."

"Not crowds. People. As in too many of them to witness us coming and going together if I walk inside with you. Plus, the DMV sucks the light out of your soul."

"Isn't your soul already black?"

"Touché," I chuckle. "I'm still not going in there."

"Oh, come on. I'm not asking you to walk in holding my hand. I mean, I am, but not physically. I don't know what to do in there."

"You hand them your identification cards, take a test, and ideally come out with a piece of paper that says you can drive on the road."

"What are you gonna do then?"

"Skate." I point to the skatepark adjacent to the little strip mall that houses the DMV. "Come grab me when you're done."

Chapter 13
Niko

It's well over an hour later that I finally make it outside and over to the skate park, and what do I find when I get there? A shirtless, sweaty Xander.

He's supposed to be my platonic friend, but as far as I know, there's no rule against ogling him for the spank bank. As long as I don't touch, I should be able to look my fill. Finding a bench underneath a tree, I sit back to enjoy the view.

Like a total creeper, my eyes track him as he moves around the park. Dark hair flapping gently in the breeze, abs glistening in the afternoon sun, Xander seems to float over the ground as the board rolls underneath him. Contrary to his normal look, his face seems relaxed. Happy even. It's kinda cute. Then without warning his eyes narrow, his lips press into a determined line, and he bends his legs to launch the board in the air, flipping and spinning it wildly before it crashes back to Earth with Xander steadily on top of it.

Now that... That was sexy as fuck.

There are at least half a dozen guys out here, coasting effortlessly over the smooth concrete, but none of them are as graceful as my dark angel. And I'm not even ashamed to call him that because it's true.

Xander may be prickly on the outside, but inside he's sensitive. Fragile almost. Yet he's making himself vulnerable to me, so I see the good in him. Not in a Darth Vader way since he's not a villain, but in a loyal do anything for someone in need way, wrapped in a moody, muscley package. A living, breathing fantasy—for me.

If only he wasn't stuck on this whole 'I'm not out' thing.

It's not that I don't empathize with his reasons for keeping me in the friend zone—I do. I can appreciate the challenge of being out and sleeping with someone who isn't, and I realize it's not fair to ask him to hide when that hasn't been his lifestyle for years. But I also feel like it's short-sighted to ignore the pull between us just because we're in two different stages of life, especially since I already admitted I was open to coming out if it makes sense.

I need time to find my place in the league and on this team before I can make any big decisions, and truthfully, it's frustrating that Xander won't give me that. It's even more frustrating that some douche from his past is the reason.

It feels like I'm being labeled as the same kind of jerk his ex was simply because I'm an athlete, and I don't like that assumption. I shouldn't—*we shouldn't*—be denied the chance to explore this because of some guy who isn't even in the equation. I only hope being his friend will get him to come around and see me for me, sooner rather than later, since it's only getting harder to be around him without taking what I know we both want.

It must be twenty minutes or more before Xander spots me, and when he does his mouth curves into a seductive grin—an actual, legitimate grin—as he stomps on the end of the board so that it snaps up and into his hand. *Pretty sure I haven't been this turned on in...ever.*

"Did you pass?" His lean stomach ripples as he walks toward me.

"What?" I force my eyes to his, but not before he guesses where they were. *Busted.*

"The test we came here for. Did you pass?" He drops his board to grab the shirt from the waistband of his shorts.

"Of course." I grin proudly.

"Well, if you don't mind sitting in the car with me while I'm all sweaty, we can do your first drive. Once I get us to a more secluded spot."

I shift uncomfortably on the bench. "I'm pretty sure it wasn't your intent, but my dick heard the words sweaty and secluded in the same breath, and now we're gonna need to hang out here for a few minutes until I can walk straight."

"Jesus, you're as bad as Tripp," he mumbles.

"I did just watch you ride around shirtless looking like some sort of skateboard god. Do you have any idea how hot you look on that thing?"

Xander shrugs his shirt on, robbing me of the incredible view. "Probably as hot as you look on ice skates."

"You've seen me on ice skates?" There's a pull at the corner of my lip, but I fight the urge to put him on the spot with a proud smile.

"I've seen you all skate. My dad has film of everybody." He's looking everywhere but at me as he talks himself into a hole. "If the TV is on at his house, it's playing some game."

"And you expect me to believe you've watched that film? The guy who doesn't like sports?" I can't stop it. A full-fledged grin spreads over my face.

"Not by choice. Hockey is the only language my dad speaks so it's basically an unavoidable subject."

"Of course. Dinner table conversation is all hockey—I buy that. It still doesn't explain why you've seen me skate, unless your dad forced you to watch my college games, since I've never played a pro one."

His mouth opens and shuts three times before any words come out. "Fine. I looked you up after the cookout. Stop gloating." He picks up his board and stalks away. "Meet me at the car when you're decent."

***

Thank God the ice rink is cold, otherwise I'd have a massive problem on my hands. Or rather, between my legs.

Xander's confession that he looked me up after the cookout has been playing on repeat since yesterday afternoon, and coupled with the visual of him riding, I've been half-hard for hours now.

While the memories are...pleasant, their timing is less so. I can't recall being preoccupied on the ice, much less by thoughts of a man. And seeing as how this is my first season as a pro, distractions are not welcome. Yet for the life of me I can't stop picturing Xander's sexy form on the board, his genuine smile when he caught me watching him.

I did that. I put that look on his face.

Yeah, I'm gloating like some schoolgirl with her first crush, which is pathetic since it's so close to the truth.

While I've had a few hookups over the years, I can't say I've ever had feelings for any of them, nor they me. Until now, everyone I've been with represented a mutual need for physical release. True, Xander started that way, though it was clear even from the first he was different somehow. He lingered in my mind long after the night was over, which had never happened to me before. Still, I didn't expect that to amount to anything since we weren't supposed to see each other again. Now that our paths have crossed, continue to cross, I have this lightness inside me that spikes when I think of him. Off the ice it's kind of pleasant. On the ice, it could be a massive detriment.

"You missed another slide," Coach barks at me as the puck hits the back of the net. "That's three today. What's up with you?" He waves me over, signaling to the other guys to get a drink so he can ream me.

"Sorry," I say lamely as I glide over." I'm a little off but I'll fix it."

"Fix what? Are you hurt? Sick?"

Saying yes to either of those things will land me in the trainer's, and while that's a better alternative than admitting the real reason I'm playing like shit, I don't want to be under the scrutiny of the medical staff. They'll dissect every little move I make to diagnose the problem, and when there isn't an actual problem, that's not good. Better to just suck it up and take my punishment now.

"No, Coach. I'm in my head a little bit today."

"What the hell for?"

"I wish I knew." I pop my mouthguard out, so it doesn't make me slur any words, as if speaking clearly will make my lies more believable. "Maybe I'm overthinking. I don't want to be the weak link, but it feels like the harder I try the slower I am."

"From where I'm sitting it doesn't look like you're thinking at all. You're not anticipating the offense, you're reacting to it. You don't need to chase players where they *are*, you need to meet them where they *will be* so you can stop their advance."

I know this already, but that's dangerous to admit when I'm not doing it. "Okay, Coach."

"You should be watching past games in your free time to get a feel for how guys are moving on the ice. Now get out there and run it again."

I grab a quick drink of water and skate back toward the goal to get in position. Before we start, Noah skates over to me for another check in.

"You okay?"

"Yeah, just... Thinking. Family stuff." I regret the lie as soon as it passes my lips, but it's better than the truth at the moment.

"Everything good?" Noah flips his helmet up with a look of concern.

"Yeah, no. I mean it's nothing, just my sister had something going on, which is hard since she's so far away. It's fine now, I just still have it in my head. Like leftover adrenaline making me jittery, you know."

Noah looks at me down the bridge of his nose. "You should be able to play through that at this level."

"Usually, I do but," I gesture to the rink around me, "I might be putting some extra pressure on myself not to screw up, which is making me screw up, and—" *I'm butchering this.* "Do you ever have those days where everything is a lot?"

His face relaxes as he drops his voice. "Yeah. I had a few days like that when I got traded to Denver. I wasn't sure if I was a failure for getting traded or a superstar because they picked me over the other guys."

"Superstar?" I cock my eyebrow.

"Phenom sounded like a little much." He bumps my shoulder with his thick glove. "You gotta find something off the ice to let the stress out and keep sane."

"What, like crocheting?"

"Huh?" Noah looks at me down his nose again.

"You know that Olympic diver guy? The one they kept showing with his knitting crap on the bleachers? Supposedly that keeps him calm and focused or some shit like that."

"If that's what you're into, sure, although I was thinking more like playing an instrument. Or sex."

There's a reason the puck bunny culture exists, so hearing Noah suggest I bang out my stress in the bedroom is par for the course. Too bad the thing he's suggesting could relieve my frustrations is also the thing causing it.

"Yeah, good thinking." I pop my mouthguard in to end the conversation and get back to practice before Coach gets on my case again. Not that I didn't deserve to get called out, I just don't want to make a habit of it.

Things go better the latter half of practice, mostly because I'm scared shitless to get caught daydreaming again. It's bad enough to lose focus, but to lose focus because I'm thinking about all the things I'd like to do to Coach's son... I wonder if this is the feeling guys describe when they meet their girlfriend's dad for the first time. I never thought I'd experience it since dads are rumored to be more protective of their daughters than sons, but I'm pretty sure the thoughts running through my mind wouldn't be appreciated by a parent regardless of gender.

Unfortunately, my second half improvement doesn't spare me the concern of our team captains, Noah and Luca, who force me and Justus to grab a beer and a bite as some sort of mental check-in.

"So, how are you both doing?" Noah rests his forearms on the table and glances between us, waiting for someone to answer.

Figuring this whole thing is my fault, I spew even more half-truths that I pray I can keep straight. "I mean the hockey part is great, but being in a city I don't know and living in a space that isn't mine takes some getting used to."

"You don't like the team condo?" Luca balks. "I thought it was great when I first got here."

The condo is perfectly fine, but now that I've opened that door, I have to walk through it. "You came here straight from high school and it was probably your first place on your own. Of course, you loved it. But my last place was all *my* stuff, and this...isn't. It made more sense to get here than move my shit across the country and what's here just isn't as comfortable."

"I get that," Justus saves me from digging an even deeper hole. "I only had to move a few hours, so I brought all my stuff. There's nothing like sleeping on a sofa that's worn exactly the way you like it."

"Oh shit." Luca cracks up as he shares a knowing look with Noah. "These two think the furniture they had before is good. Wait until you start buying the good stuff, boys." His shifts his gaze back to us. "You have no idea what comfortable is until you've bought a fifteen-thou-sand-dollar couch."

"Fifteen grand!" Justus' eyes grow wide. "I could never spend that much on a couch."

"That's on the low end, right Noah." Luca grins.

"It seems foreign now, but you'll both be making enough to buy some nice things."

"I just want to play hockey." Justus dips his head bashfully.

"Same." I try to save him the way he saved me. "I wouldn't mind my own place though."

"What's stopping you?" Noah asks.

"I need a few more paychecks for one. And I don't know where to buy yet. Or what to buy."

"You need a realtor," Justus says as the waitress delivers a pitcher. "I can give you the one I used to find my apartment."

"An apartment? Why would you get one of those when you can get a whole house?" Luca stares at him like he's made a colossal error, giving me the impression he's the kind of guy that gets the biggest and best no matter what.

"I'm just one guy, why do I need an entire house?" Justus returns the look.

"A weight room, a movie room, a few guest rooms, plus the game room where you hang all your jerseys and stuff." He raises a finger with each item he names.

"Maybe when I've been in the league as long as you, sure. I haven't even played my first game yet." I swear Justus' cheeks get a little pink as he points that out.

"Getting back to the issue." Noah steers us on course, proving why he's a captain. "What can we do to make sure your minds are right? Niko, you mentioned a sister. Do we need to get her out here?"

I don't know what I thought he was going to say, but it wasn't that, and for a moment I'm not even sure how to respond. "You would do that?"

"The team would, yeah. If it'll make your transition easier."

"That's... I mean I wouldn't say no to that." With a few more pay-checks I could do that myself, but to date I've only received one—my first ever—so it represents the sum of all the money I have. And while Xander thinks I'll be able to buy whatever car I want with it, I'm not looking to blow all my money on one purchase. I want to be smart with what I'm spending, which is why a plane ticket wasn't top of the list no matter how much I miss Anna. But this... The idea of seeing her sooner rather than later... I have no words.

"I'll talk to Coach. Maybe we can get her out here for the first home game," Noah suggests.

"Deal, yeah." *What would Xander say if he could see these dimples? I feel like my face might break.*

"What about you, Justus? Anything we can do for you?"

"My grandpa would probably love to be here. My parents too, but they already have plans to come closer to Thanksgiving. Having my grandpa at the first home game would be pretty incredible."

I feel a little pang of regret that I didn't mention my parents, but I don't want to be greedy, and they're already planning a holiday trip for several weeks so they can stop in and visit my mom's relatives in upstate New York. They wouldn't be able to get away twice in as little as three months. Anna might not be able to swing that either, but as a student she can probably arrange to keep up with her classes online.

"Okay, I'll see about flights for the families, and Justus will get Niko the name of his realtor." Noah lifts his glass for us all to clink.

"What do I do?" Luca asks.

"Pay for our tab." Noah hits him with a sharp elbow, causing him to wobble in his chair. For a second it looks like he's going to object, then he seems to think better of it.

"Deal."

We toast and spend the next couple hours bullshitting about the game, the competition, and where I should look for a place. I don't even have to tell a white lie about what's on my mind the rest of the night.

Chapter 14
Xander

Niko pecks away at the keys on the laptop sitting between us on the kitchen table, his long, strong fingers moving more delicately than their size would suggest they should. Since his arm brushes against mine as he types, shooting a wave of electricity throughout my body, it's a struggle to focus on the screen instead of the erratic thumping in my chest.

Why did I agree to help him look at cars again? Oh yeah, my mouth has a habit of forming words around him before my brain can stop it.

"What about this one?" He pulls up an image of a Jeep Grand Wagoneer. "Derek Jeter drives it."

It takes a herculean effort not to roll my eyes. "Okay, first, he's been retired for years so how do you even know who that is? And second, you understand how commercials work, right?"

"I know who he is because my roommates in college told me. And yes, I understand he's a spokesperson, but why would he do that if he didn't believe in what he's pitching?"

"Uh, money."

"He's got plenty of that." Niko waves a dismissive hand in my direction, flooding my nostrils with the scent of his mountain-air smelling soap. "He wouldn't need to lie on TV just to make more."

I exhale to expel the aroma as I mutter, "I can't wait to see how you handle endorsement deals."

"Hockey players don't get many of those," he retorts without missing a beat.

"They're getting more and more, and they can add millions to your annual pay."

"There's fewer than ten guys making millions from endorsements. Most players get hundreds of thousands."

"Whatever the amount, would you turn it down just because you didn't drive the car they want you to sell?"

Niko chews his lip thoughtfully, which I have to look away from because it's so fucking plump I can't help picturing what it would look like around my cock, and shocks me with a surprisingly thoughtful answer.

"No, but only if I believed in the product. Like, if I already have a car I love and they want me to pitch a different car, I'd do it if I thought that car was a good buy overall. If the car's a piece of shit I wouldn't do it."

"Why not?"

He blinks at me like he can't believe I asked the question. "I don't want my name ruined by tying it to things I wouldn't use."

"Not every spokesperson has the same integrity you do." I'm trying to find something wrong with him. Something that will make it easier to keep him in the friend box he belongs in. Too bad he's such a fucking golden retriever, whose leg is brushing against mine as it bounces under the table, making it hard to concentrate.

He pinches that tempting lip between his thumb and forefinger. "I don't want people to question whether I'm trustworthy or not."

Dammit, he's really too good to be true.

"My father said you were off your game the other day." I change the subject to something a little less likely to make me think of him as a good guy.

"I thought you hated talking hockey with him?"

"That's true, but it's also the only thing he talks to me about, so... Why were you playing like shit?"

"You."

"Me?" I point to my chest despite the fact I'm clearly who he's referring to.

"Yeah."

"I wasn't even there. How could I possibly be responsible for you sucking ass?"

"A, no one said sucking ass, unless there's something you're not telling me," he waggles his eyebrows, "and if so we're gonna need to circle back to that because I'm in. And B, you didn't have to be there. You were here." He points to his head.

My heart feels like it takes two beats in the time it should only make one, but I manage to keep my expression blank and my tone sarcastic. "Did you get hit in the head with the puck?"

"No."

"Then why were you hallucinating?"

"I wasn't. I was daydreaming."

"About?"

"You don't want to know." His raspy voice is barely audible over the heavy exhale.

I don't see any dimples so he's not trying to bait me, which only makes me more curious.

"If you're blaming me for playing like shit then I think I'm entitled to know."

"I'm not blaming you. It was my fault because my head was on you instead of the game. Still want to know specifics?" Those gorgeous blue eyes lock onto mine as he arches a brow, dousing me in a wave of heat that should be a signal to say no. Only I don't.

"Um..." My throat bobs as I swallow down another wave of butter-flies. *What is happening to me? I don't do giddy.*

Apparently, he takes my silence as an invitation to continue.

"I was thinking that if you looked me up *after* the cookout, you weren't being truthful when you said you don't do friends with ben-efits."

"Being curious about someone I've slept with doesn't inherently mean I want to do it again. I really am more of a one-night guy."

"Mmhmm." He nods in a way that suggests he's only pretending to agree. "I was also thinking about how sexy you move on that skate-board."

"We've been through this," I dismiss. "I look like you just on wheels instead of blades."

"Yeah, but I'm covered in bulky pads while you're shirtless." He closes his eyes and leans his head back, licking those plump lips before continuing. "Then I started thinking about that dick of yours. The way it slapped against your stomach while I fucked you. Fortunately, the rink was cold, otherwise I might've gotten hard. It's damn near impossible not to when I think of that beautiful cock."

"Then stop thinking about it," I snap.

Cracking his eyes open, he glances at my lap. "That'd be a whole lot easier to do if it wasn't straining to get out of your pants and into my hand."

I don't have to look down to know he's right, but I'm determined not to give in to my more carnal urges. "Dammit, Niko. We're sup-posed to be platonic friends, remember?"

"We said we'd try that first, remember? And I think we're doing pretty good at it. We laugh, we have fun, we're honest with each other. Are we really not on the same page here?"

"We're not even in the same book. I read yours already and it didn't have a happy ending."

Niko presses his lips into a firm line as his brows draw together, and it's a full thirty seconds before he finally speaks. "I'm not him."

"What?"

"I'm not him. The guy who ghosted you. I'm not him. The whole point of the friends thing is for me to prove to you that I'm different. Have I not proved that?"

I roll my eyes with a heavy sigh. "We'd have to do more than just practice driving together for you to prove that. We'd have to actually go out. In public."

"Fine, let's go."

"Where?"

"Anywhere." He lifts his shoulders. "Wherever you need to go to believe I won't disappear on you."

"What would that change? You'd still be in the closet."

"For now. Not always. How many times do I have to tell you that?"

"Probably as many times as I tell you I'm not doing this. I'm not getting involved."

"Then why are you here?" He gestures to the room around us. "If you aren't interested in being friends or lovers, you might as well go."

He's not wrong, but hearing the words hurts more than I expected. I guess somewhere in the back of my mind I wanted to believe his pursuit of this *friendship* was his way of working up to something more. Something beyond the closed-door sex I know he prefers. At least we're coming to this decision now, so what I feel is disappointment as opposed to pain.

"Fine." I stand and turn for the door, intending to leave without dragging out some pathetic goodbye. But I only take one step before a warm hand wraps around my wrist, holding me in place. I look over my shoulder to find Niko shaking his head with an almost defeated look on his face.

"I can't do it. I can't let you walk out that door."

My body tenses, bracing for battle. "Why?"

His head continues its back-and-forth motion, eyes staring unfocused on the floor. "I don't know. I don't know why this is happening or what it means. I just know that when I'm not on the ice, I want to be with you. And when I'm on the ice I'm thinking about you. The timing fucking sucks because I have so much to prove right now, and even if I was out getting involved with someone year one is about the dumbest move I could make. I know that. But I can't stop thinking about it."

Getting involved? This just went from secret hookup to serious in a matter of seconds. I lick my suddenly dry lips. "Getting involved? Since when was that your intent?"

"I'm starting to think it always was."

"So the whole friends thing wasn't just a means to get into a friends with benefits thing?"

His fingers slide down to my hand and lock around mine. "I mean, I've been dying to get you back in bed since the cookout, but if I'm being honest, it wasn't just about the sex. That was incredible, obviously, but I never felt a connection with anyone like I do with you. Right from the start everything was just...*more*. I can't get it out of my head. I can't get *you* out of my head."

"What are you saying?"

"I want you, and I think you want me."

"I don't." I shake my head firmly.

"Kinda feels like you do." His thumb slides over the back of my hand.

"I don't want to, though."

"Why?"

"Jocks aren't my type." We both know it's a lame excuse, but it's the only one that comes to mind right now.

"All jocks, or just this one?" He points to his face with his free hand. "Because this one is over six feet, has blue eyes, dimples, and..." His eyes drift lower even as his brows lift. "If I remember right, that's everything on your wish list."

"Physically, yeah. But..."

"You need more than physical to get past the jock thing." He finishes my thought for me. "I get it. Look, I know I'm not in the same book as you right now, and no matter how much I want to open it I can't. Not yet. But I feel like this could be something, and I don't want to throw it away before it starts."

He finally brings his gaze to meet mine, and I find myself in awe. *He's giving me puppy dog eyes and I'm starting to crack.* "What are you asking of me?"

"I'm asking if you feel it too. If you don't, it's okay to leave. I won't stop you. But if you do..." His voice falters as he trails off, speechless for the first time since we met.

Fuck yes, I feel it. That's why I didn't want to be friends. It's also why I agreed to it. I can't let go of him any more than he can let go of me, and trying to keep us in the friend zone is torture. The only reason I haven't fully caved to his charm is the knowledge of what heartbreak feels like, because there's no doubt in my mind that this man will break me for good if he turns out to be like my ex. Yet despite that knowledge, I'm still here, willingly putting myself in his orbit.

When I don't answer he continues. "My theory is you're drawn to people who smile because you don't and...dimples." He flashes those adorable divots at me for a brief moment before he turns serious. "I think I could make you smile, Alexander. If you let me."

I don't know if that makes me a masochist or a romantic. Maybe a bit of both. Either way, the raw honesty of his words makes its way through the tiny crack he created, and before I can fully weigh the consequences, I yank him from the chair and crush my lips to his.

The force of our collision nearly sends me stumbling backwards, but Niko wraps an arm around my back to steady me, pulling us chest to chest in the process. My hands find his pecs as his clutch my waist, both of us angling our heads so our tongues can meet, and when they touch...

The tension that's been growing for weeks unleashes as we finally give in to the attraction we've been trying to suffocate. Neither of us are particularly passive, and though he's got a few inches and probably over forty pounds on me, I give just as good as I get, forcing my tongue in his mouth despite the burn of his stubble scraping my cheek.

Unlike the first time, when I was a little wary about kissing, this time I'm eager for it. Desperate even, after weeks of staring at his full lips and wondering if they'd feel as soft as I remember. They do, flooding my body with the anticipation and arousal that can only come from sharing another person's air and sending it straight to my dick, which swells behind my zipper.

"Been wanting to taste these lips again for weeks," Niko growls against my mouth. "Been wanting to smell the rosemary mint on your body." He recalls the scent of my soap as he nuzzles my neck.

"You remember that?"

"It's my new favorite scent. Doesn't smell the same if it's not on your skin though." His hips rock forward, grinding our hard cocks together, and I swear I fucking tremble in his arms. And not just because he's rubbing my boner with his, but because his words are... sweet. I'm still not totally comfortable with sweet, though.

"You don't have to feed me lines. Pretty sure you're gonna get laid anyway." I brush the tips of my thumbs over his pebbled nipples.

"No lines." He pushes his tongue in my mouth and rolls his pelvis against mine. "I smell it and my cock goes rigid. Thank god no one uses it in the locker room or I'd never get my pants on."

Niko's hands find my ass, kneading the full globes in his palms as his tongue finds mine again. Coupled with the way our hips are thrusting, our cocks searching for friction despite the denim barriers between us, we're practically humping upright. It's everything and not enough, making me wonder if the groan that rumbles up my throat is from satisfaction or desperation.

Regardless, it pulls a similar sound from Niko, who hauls me into his arms, guiding my legs around his waist just like he did that first night. Once again, the caveman treatment sends my libido into overdrive, making me wonder if he's awakened some new kink.

I ride him over our clothes as he carries me to the bedroom, stumbling once when I circle my hips and really grind against the sensitive underside of his cock. Setting me down at the foot of the bed, he rips my shirt over my head and runs his hands over my torso.

"Missed this body," he pants between kisses to my neck, my shoulders, my chest. Tiny fireworks erupt on my skin everywhere his lips touch, shooting chills through my limbs while making a strange warmth radiate from my core. It's a sensation I can't make sense of since I've never experienced it before, but even though I don't understand it, I want more.

I tilt my head, giving him better access. He trails his lips over the peaks and valleys of my pecs as his fingers dance over my abs, the touch surprisingly light considering their size and obvious strength. I take a shaky breath, trying to calm the rapid rise and fall of my chest.

It doesn't help, his touch is too electric for my body to temper its response.

Niko tugs my pants open as I reach for his shirt, searching for the warm muscle I remember mapping with my fingers months ago. He lets me go long enough to whip the shirt over his head and undo his own pants, freeing both our cocks and wrapping his large hand around them.

"Missed this cock." His fist contracts gently as he gives a languid pull of our lengths. "Been wanting to feel it next to mine since I saw you at the cookout."

Leaning his forehead against mine, we both pant heavily as he strokes. Sandwiched between his own rigid dick and his fist, I can feel my cock throb rhythmically, like a drumbeat keeping time until the music starts. Once again, it's everything and not enough, and I find myself torn between wanting to hold still and bask in the steady hum of arousal or buck my hips to chase an even greater high.

Niko swipes his thumb over our crowns, mixing our precum. The dampness is cool on my heated skin, sending a tiny shiver up my spine as he squeezes our cocks in his fist. Then it's back to my cockhead, where he teases my slit with the barest of pressure, causing me to leak even more. Over and over again, he chokes our dicks in his hand then gently coats us in our own arousal, forcing me to grip his shoulders for support when my knees buckle.

"Jesus your cock feels good next to mine," he says breathlessly. "So hard. So full."

I slide my hands from his shoulders to his hard abs, and down between his legs. Curling his balls in my hand, I roll them, feeling their weight.

"Holy shit." His shaky breath fans across my face. "That feels incredible."

"You like when I play with your sac?" I give it a little tug as I lick the base of his neck, chasing it with a featherlight kiss.

"I like when you touch me, period." He takes my mouth in a searing kiss that leaves my chest heaving as I pant for air. "But yeah, I especially like your hands between my legs."

Niko's hand starts to slide over us in light, feathery strokes as he plunges his tongue in and out of my mouth. His raspy moans play like a soundtrack that echos in the sparsely furnished room around us. It makes my dick swell so hard it'd rival a steel pipe, and I rock to my toes to chase his hand as it travels over my length.

He lets go of his own dick to hold mine, pumping it a little faster though the grip remains soft. A tease. "So fucking hard. Why so pent up?" He squeezes me, firmly, and a high-pitched whimper pierces the air. "Is it me, or have you not been taking care of yourself? Tell me it's me." He nuzzles the spot where my neck meets my ear.

"Both," I whisper on an exhale.

"Then you haven't been touching yourself while thinking of me?"

"Been trying not to." I rise to my toes to chase another firm stroke.

"In that case..." He lets go of my dick and strides toward the nightstand, his own bobbing with each step where it pokes out through his open fly. "We better leave your cock alone for a while so you can give me what I want."

"What's that?" It's a struggle not to drop to the bed with all the blood in my body residing below the belt.

"All night." He winks at me as he stalks back with a bottle of lube, those sexy dimples prominent even in shadow. "Pants off. Face the mirror."

As he strips down, I notice the large mirror sitting above the dresser that stands opposite the bed. In the dim light I can make out the slight flush in my cheeks, the flat planes of my stomach. And the roughly seven inches standing proud, begging for attention. *I actually look kind of hot. Wait, why am I looking at myself? Am I supposed to watch...me?*

Distracted by questions over what Niko has planned, I don't realize he's moved behind me until his strong arm wraps around my waist. "I need you from behind, but I don't want to miss that beautiful cock smacking against your abs."

My weight falls back against him as he takes me in his fist and pulls with lazy strokes, a subtle warmth spreading from my center down to my toes with each tug. My eyes roll back in my head as he straight up fondles my dick, coaxing it to a stiffness I didn't know was possible with such a light touch. *The man is magic with his hands.*

"Is that some sort of kink you have? Seeing a guy's abs while you fuck him?"

"It never was before." Niko strokes over my stomach with the other hand, lovingly tracing the lines of muscle. No, not lovingly. Tenderly? Possessively? Regardless, it's kind of soothing and arousing, putting me in a fog of blissed-out lust that makes it hard to think. Only feel. "But you... The cut of these muscles on your lean frame..." He nestles his cock between my thighs with a contented sigh. "Fuck, it's sexy. And with this gorgeous dick." He pumps me gently. "Yeah, I guess maybe it is a kink."

A needy little mewl—a *fucking mewl*—passes through my lips as he lets me go and pulls away from my thighs, though the sudden absence of his warm hands is soon forgotten as I feel his slick fingers probing my hole.

Leaning against him for support, I relax as much as possible while still using my legs to stand. I shiver as he pushes a finger inside, both from the cool lube and the slight burn of his finger stretching me, though that quickly turns to a pleasant fullness as he gently works the digit in and out. Rocking back to take him deeper, my cock bobs and twitches as he nudges my prostate.

"So fucking hot." He growls in my ear as his eyes rake over my body in the mirror, finger thrusting steadily. "Ready for another?"

"Please."

There's a brief sting as the pressure increases, but it fades just as quickly as it comes on, leaving only desire in its wake.

Niko stretches my hole with one hand while the other ghosts over my pecs, my abs, a soft touch that's somehow possessive at the same time. Admiring yet also seeming to mark me as his, as if I hold the key to his pleasure.

It's a heady thought, the notion that I could belong to him, and one that would normally send my mind into overdrive. But my mind has checked out, giving total control to my body, and my body wants Niko.

I arch into his hand even as I push against his fingers, wanting to feel him everywhere. Needing more. As if he can read my mind Niko lets me go once again, gifting me with the sound of a foil packet being ripped open. Then his thick cock is pressing against my hole.

"Okay?" he rasps.

"Yes."

The invasion is slow but relentless, coming to a halt only when he's seated fully inside me, and we're both desperately trying to catch our breath before we move.

"Look at us, Alexander. Look how well we fit together." Niko's face hovers behind mine, hungry eyes watching in the mirror as his hands drift along my arms, over my torso, down my thighs. "You feel it, right? You feel how good we fit?"

I nod my head, unable to form the words.

"Say it, Alexander. Say how well we fit."

My heart nearly stops when his eyes meet mine in the mirror, and before I can stop it, I find myself replying, "We fit perfectly, Nikolas."

He leans forward to bite my earlobe, growling, "Damn right we do." Then his dimples take on an almost sinister quality as he smiles mischievously and starts to move.

Chapter 15
Niko

I'm not gentle. I can't be. I've waited too long, fantasized too often, and now that it's happening... I'm a slave to my primal urges, damn near unhinged, and the way Xander is writhing that tight little ass on my dick says he's into it.

"Love how tight you are." I grip his hips for dear life, pumping long and deep. "Love the way that heavy cock smacks against those sexy abs."

I'm babbling, but I can't help it. His tight channel is virtually strangling me, and the view... I never knew it until him but the image of a rock-hard dick swinging so fast it defies gravity to smack his stomach is probably the filthiest thing I've ever witnessed. I love it.

"God, look how hard that cock is." I slam into him. "I don't know what I want more, to feel it inside me or watch it burst."

"Touch it," he pants. "Please."

"Not yet." Xander reaches for his cock, but I swat his hand away before he can make contact. Am I torturing him a little for refusing to touch my dick until the last second when he fucked me months ago? Maybe. I also just really like looking at his cock. "Grab my ass if you need to hang onto something."

His hands clamp down on my ass just as I instructed, and damn if that doesn't send another jolt of lust to my balls, which are swinging heavily between my legs with each thrust.

"Nikolaaas." My name is a desperate plea on his lips that coils around my balls and caresses them as thoroughly as if it were his hand. *Holy hell, I want to hear that again.*

"I know, baby." I piston my hips back and forth. "Just a little longer and I'll give you what you want."

Baby? Never in the history of sex—my history of sex—has that word ever passed through my lips. I have no idea where it came from, but somehow, it fits, just like our bodies do. A snug, seamless fit, blurring the lines between where I end and he begins, and erasing boundaries that words like *baby* would normally fall outside of.

Looking at Xander in the mirror, chest glistening with exertion, jaw locked tight as he struggles to hold back his release, the endearment feels right. Especially considering I want to give him as much pleasure as possible since he's so unselfishly letting me take mine.

As I push us toward the edge, I can feel Xander's thighs shaking under the strain of trying to stay upright, and I know he can't hold out much longer. Digging my fingers into his hips hard enough to bruise, I plunge my cock as deep, and hard, and fast as I can, trying to quiet my breath so I can hear the deliciously carnal sound of his cock slapping against his stomach.

When he wails my name again, I know he needs his release, and I wrap my hand around his length, holding it tight so the power of my thrusts increases the friction.

"Fuck my fist, baby. Drive that cock deep and take what you need."

Impaled on my length, Xander can't really fuck my fist. But I know from our first night he likes dirty talk, and if that'll make him detonate, well, I'm great at it.

"That's it. Fill my hand with your cum. I want to lick it off my fingers."

Two seconds later, his ass clamps down like a vice, clenching and pulling at my dick as his body unleashes all that pent-up pleasure. A few contractions are all it takes for me to follow him over the edge, and soon I'm twitching inside him the same as he's pulsing in my hand.

Sparks of pleasure ripple along my length as I come undone, and while they radiate through my center to my limbs, it's the epicenter, the place where we're joined, where I feel wave after wave of pure, carnal bliss.

Holy fuck.

Though my hips stop working the moment I blow, leaving me helpless to do anything but hold myself deep as I fill the condom, my hand retains enough function to stroke Xander's rigid length until every last drop is spent. Only, I don't let go when he stops leaking. I can't. I like the feel of him in my hand too much, so I make no effort to move. I just hold us together, his back to my front, softening dick in my palm, until our breathing returns to normal. Even then I don't step away, certain that without me to hold him up, he'll topple over.

"Lie down." I guide us to the bed, only then pulling out and taking off the condom, which I knot and toss on the floor to deal with later.

Crawling on shaky limbs, he manages to get his head to the pillow, collapsing with an adorably heavy sigh. It makes my chest swell with pride to know I'm the one who wrecked him so thoroughly. Instead of boasting about my prowess or gloating that I was right about us, to lighten the mood and make sure he's not overwhelmed with the intensity of what just happened, all I want to do is lie next to him and pull him into my arms. So, I do.

"What comes next?" he mumbles as I cover us with a thin sheet, and I say a little thank you that he's too out of it to see the goofy smile those words put on my face. I knew there was a softie behind that moody exterior, but to remember my exact words from our first encounter and say them back to me? If I didn't already think there was something worth exploring between the two of us, those words right there would've done the trick.

Still, thanks to his delirium, I don't know if he's asking about today or long-term. And while we jumped into bed before working out all the kinks, now is not the time for a heavy discussion.

"Right now, we rest." I plant a chaste kiss on his forehead. "Then we'll figure it out together."

I'm not even sure he hears those words before he's sawing logs—metaphorically, since he doesn't actually snore—but I can tell the exact moment he wakes up from our post sex nap.

His body—still tucked against mine with his head in the crook of my shoulder—seizes up, and the breath that was drifting rhythmically over my chest suddenly stops. I freeze myself, waiting to see if this is just an *I forgot where I am for a second* stillness or a *what the fuck did I just do* moment. When he jerks upright instead of relaxing back in my arms, I have my answer. *Shit!*

I'm not naïve enough to think everything would magically be perfect after one epic fuck—okay three if you count that first night—but I was hoping to bask in the afterglow a little longer.

"I should go." Xander tries to scoot off the bed, but I grab his wrist to stop his momentum.

"You aren't leaving. Not yet."

He looks at the arm I have trapped in my hand, those beautiful brown eyes nearly black with a mixture of fear and anger. "Are you holding me hostage?

"No, but I am forcing you to talk to me before you storm out. An hour ago, you were on board with this, then we have the most amazing sex I've ever had, and now you're panicking. Why? Walk me through what's going on here."

"I fucked up and I need to leave. Let me go." He tries to jerk his arm from my grasp.

"Not good enough."

"Excuse me?"

"Not good enough," I repeat. "Something made you freak out, what is it? You've slept next to me before so it can't be that. And I know it can't be that I'd ghost you because we've already been over how that's not my style. So, what's got you so riled up you need to race out of my bed?"

"I'm not racing." His too long hair swings over his eyes as he shakes his head.

"Bullshit. If I didn't have a hold on your arm, you'd already be out the door. I may not have a lot of experience with whatever this is between us, but I also know it won't work if you keep shutting me out. Now talk."

His lean chest rises and falls several times before he finally speaks, staring at where my hand holds his wrist the whole time. "I could fall for you. If I do, and you...and this ends..."

"I could fall for you too. Why do you think I'm trying so hard here?"

"Exactly." He lifts his eyes to mine, and while they're still nearly black, the anger is gone, replaced by a wariness that gives me a funny pain in my chest. "There could be something here, and if it ends... I can't do it. I can't go through that again."

"Look." I sit up and wrap my hand around the back of his neck, forcing him to meet my eyes. "I can't sit here and promise you a happy ending no matter how much I might want to. There are too many factors at play, and only one of them is me being in the closet. We could find the separation of away games too much of a hassle. I could get traded..."

"I notice none of those things is me deciding I don't like you."
There's my sarcastic dark angel.

"And none of them is me ghosting you either. The point is we don't
know what could happen. There's always that risk, with everything in
life. But I'm not interested in missing out on things just because there's
a chance they might not work."

"That's easy to say when you haven't had your life turned upside
down by someone you thought cared about you." He pulls out of my
reach, letting his gaze fall to the bed.

"Fuck, that guy did a number on you."

"Not just him," Xander mumbles, but not so softly I don't hear it.

"What? Who else hurt you?" I don't know where it comes from or
why, but the urge to protect the man that I'm really wanting to be
mine is so overwhelming I'm ready to chase down anyone who ever
caused him pain.

"Nothing." He shakes his head with a heavy sigh. "It's nothing."

"Alexander," I warn, noting how the firm use of his name seems to
make some of the tension leave his body. "Tell me."

"It'll just make things worse for you."

"For me?" I point to myself. "How could an ex douche of yours
make things worse for me?"

"Not an ex." He shakes his head. "My dad."

"I thought you said he doesn't have a problem with the gay thing?"
I guess Xander was just trying to make me feel better before. "Damn,
no wonder you freaked about me wanting to wait to come out. You
think I never will."

"He doesn't have a problem with the gay thing." Xander licks his
lip, and damn if that doesn't make my cock start to stir again. *Not now
buddy.* "He has a problem with me. I wasn't the star player he dreamed
of raising."

Though his expression is blank, I think I know Xander well enough to say that's a mask, designed to hide how much that statement hurts. And I definitely know he'd rather shut down than appear weak, so to give him a little dignity I lay down and pull him with me, tucking him against my chest. He resists at first, going stiff again, then slowly relaxes into my hold. And—fuck me—he actually starts talking again.

"I'm not a miniature version of him. I don't even like sports, although that might be more of a rebellion thing than an actual preference." I feel his brow wrinkle as he seems to absorb that statement, like the truth of it just occurred to him. "Once I quit hockey the person who was supposed to support me unconditionally just...stopped. He wasn't mean or angry or anything, just indifferent."

His earlier comment about making things worse for me falls into place, and I realize he wasn't trying to shut me out so much as protect me from developing a poor opinion of the guy I'm supposed to give my all for. And yeah, part of me does want to be pissed at Coach for making Xander feel this way, but a bigger part of me is giddy over the fact that he shared something so personal. That's a good sign. Now I just have to keep him talking, and maybe we can put this panic behind us.

"How old were you?" I sift my fingers through his silky hair.

"Middle school. Thirteen maybe?"

"Old enough to start thinking for yourself but still young enough to want to please your dad."

He nods against my chest. "Yeah."

"So, first your dad stops noticing you, then the ex ghosts you, then I come along and want you to be my little secret." I hug him to me, so the words don't make him pull away.

"Yes." It's barely a whisper, and while a dozen responses to make him feel better run through my mind, the only one I act on is the desire to kiss his forehead.

I never stopped to question what made Xander dark and brooding—I simply reacted to the physical pull I felt. But these revelations help me to see that the bad boy exterior isn't just hiding a softie, but a truly vulnerable guy, and while I have the urge to protect him, I'm also now realizing I'm the one he needs protection from.

Reaching for his hand, I thread our fingers together and rest them on my chest. "I'm sorry."

"For what?"

"I didn't realize the magnitude of what I was asking you to do by keeping this a secret. I mean, I knew you'd had a bad breakup, and I knew he picked his career over you, but it didn't occur to me that he wasn't the first person to do that, or that I was doing the same thing. In my head I'm not since I'm just waiting for the right time to—tell my story or whatever. But I can see how telling you that is just a bunch of words until I follow through."

Xander's throat brushes against my pec as he swallows. "That's... Thank you."

"Why are you thanking me?"

He's quiet for so long I wonder if I've pushed him too far too fast, asking for details he's not ready to share. Then I feel the tiniest, softest kiss just to the side of my nipple, right where his head is resting against me.

"For understanding." It's all the explanation I get, though it doesn't clear things up for me.

"Well, I may follow where you're coming from, but I'm not sure I can say I follow where you're going. I mean, considering everything

I've learned, I have no idea why you're giving this a chance. I literally have to be your worst nightmare."

"I thought you would be," he agrees, "but it turns out you're also everything I want. Except for the jock thing and the being in the closet thing."

"But those are big things for you."

"Huge." His hair brushes over my chest as he nods. "But I can overlook them, at least for now, since you're being honest."

"Honesty is as important as dimples?" I tug him a little closer and drop a kiss on the top of his head, trying to keep things light so he keeps talking.

"Don't joke." He lets go of my hand and pinches my nipple—hard—before reaching for my fingers again.

"Ow. I've been sufficiently warned." I rub our joined hands over the tender bud. "I don't understand how honesty outweighs the other shit though. Don't get me wrong, I'm glad it does. I just haven't done anything special."

"You've been clear about what you wanted, how you feel—even if you don't know exactly what that is—and about what I can expect."

"I said I couldn't promise anything. That doesn't really make me a good boyfriend."

"You think you're my boyfriend?"

I really need to get better about thinking before I speak.

"Uh, maybe?" Xander's head bobs slightly when I try to shrug the shoulder it's resting on. "I've never had one of those before so I'm not sure I fit the criteria, but I'm not opposed. What is the criteria, anyway, besides mind-blowing orgasms?"

"It's different for everyone, I think." He goes quiet again, though since I can feel him thinking in my arms, I know he's got more to say. He just needs to figure out how to say it. When he's finally ready, he starts rubbing his thumb over the back of my hand as he speaks. "For me, it's honesty, respect, trust, and just a general feeling that I want to be with that person more than anyone else. What would it be for you?"

I'm not expecting the question since we've already established my ignorance in this area, yet I'm well aware this entire conversation is probably a massive breakthrough for Xander, so I need to take it seriously.

"Like you said, a general feeling that I want to be with that specific person more than anyone else. And comfort is important. I want to feel like I can be *me*. The jock and the nerd and...all the other quirks and shit. Most of all I think I'd want support. Not the taking care of me kind but the willingness to accept my limitations kind. And I'm not talking about being in the closet, I'm talking about the pitfalls of my job. The travel and the long hours and stuff that would take up more time than a boyfriend would probably want them to. And holy shit–now that I say all that out loud, I am a truly awful catch."

There's a hint of humor in my voice, but only because I force it, not because I think this is funny. My closely guarded sexuality is really only the tip of the iceberg in terms of obstacles any boyfriend of mine would have to overcome, and I wouldn't blame Xander for thinking I'm not worth the trouble.

"Yeah, you really should come with a warning label," he laugh-snorts.

"Did you just make a joke?" I grab onto his comments like a lifeline, hoping there's a chance he doesn't see my obstacles as a deal-breaker. "What would my label say? Dick is too shriveled up by the ice he lives on to be good boyfriend material."

"I was gonna say 'Will sweet talk you into bed and give you orgasms so good you lose your mind.'"

Though his tone is almost playful the words make it hard to breathe. *Does he really think I've only been after sex this whole time?* "If that's what you think, how can you say I'm honest?"

Xander props himself on an elbow to look at me, his bottomless brown eyes holding a note of sincerity I haven't seen in them before. "The honesty is the sweet talk, Nikolas. You being you, no false promises... Those are the words that drew me to your bed. And yes, the orgasms make me lose my mind, but in a way that gets me out of my head and into the moment, not in a way that I regret."

"You're sure?"

"I wasn't at first. You made me talk through it, and now... Yeah. I'm sure. I'm willing to take the risk."

I unravel our fingers to bring my hand to his face, stroking my thumb over the five o'clock shadow sprouting on his cheek. "I've wanted to hear you say that for weeks, but now... I have this strong urge to protect you, even from me, and it makes me want to say we shouldn't date."

"Is that what you want?" Xander's beautiful face is once again expressionless. Another mask. I'm already hurting him, all the more reason to say yes.

"Fuck no," I blurt before my own sense of morality can get in the way. "I want you now more than ever. I just don't want to disappoint you."

"Keep being honest and you won't."

I'm pretty sure we both know it's not that simple, but with our faces inches apart, and his gaze drifting to my mouth, it's hard not believe it could be. With a gentle tug I bring him closer, so our lips just barely make contact, and even though it's hardly my first kiss, in many ways it feels like it is.

I've never done the sweet thing. The tender caress where you just barely make contact. I've peppered soft kisses on necks, stomachs, even cocks, mostly as a way to slow things down in the heat of the moment so I don't get ahead of myself.

Up until this point, I've always felt an urgency with Xander–a need to be closer until it's impossible to resist. Now, it's different. The need building inside me isn't hunger that craves to be satisfied. It's a calmness that just wants to be closer to him in any form of the word. Mentally, physically, or *both*. These kisses aren't given out of sheer lust but rather a promise of what we could be.

Our movements are unhurried. Indulgent. We savor every second. The feel of soft lips rubbing together. The scratch of stubble against stubble. The friction of tongues shyly sliding along one another each time our mouth's part.

This kiss is unlike anything I've ever experienced, which sort of makes me wonder why I've never done it before, yet at the same time I can't fathom doing this with anyone but Xander. It's too—*fuck me*—too meaningful to share with anyone else.

That thought makes me feel like a giant turd—not exactly how I was expecting to feel when my persistence finally won him over. I have zero intention of hurting him, but my lifelong dream is more real than it's ever been, and I don't want to throw it away by painting a target on my back as the first openly gay rookie. And yet, it's getting harder and harder to think of hockey as my lifelong dream if it would mean I have to give up Xander to achieve it.

Am I deluding myself by thinking I could have both? That he'll wait long enough for me to be comfortable coming out, or that I can come out without any backlash? God I hope not, because right now, pressed against him and sharing the most profound kiss of my life, I'm sort of thinking he can make me just as happy as hockey always has.

Xander's tongue licks tranquilly along my lip before he gives me the most sensitive little kiss, letting his mouth hover against mine as he whispers into it. "Boyfriends, then?"

I smile against his lips, unreasonably giddy despite my lingering fears that I might somehow screw this up. "I mean, you did say I'm everything you want."

"I knew I was going to regret that." I swear I feel him crack a smile in return. "Fine. Yes. Your incessant happiness balances my grouchiness and I like being around you. You make things...fun."

"Fun?" I pull back just enough so he can see me waggle my eyebrows. "Did my dark and brooding angel just admit I'm fun? And he likes it?"

"Angel?" he deadpans. "Of all the pet names to choose from, that's the one you're going with?"

"Hey, it's actually pretty accurate. Obviously, you're a moody fucker, but you don't have an evil bone in this gorgeous body, and you're giving us a chance despite me still being closeted. So...angel."

"I guess that makes you dimples then." He lifts his brows, daring me to object.

I try not to. I really do, but...eew. "Okay, you win. No pet names, except boyfriend."

"Boyfriends," he agrees, and even though I fucking love seeing that smile on his face, I can't stop myself from kissing it off.

Chapter 16
Xander

He's still sleeping soundly when I wake the next morning, chest pressed against my back with his arm draped over my stomach, and despite the tiny tremor of anxiety his proximity causes, I make no effort to move.

I've never been the little spoon. Not even with my ex who, while bigger than me, never shared my bed for longer than it took to fuck. Looking back, I suppose that should've been a major red flag, but love is blind and all that. Not that what I'm feeling for Niko is love—it's too soon and my walls are still too high—and I'm not turning a blind eye to the flags that do exist. But I am trying to look at Niko without seeing the scars from my past. Scars that he didn't inflict.

I still don't love the idea of hiding, and I won't do it indefinitely. But I can give him time to adjust. After all, he's embarking on a lifelong dream, in a new city with all new teammates, and as he pointed out, that's not great timing to start a relationship. Not with his career. That'd be true even if he were straight, or out, so I'm comfortable giving him some time to get his bearings. And if I'm being totally honest, I've rejected the idea of dating for so long I might need a little time to adjust myself. To remember what it can be instead of focusing on what it wasn't. Like waking up wrapped in someone's arms.

Boyfriends.

Did I jump into that too quickly? Caving to his charms instead of holding firm to my own needs? Maybe. Probably. Yet, I can't deny I like the sound of that, even if it's not exactly what I want it to be. Not yet. It will be, though. He said so. He's not opposed to coming out, he just can't do it *yet*.

True, I've heard that line before, which is the main reason I tried so hard not to get to this point. But *this* point, waking up next to a man after sleeping in his arms all night, is unfamiliar territory. It's something my ex never allowed. That gives me hope that despite the similar circumstances, the outcome will be different with Niko.

Warm breath hits my neck just before soft lips brush against it. "I can feel you overthinking." Niko's voice is scratchy, thick with sleep. "Get out of your head and just enjoy the moment."

"What makes you think I'm not enjoying the moment?"

"If you were, you'd notice my cock twitching against your ass, and you'd start rocking against it."

As soon as he says it, I feel the steel length jolt where it's sandwiched between us, which makes me realize I'm half-hard myself. And before I can come up with a response, my body presses into his like it's compelled, incapable of resisting the call of his desire.

"That's more like it," he grumbles, nipping at my earlobe as his pelvis moves against mine in a slow, sensual dance beneath the covers.

Cradled in his arm, our hips swiveling in a lazy grind as he peppers kisses over my shoulders, I sink into a fog of pleasure. There's no 'what-ifs' ringing through my mind, no nervous tensions settling in my stomach. There's only the steady drumbeat of Niko's heartbeat thumping against my back, the pleasant hum of arousal that simmers beneath the surface of my skin. A feeling of contentment unlike anything I've ever experienced, and one I could see myself getting used to.

Niko's fingers trace a path down my stomach, over my thighs, brushing against my engorged dick before repeating again. "Boyfriends have morning sex, right? I'm not sure I mentioned that specifically, but it's on the list of things I want."

"I would've thought you'd want it morning, noon and night," I say as wryly as I can. His hand wraps around my dick and gives it a long, languid tug.

"Well, yeah. But I've never had morning sex. Unless you count jerking off in front of each other last week, which I don't."

"What would count then?"

"You sitting on top of me and jerking us off together. I want to see your hand wrapped around our cocks." He swipes his thumb over my slit before giving me another leisurely stroke, and my whole body shivers with desire. "Feels like you like that idea."

Wriggling out of his hold, I spin and push him to his back, straddling him so that our dicks rub together when I circle my hips. He inhales sharply when the sensitive crowns make contact, eyes glazing over with lust as they slide along each other.

Following his gaze, I admire the sight. Thick. Rigid. Unyielding. I'm reminded of something he said the night we met, choosing a jedi for his fantasy basketball team, and before I can process the absurdity of it, I twist my hips so my junk smacks against his.

"Did you just swordfight me with your dick?" He blinks rapidly as his jaw falls open.

"Lightsaber."

A wicked smile spreads across his face, those luscious dimples issuing a challenge. Then he clamps his hands on my thighs, holding me in place as he rocks side to side, trying to slam his cock against mine.

We grapple for control, both of us twisting and contorting ourselves to gain advantage as the faint sound of skin slapping against skin echoes around us. Despite being trapped between my legs, which should be a disadvantage, Niko's strong arms hold me damn near immobile, so being on top doesn't give me nearly the leverage it should.

That doesn't stop me from throwing my weight from side-to-side in a desperate attempt to overpower him, which is totally ineffective as a combat strategy, but makes my cock leak with desire.

"You're cheating. This is a lightsaber duel, not a wrestling match," I grit as I try to break his hold on my thighs.

"There are no rules in lightsaber battles." He bucks his hips, trying to throw me off balance, which he nearly does. But it's not the power of his thrust that topples me, it's the way his abs ripple. The image pulls a needy groan from my throat as his dick slaps mine.

"I win," Niko boasts triumphantly.

"Says who?"

"That sexy moan you just made." His dimples cut deep as he smiles coyly.

"Moans don't determine the winner." I shake my head.

"What's the tie breaker then?"

"Whoever comes first takes all." I trap our cocks in my hand and start pumping. Not the slow, sensual strokes Niko woke me up with, but fast, firm pulls that have us both thrusting into my fist in a race to the finish.

The room fills with strangled grunts, the rhythmic thumping of the headboard hitting the wall as we test the strength of the frame. For a moment I feel a slight twinge of regret that instead of making my first boyfriend sleepover an intimate moment I turned it into some cheesy sci-fi fuck-fest, but the youthful joy in Niko's eyes when I started goofing around, followed by the heated look in them now, makes me think this is perfect.

"Fuck yes," Niko groans as I take us to the brink. "Just like that. Make me come all over your dick."

His words send a shiver racing down my spine and my grip falters, but only for a moment. As a new surge of strength ignites within me, I hold us tighter and stroke faster. Niko's chest rises and falls erratically as he chases his release. The tendons in his neck stretch tight, trying to break through the skin as his jaw locks in concentration. Then suddenly it falls open on a soundless scream as he spasms in my hand, and his cum drips along my cock and floods between my fingers.

This isn't the first time I've watched him come, but the sheer awe on his face as his body convulses sends me over the edge. My balls draw up to the point of pain and burst, mixing my jizz with his as it spurts from my tip and slides over our skin. Through it all I keep pumping, pulling out every last drop until there's nothing left to give. Only then do I collapse onto his chest, reveling in the sticky, sweaty remnants of one of the best orgasms of my life.

"I win," Niko pants as he wraps his arms around me.

"If you say so," I rasp against his glistening skin.

"I came first. Even if I didn't, you played lightsaber dicks with me. You did something fun without me making you do it first. Total win." I can hear the smile in his voice, and instead of feeling embarrassed or grouchy for doing something so ridiculous, I actually feel sort of happy.

Still, I can't let him think it's that easy. "You ambushed me with sex talk before I was fully awake. Don't let it go to your head."

"Wouldn't dream of it." He kisses my cheek before relaxing back into the pillows. The languid stroke of his fingers over my back makes me fight to keep my eyes open. It's the most tender moment I've ever experienced with another man, both because it's so intimate and because it follows sex that I laughed during. That's never happened, yet I kinda like it.Several minutes later, Niko breaks the comfortable silence. "How did you know I always wanted to do that?"

"Do what?"

"Use my dick like a lightsaber."

I smile against his pec. "Pretty sure every guy on the planet imagined doing that as a kid when they discovered it gets hard."

"Yeah, but don't they outgrow that like a decade before they're twenty?"

Resting my head upon my fist I stare up his chest and give him a wry grin. This smiling thing is almost starting to feel normal, especially when those blue eyes stare back at me. "Maybe. But you also picked me up using Star Wars references and you smile so damn much you remind me of a little kid with a shiny new toy, so I figured you'd enjoy some light role play."

"Little kid? With this body?" He wraps his arms around me as he flexes, demonstrating how *'not little'* he is.

I shift my hand so I can reach his nipple and give it a firm pinch. "Little kid at heart, dimples."

"Didn't we agree not to use that nickname?" He rubs the sting away with an exaggerated pout.

"Sorry, couldn't resist. And while we're on the topic, I can get on board with lightsaber dicks, but I draw the line at cosplay."

A slight crease mars his brow. "What's cosplay?"

"Dressing up like fantasy characters."

"You don't like Halloween?" A look of pure horror washes over his face. "That's one of the best holidays. Even Swedes celebrate it. Not on the same day, but we do the whole dress up thing. It's awesome. My sister and I went as Luke and Leia Skywalker one year because—twins. And I went as Peter Forsberg one year—I'm assuming as the son of a hockey coach you know who that is—and we go door-to-door for candy. Not enough people give out dark chocolate, which sucks since my coaches didn't want us to have too much sugar, but it was still fun."

I have to force myself not to roll my eyes at his childlike excitement. He has no idea how easy he is to read. "I like Halloween just fine. Fantasy conventions in costume I don't like."

"Conventions?"

"It's a thing comic fans do. Or fans of sci fi or fantasy. They have big gatherings where the actors sign stuff and people sell movie swag and most of the crowd dresses in elaborate costumes like their favorite characters."

"How could you not love that?"

"Hmm, maybe because I'm nearly twenty-four, I hate crowds—people in general, really—and my appreciation for good entertainment stops well short of obsession."

"No wonder you're drawn to me." Those dimples are damn near craters, and his smug grin is so big as he looks at me down his chest.

"Why's that?"

"I'm going to keep you from becoming a grumpy old man in your twenties."

"Isn't brooding your type? You should be enjoying my grumpiness instead of trying to convert me to the light."

"Brooding is sexy, but not as sexy as when I can get my dark and grouchy man to smile just for me." Niko waggles his eyebrows, and damn if that doesn't make the corner of my lip tic upward. "Just like that," he whispers as he pulls my mouth to his.

***

The hollow scraping of wheels rolling over concrete echoes around me as I propel myself forward, picking up speed as I roll toward the spine in the center of the capsule. Just as the slope turns vertical, I bend my knees and pump my arms to gain more air, gripping the skateboard as I spin five hundred and forty degrees, landing right back where I started and rolling cleanly out of the trick.

"It's criminal how easy you make that look." Tripp kicks after me until we're rolling side-by-side toward the far end of the park. "Especially since I taught you that trick and you look better than me doing it."

I'd been skating a few years before I met Tripp in college, but YouTube was my primary teacher since I wasn't exactly a popular kid. When we both happened to be at the park one day Tripp pointed out how I could better execute some of the tricks I'd been working on, and it took my skating to another level.

He likes to give me shit about passing him in the skills department, but what he doesn't understand is loners have a lot more time to practice than guys like him who are happy to be the center of attention. As it is, he only rides once a week, whereas I'm here at least three. I'd come more than that, but he usually forces me to go see a band instead of skating, which is funny since he tends to complain about how boring I am when I do go to concerts with him.

Truthfully, while we have some things in common, I've often wondered why he tries to be my friend. God knows, I don't make it easy even though I like him more than most people.

"Did that band like the video you made for them?" I steer us away from skateboarding so he doesn't dissect why I make it look easy, which would only lead to a reprimand about me needing to play nice with others.

"The lead singer thought I made him look hotter in the video than he is in real life—duh—and now he's hired a trainer and nutritionist to make sure his body is just as good as the one I gave him. The other's aren't quite as vain and they loved it without getting an inferiority complex."

"This is why I don't like working with musicians. Or actors. Too much drama." I roll to a stop and kick my board into my hand so I can carry it over to the table where we've set our drinks.

Tripp mirrors me from a few steps behind. "Yes, but the videos they want are so much more cutting edge than corporate teasers and commercials. Don't you want to push the envelope? Test your design skills?"

"I want to go home at the end of the day and not think about work anymore."

"So, you don't care at all about making a name for yourself?"

"I like my anonymity." That might be the result of having a sizeable trust fund which means I don't have to forge my own success, but it's just as accurate to say that I like to fly under the radar since there are fewer questions about why I didn't follow my dad's footsteps that way.

Obviously, my secret boyfriend will throw a wrench into that plan when he eventually comes out, and the hockey questions will come up again. I'm dreading that part of dating an NHL player, but I'm hopeful after the initial reveal things will die down and I'll fade into the background again. Besides, if things do work between us, we'd probably drive each other crazy if we both take work home with us, and since I know how consuming hockey can be outside the rink, I'm more than happy to be the one who can completely unplug once I'm off the clock.

"If you like it so much, why are you frowning? I mean, I know that's your face, but it's different now. More like you're deep in thought than angry." He uncaps his water bottle and starts chugging, a trickle escaping from the corner of his mouth as he waits for my reply.

Sometimes I hate how observant Tripp is, but I suppose this is a good opportunity to try being his actual friend.

"At some point in the future, sometime this year probably, I'm going to lose my anonymity. At least temporarily."

"You got some big project I don't know about? And if so, why aren't I working on it with you? You know we're the two best artists in the whole office, and I want the fame and glory."

"This isn't about work, and it won't earn me any glory."

"Fame then?" His eyebrows skyrocket as he starts imagining the possibilities.

"Hopefully not." I squeeze my eyes shut to get the next part out. "I'm sort of maybe seeing someone. Someone who's currently in the closet."

"The baby gay hockey player who took you home from the concert?" he deadpans.

I crack an eyelid open to study him, hoping to see some sign that he's teasing me, but it's not there. Instead, he has this sort of bored look that says *duh*.

"Okay, A, he's not a baby gay he's been gay his whole life, he just hasn't told anyone besides family yet. And B, why would you assume it's him?"

"By my definition, anyone still in the closet is a baby gay, and my blond hair is a dye job–" he points to his head "-not a state of mind. I'm way too savvy to miss the tension crackling between you two. Plus, ever since he moved here, I've caught you almost smiling at least half a dozen times, which only happened twice in all the years prior. All I can say is it's a good thing you aren't a spy or anything because you suck at discretion."

"*I* suck at discretion? I haven't told you about a single hookup of mine, meanwhile you boast about yours in so much detail I could probably pick out the dicks of everyone you've ever slept with from a lineup."

Tripp shakes his head with an exaggerated sigh and points to his eyes. "Twenty, twenty. As an artist, you should know you can see a picture more clearly by looking at it than hearing the words used to describe it."

"You're a philosopher now?" I arch a thick brow in his direction.

"I don't need to be to understand you. Something happened to you, something that made you build a wall to keep everyone in your life from getting too close. Then right about the same time Mr. Tall, Dark and Hockey followed you to the bathroom at your dad's house the wall started to crack. I did not need a magnifying glass and a trench coat to piece that shit together."

"That's your evidence? He followed me to the bathroom?"

"If you recall I pegged him as your mystery guy before that, but I let you think I bought your denial since it clearly freaked you out to admit you were into him. You're lucky I'm so good at reading you otherwise I'd have never let him take you home from the concert which, by my math, is when things really started to get rolling between you two. You're welcome. Now, explain how this might result in fame you don't want, because I for one would be happy to be the arm candy of a hockey god."

Opening up still doesn't come naturally—it's been years since I've voluntarily done it—and the fear of my words and feelings being used against me is present even now, despite the fact that Tripp has never done anything to betray my trust. Yet I also have the urge to think out loud, with someone, instead of holding everything inside.

Whether that's Niko's influence, an internal desire to change, or the fact Tripp's already put most of the puzzle together I can't say. I just know I'm tired of working so hard to keep people at arm's length.

"Isn't that obvious?" *Apparently, my way of opening up still skews toward defensive, but I guess it's a start.* "Neither of us wants Niko to be known for his sexuality rather than his talent, and as the son of the coach, our relationship would raise questions about favoritism."

That's a side effect Niko and I haven't discussed, though I'm sure he's thought of it, same as I have. It just takes a back seat to the whole 'first gay rookie in the NHL thing.'

Tripp waves a dismissive hand. "The son of the coach thing is bullshit. Do you know how many NFL coaches have their kids working for them?"

If that's a thing it's news to me. "Do you?"

"Yes. At least half a dozen. And that doesn't include college ball. Sports can turn into a family business, just like anything else, so the whole nepotism argument doesn't hold any weight."

"How do you know this?"

"I keep up with pop culture." His shoulder ticks up casually. "That includes sports."

"Huh. Well, even if it's not unheard of to have family relationships cross over to work, we're talking about my dad. You know how protective he is of his players. He banned you from his house for flirting with them. He'd kill me if he knew I was dating one. And it's Niko's first year on the team—dating me wouldn't put him in my dad's good graces."

"Even if you two were in love?"

"Who said anything about love?" I prop my ass on the table like I'm tired of standing, though the reality is my legs feel like they could give out any moment. The 'L' word hasn't been a part of my vocabulary for a long time and I'm not ready to bring it back yet.

Tripp cocks an eyebrow in this artfully exaggerated way that makes him look all-knowing. It's part creepy and part impressive, though I'd never admit that to him.

"How many years have we known each other? Five? Six? And in all that time you've never confided in me about your personal life. Not once. Until Mr. Hockey."

"That's because one-night stands are hardly worth talking about."

"Sex is *always* worth talking about." His mouth ticks up in a suggestive grin as he takes another sip of water.

"I'm not talking about sex now."

"I know, and I wish you would. Mr. Hockey is hot. I bet he's sort of innocent too, since he's not out. You can mold him into your perfect sex toy. Damn, that gives me goosebumps. I want a Mr. Hockey." Tripp closes his eyes as a shiver pulses through him, his toned abs rippling in a way I'm sure has his partners drooling, though his theatrics leave me rolling my eyes.

It wouldn't be accurate to call him flamboyant, just showy. Always pushing the envelope to see what type of reaction he can elicit. And now that I think about it, he's probably over-the-top with me since I work so hard not to show any reaction.

"Still not telling you about sex with Niko." I hold firm, not because I object to Tripp's curiosity but because I don't want to share that side of my boyfriend.

I have a boyfriend!

"You're doing it again." Tripp's eyes grow wide as he watches me.

"What?"

"Smiling. It must be good then. That's a relief. I'd be pissed on your behalf if he wasn't at least giving you good dick, considering he's pulled you into the closet with him."

That statement has me instantly sobering. "I'm not in the closet."

"No? So, where'd you go on your first date?"

"I... It's not like that. He needs time to secure his status on the team before coming out." *Jesus, now I'm defending the very thing I swore never to tolerate? Maybe the 'L' word isn't out-of-line. No, wait. It's too soon for that, isn't it?*

"I'm not judging." Tripp holds his hands up in surrender. "I'm just pointing out the obvious. If one half of a couple is in the closet, then you both are. It's inevitable."

"Shit." I scrub a hand over my face as I realize the truth. *Why didn't I see it before I agreed to...* Okay, that's a lie. I saw it, which is why I didn't want to be in this position. Yet, here I am, willingly putting separation between my public and private life.

"Still want me to believe you aren't in love with him?"

"I mean, I could see that happening. I didn't think it already had."

I must look panicked because Tripp starts babbling. "Maybe you aren't. I'm hardly the right person to make that call. I've never been in love. Pretty sure I'm not capable of it. Don't let this lean body deceive you—I'm a buffet kind of guy. The more options the better. On occasion I'll go back for seconds or thirds, but mostly I'm a 'get my fill and move on to the next dish' person. I..."

"So, you'd never go back in the closet. Under any circumstances?"

"Personally?" He splays a hand over his chest. "I can't see that being a situation that would apply to me, no."

"I'm being an idiot then." I press my lips into a line before I go into a tirade about knowing this was a bad idea.

"I didn't say that."

"You're thinking it. What kind of guy goes back into the closet after being out for over a decade?"

"The kind who found someone worth making sacrifices for." Tripp's perpetually mischievous look turns serious. "I'll deny it until my dying breath, so don't get any crazy ideas about me being a romantic or anything, but since Mr. Hockey got here you've been different. Happy. He did that. He gave you that. So, even if it means going back in the closet for now, maybe what you can give him in return is the support he needs to come out."

"I want to believe that. Hell, I think I already convinced myself it would go down that way. I've been wrong before though..." I don't have the strength to finish that thought.

"Is that where the wall comes from?"

I close my eyes and nod sharply.

"You need a new type." He shakes his head with an exaggerated eye roll.

"Subtle as always," I mumble.

"Oh, come on, let me have a little fun with this. I deserve it after years of you being such an impenetrable vault."

"Fair." I blow a stray hair away from my eye on a heavy exhale.

"Can I assume Mr. Hockey has some redeeming qualities that make him worth the trouble? Other than the cock I'm betting is just as gorgeous as the rest of him?"

It's on the tip of my tongue to say honesty, though as Niko himself pointed out, his words are just that until he acts on them. Until then, who's to say if he's as honest as I want to believe? There's his boyish amusement with everything life has to offer, his love of all things superhero and sci-fi, but those aren't redeeming qualities, just things that make me like him.

The longer I'm silent the longer I wonder if there's any real substance behind my feelings, or if it's all an illusion. A handful of similarities wrapped in a sexy package that I've confused as someone I could love instead of someone I lust after. How do I tell the difference? Would Tripp know?

Then a memory wriggles through the fog in my brain. The one where I lashed out at Niko for forcing me to keep his secret, and him telling me I should confide in Tripp. Telling me he trusts me enough to know who it's safe to share that secret with.

"He told me to tell you. About us. He said he trusts me to share his secret with people who would respect it." I search Tripp's face for signs that he sees that as a redeeming quality, and my breaths seem to come easier when he gives me a curt little nod.

"I suppose if he was opposed to coming out, he wouldn't have made that concession," Tripp muses.

"That's my hope."

"Is it really that big a deal to be gay in sports?" he asks.

We both know the answer, but I suspect this is his way of trying to cheer me up. I appreciate the gesture, even though it's a futile one. "You're the pop culture guy, is it?"

He chews on his lip a moment before responding. "Most people do seem to wait until retirement to come out. And this is your guy's first year."

Now we're back to what's been my biggest fear all along. Not whether Niko will come out—because I do believe he will—but when.

"How long is the average hockey career?" Tripp tilts his head to the side thoughtfully.

"Average is around five, but some guys play fifteen years or more. They're the exception, but it happens."

"Could you—"

"No." I complete his thought before he can finish it. "I couldn't live in the closet for fifteen years or more."

"What about five?"

"I'd rather not, although if it's only five I'd still be under thirty by the time he comes out. Plenty of time... Shit." I shake my head with a humorless laugh. "We're talking like this is a sure thing when I only started dating him last night."

"You wouldn't be dating him at all if you didn't think it was a sure thing. Not with him still in the closet."

He's not wrong, but I'm curious why he's so sure about that considering how little I've confided in him over the years. "What makes you say that?"

"You live your life like the glass is half empty. If you believed that about him, you wouldn't waste your time. Remember," he points to his hair when my jaw drops, "dye job, not a state of mind. So, is this our last weekly skate?"

"What?" My brows fall into their trademark frown as I gape at him. "Why would you say that?"

"Closets and whatnot." He waves a nonchalant hand, though his posture is uncharacteristically stiff.

"Dating a guy in the closet doesn't mean I can't have gay friends."

"It shouldn't, but sometimes people get weird about that shit. And, no offense, but you weren't exactly the friendliest son of a bitch to begin with."

I give his shoulder a firm shove. "The only thing this changes is no PDA."

"You didn't do that anyway," he snorts.

"Exactly. So, nothing changes."

"In that case, congratulations on chaining yourself to a set of balls. Please direct any and all sexy guys you can't have to me." He holds a hand out and I take it, thinking we're just going to shake. Instead, he pulls me to him so our shoulders bump and pats his hand on my back. Then he drops my hand and pushes me away. "You're still too moody for a bro hug. Feels weird."

"Yeah, let's not make a habit of that." I grab my board and head back over to the park, taunting him over my shoulder. "If you make the five forty look as pretty as I do, maybe I'll give you a fist bump."

He grabs his board and jogs after me. "Oh, hell no! You know fist bumps are even more lame than jazz hands. Please tell me you didn't learn that from Mr. Hockey. It'll ruin the fantasy if they jumped on that bandwagon."

I have no idea whether Niko and his friends fist bump or not since I've only seen them together at the concert I barely remember, but to spare Tripp I tell him what he wants to hear. "Of course not."

"Oh, thank god." His chest relaxes as he exhales. "The Thor look-alike can stay on my to-do list."

"Pretty sure he's straight." I roll my eyes at him.

"Like that'll stop me from trying." Tripp grins as he drops his board and pushes off, missing how I smile at his antics for the first time.

Chapter 17
Niko

"Putt putt is like hockey on dry land. How do you not have an unfair advantage?" Xander asks as we collect the balls and putters.

"It's like a disco in here, I can barely see what I'm aiming for." A Google search for things to do turned up this event center that has everything from mini golf to bowling and laser tag

Plus, after nine it's adults only so it becomes equal parts bar hangout and activity space. I picked it thinking the dim lighting might help us stay relatively anonymous, not because I'm here with Xander, but because I want to be interrupted as little as possible.

When our preseason games started and the media coverage ramped up, so did the chatter about me. I'm far from a household name, but die-hard fans might spot me, and I'd rather not get stuck in a conversation with them when my focus should be on my boyfriend. As much as it can be when we're trying to maintain the illusion that we're just friends.

"If you can follow a puck traveling at a hundred miles an hour, I'm sure you make a hole in the ground from twenty feet away."

"I guess we'll find out." I drop my ball onto the little mat with three holes and step back to study what might be the best path. There's no clear answer, angled walls mean the ball will have to ricochet a few times to get to the hole, and geometry was never my strength. Figuring a solid whack is as good a solution as any, I give the ball a solid hit and watch in ping pong back and forth on its way toward the hole. It doesn't drop, but it gets damn close.

"You were saying?" Xander remarks dryly.

"Beginners luck."

Nine holes later I've got a commanding lead, which makes me feel both guilty and amused. I really didn't expect to be good at this game, but it's sort of funny that I am. It's even funnier that Xander's so bad, though it's fitting considering silly games like this are way outside his element. He gets points for being a good sport though.

"We need to loosen you up. You'd do a lot better if you weren't so stiff." I let my putter fall to the ground and grip his shoulders from behind, squeezing the muscles in my hand once before abruptly letting go with a quick glance to see if anyone saw me.

"I'd do a lot better if I wasn't matched against someone who hits things with a stick for a living. I told you that you'd have an unfair advantage."

I pick up my putter and stride to collect my ball. "We could do laser tag instead. Neither of us should have an advantage there. Or bowling. Definitely bowling. I like the idea of watching you strut up to the line to roll your ball." I sneak a quick peek at his tight ass before I can stop myself, then shake my head to clear the image.

"That kind of talk will give you a boner, and you're not supposed to sprout those with your friends." His tone isn't accusatory in the least, it's actually almost playful, but it still makes me feel like an asshole.

"It's my first secret date. I'm still getting my bearings."

"Let's grab a drink then. We can't get into much trouble sitting in the bar."

We return our equipment and grab a booth in the corner of the mostly empty seating area. Even though the crowd is light since it's a weeknight, we both seem to gravitate toward the spot that's out of the way. After ordering and receiving our beer—without having to show ID, fortunately—I broach the elephant in the room.

"So, I guess this can be considered a fail."

"How so?" Xander's expression doesn't give anything away, leaving me to go out on a limb.

"You don't seem to be having much fun and I'm not sure how to act. It feels like we're strangers."

His brown eyes seem to soften a bit after hearing my confession. "This isn't just your first secret date, it's your first date, period. Isn't it?"

I nod my head.

"Well, the good news is first dates are notoriously awkward, at least in my experience. The bad news is things will never be as easy in public as they are in private. Not in our situation."

"Fuck." I scrub a hand over my face. It's not like some part of me wasn't aware of this, though I did think the intense connection Xander I have would make it less of an issue. "I guess you probably think I'm pretty naïve."

"Not naïve. Optimistic. You didn't know what to expect exactly, but you were hoping for a different experience."

I spin my glass on the coaster beneath it. "Why does it feel like we're strangers though? Normally, I feel so comfortable with you, but right now I feel...off-balance."

"Because you're trying to be something you're not. You're the adorkable jock who lives life to the fullest, not the stoic, straight guy who has to act tough. That may be a role you've played in the past, but never with me. That's why you feel off."

My lips start to curve into a smile but pause when my brain gets stuck on a single word. "Adorkable? Please tell me I heard you wrong and you didn't just Clark Kent me."

"What's wrong with Clark Kent?"

"I'm way sexier than him," I mutter under my breath. Then I catch Xander's smug grin and crack one of my own. "I walked right into that one, didn't I?"

"To be fair, I wouldn't have been able to bait you like that if I wasn't also a comic nerd."

I chuckle softly before the original conversation sobers me with a sharp pain to my chest. "This isn't gonna work, is it? I can't have you and keep you a secret at the same time."

"It's only been one non-date. It could get better."

"When did we switch roles? Usually, I'm the one trying to convince you to give things a chance."

"I mean, I figure if I agreed in the first place, I should at least give you two non-dates before I give up." I swear those chocolate eyes almost look hopeful, like he really does want this to work. That's both encouraging and depressing, since I'm pretty sure *I'm* the reason it wouldn't.

"What now? I really don't want to hide you away, but I don't know how to act like you're just some guy I like to hang out with in public. I thought I could but... It feels wrong."

"It feels wrong for me too, but I'm not sure it would feel right to act any different."

"What do you mean?"

"Brooding asshole, remember?" He points to himself. "I'm not exactly the poster boy for PDA, so I'm not sure what level of affection I'm comfortable with in public. It feels wrong to be guarded around you, but it also doesn't since I'm always guarded, if that makes any sense."

"It does." I nod thoughtfully, because I can see how this is just as new for him in his own way as it is for me. "It doesn't make things much clearer though. How can I be with you and not be *with* you? I mean, not to sound like a cliché dickhead, but you deserve better."

"We both deserve better. Every gay man on the planet deserves better. The reality is it doesn't work that way. Look." He runs a hand through his already disheveled hair. "I don't love the situation we're in, but I understand why we're in it. If we want to give this a chance, then we either have to put on the buddy act or only see each other behind closed doors."

Though I'm relieved he didn't say 'come out,' I'm also a little surprised. On the surface that's the easiest solution for him since it would mean he doesn't have to live a lie for my career. The fact that he actually took my career into account, at his own expense, damn near makes me choke up.

"I feel like that's a bigger sacrifice for you than me, though. You haven't had to put that act on in years."

"At first, I thought the same thing, but after talking with Tripp I'm not so sure. I may be out, but I'm not overly loud about it. I don't have a reputation as a playboy or anything that would create instant speculation about us if we're seen together. And as long as there isn't any joint Ubering no one will really know where we're sleeping."

"It's still denying a big part of yourself. Do you really think I'm worth that?" I bring my eyes to his, bracing for him to shake his head.

"Do you think I'm worth losing your career?" His gaze doesn't waver.

I'm tempted to say yes, but since he didn't answer I don't either. We've had enough revelations for one night. Instead, I hold his stare and say, "I think we've got a lot of takeout and Netflix in our future. Unless you want to give bowling a try." I tip my head toward the lanes, and the faint echo of wood crashing against wood, hoping to steer things in a lighter direction.

"Are you asking if I want to roll a ball over the ground or whether I want to stick my pin in your ass?"

Xander's face is perfectly straight, meanwhile my jaw drops so far it's a wonder it's still attached. "You just made a joke. A sex joke. I didn't even think of that one."

"I guess that means you aren't the only one with a dirty mind."

Licking my lips, I fish for the wad of bills in my wallet. "I have never wanted to kiss you as bad as I do right now. We need to go. Stat."

"Stat?" He arches an inquisitive brow.

"It means fast. Emergency level fast."

"I know what it means. What I don't know is anyone who says it, excluding hospital staff."

"Now you do." I lean forward, intending to give him a quick kiss, though I divert at the last second and virtually launch myself out of the booth, bracing a hand on the back of his seat to keep from toppling over. *Suave. Thank God we picked seats in the back corner.* "Ready?"

Xander bites back an amused grin. "Only you could have more grace on the ice than dry land."

"Take me back to your place and I'll show you how much grace I have in the bedroom."

I give myself a mental high-five when he sucks in a ragged breath and mumbles, "Follow me."

***

Xander's apartment is on the fourth floor, with a sliver of a mountain view out the balcony of the living room. It's small but open, so the kitchen and dining area and living room all blend together, and the bright counters over dark cabinets make it feel more modern than mountainous. But aside from that quick glimpse, I don't waste time checking the place out. I've got a sexy boyfriend to check out instead.

"Come here," I command, pulling him to me by his t-shirt until he's close enough to wrap my arms around his waist. "Do you have any idea how hard it is not to do this whenever I want?"

He gives me one of his *you-can't-be-serious* looks.

"Okay, bad word choice. Do you have any idea how hard it is to finally have someone I *want* to do this with and can't? I mean, secret hookups weren't hard to maintain when that's all they were. When that's not all I want then..."

Xander sets his hand on my hips with a swift nod. "I wanted you to kiss me tonight. When you nearly did and almost face-planted next to the booth. I wanted it so bad I'm not sure I would've stopped you if you didn't stop yourself."

"Feels like you still want it," I say as I realize my dick isn't the only one that's hard.

"Always."

"What else do you want?" I rock my hips forward, loving the way it makes his eyelids flutter.

"Your cock. In my mouth."

"Take it out then."

Slowly, delicately, Xander unbuttons my jeans and slides my zipper down, opening the flaps enough that he can work the denim and the waist of my boxers to the curve of my hip. Then he tugs the front of my shorts down, exposing my rigid length.

The blast of cool air followed immediately by the warmth of his fist pulls a needy groan from my throat, and as my head falls back in rapture, he peppers kisses along my neck and over my collarbone.

"Take your shirt off." Xander nuzzles along the neckline.

"You planning to lick my abs on the way down?"

"Maybe. But tight as this shirt is," he plucks it away from my body with a sly grin, "it's still gonna make it difficult to watch me swallow—"

He doesn't get to finish that thought before I'm whipping the material over my head, eager for an unobstructed view of his perfect little mouth wrapping around my girth.

"That's better." He pinches one nipple between his fingertips as he flicks his tongue over the other, the mix of pleasure/pain sending a bolt of lust straight to my balls, which makes my cock bob greedily in the loose grip of his hand.

"Patience," Xander murmurs as he teases the firm buds on my chest, pinching and flicking one as his tongue swirls around the peak of the other, sucking it hard into his mouth.

"Can't help it. My dick *really* wants to get wet." As if in agreement it strains in his hand again. He gives it a gentle squeeze, and an even softer tug, as he kisses over my pecs, making no move to go lower.

"Alexander," I groan, rocking to the balls of my feet so I can push my cock further into his grip. He chuckles and drags his tongue down the center of my torso, licking and nipping at the ridges of my six pack along the way.

Despite the pleasant tingle of his mouth trailing over my body, my dick throbs with the need for friction. Every muscle in my body is coiled tight and primed to explode if I lose the precarious hold I have right now.

"Baby, please," I moan. We never talked about whether that term is okay, but he's never objected to it outright like he did angel, and saying his full name didn't get the results I want. Namely, my cock between his lips. Which I need about as desperately as I need air right now.

"I love it when you beg." Xander drops to his knees as he places featherlight kisses on my hipbones, over the thatch of hair between my legs, all while just barely stroking his fingertips over my length.

"Such a tease," I grumble as he rubs his nose over my balls, inhaling my musky scent.

"This isn't teasing." He flicks his tongue over my slit, circling the crown once before pulling back to stroke me. "This is getting you ready so I can bounce on your dick."

My lewd retort gets stuck on my tongue when he takes me to the back of his throat, humming like my dick satisfies some erotic craving. God knows that's how I feel about his mouth.

And then it's gone. Cool air rushes my shaft as he pulls back, circling the velvet tip with his tongue. Lightly. Delicately. Playfully, with no real purpose other than to keep me wanting.

Xander toys with me as his fist lightly strokes over my shaft, pulling out of reach each time I try to thrust forward. The devious bastard forces me to hold still to feel him, testing the ability of my stomach muscles to stay flexed in restraint as he has his way with me. And yeah, Xander in control is hot, but in my current state it'd be hotter if that control ran more along the lines of "fuck my face" than "hold still."

I really want him to bounce on my dick later though, so I clench my fists at my sides and hold my breath. It takes everything I have to be patient while he laps at my junk when what I really want is for him to slurp it like a straw.

Then, mercifully and without warning, he takes me so far, his nose brushes against my pubes, and a feral growl rumbles from my chest.

"Sounds like you enjoyed that." He looks at me from under hooded eyes, so dark with desire my tip starts dripping from his gaze alone.

"Fuck yes I did."

"Mmm." He does it again, taking half my length this time and letting it go with an audible pop, and issues a warning. "No coming until you're inside me."

Hands braced on my denim clad thighs, Xander bobs his head over my length, running his silky tongue from root to tip as he moves. Gone is the gentle suction, the languid pace. Instead, he moves furiously, relentless in his pursuit of my pleasure.

Squelching noises filter around us as I push into his mouth, and my body shivers as I feel him coating my length with his heat. *Damn it feels good to have my dick slippery wet.* So good, I physically can't stop my hips from rocking forward, chasing the carnal high he's giving me.

"That's it, baby. Suck me all the way down. Get me nice and wet so I can fuck that tight little hole." I manage to thrust right through my comments as if I didn't just step way outside the lines, and if Xander notices, he doesn't let on. But now that I've said it out loud, I'm positively buzzing with the thought of getting inside him bare.

I've never done that before, never wanted to, yet now I've got this overwhelming desire to know what it would feel like. As wet as his mouth? As hot? Silky smooth or... "Ugh, God," I grunt, as he cups my balls, rolling them around his palm.

He pulls off me, lips deliciously swollen and pink, and gives me a nice, firm tug. "I think this will do. Go sit on the couch."

I do not need to be told twice.

Chapter 18
Xander

Shirtless, with his pants just low enough to expose that beautiful cock, Niko leans against the back of the couch, one arm slung over the cushions while the other leisurely strokes his length. Looking at me from under hooded blue eyes, muscles clenched in an obvious attempt at restraint, he's the epitome of raw sex appeal.

Gorgeous.

Feral.

And all *mine*.

I suppress a shiver as that thought goes through my mind. I've never been the possessive type, nor have I ever felt pride in capturing a man's attention. With Niko I want to bask in the knowledge that his body belongs to me, and I'm the only one who can satisfy it.

"You gonna stare at me all night?" Niko challenges.

"I do like the view." I lick my lips as he fondles himself.

"I'd say the same but... Mine's obstructed."

"What do you want to see?"

"Everything." Those baby blues darken with lust, a silent command to bare myself for his enjoyment, and I waste no time shedding my clothes to give him what he so desperately wants.

Naked, exposed, my cock is a steel rod pointing directly at him, and he traps his bottom lip between his teeth in anticipation as he lifts his arm from the back of the couch and crooks a finger at me. I stalk slowly toward him, skin warming under the heat of his eyes, and kneel with my legs on either side of his hips. Close enough that I can feel his breath caress my crown each time he exhales.

Fisting his own cock with his right hand, he tenderly drags a finger over mine before cupping my balls, gently massaging the globes in his palm. Pleasure radiates through them, spiraling outward to my extremities and making my length bob heavily in front of his mouth. Leaning forward, he swipes his tongue over my slit, capturing a drop of precum.

"God," he sighs. "Seeing you this hard for me..." He takes his hand off my balls and rubs it slowly along my shaft. "I'll never get tired of this."

"I hope not." I hand him the foil packet I took from my pocket before losing my clothes. "Think you can put this on while you suck me?" I tilt my hips forward just enough that the sensitive skin of my cockhead ghosts over his lips.

"Please," he scoffs, taking it from me and letting his mouth fall open.

Slowly, tentatively, I push my crown inside, rubbing it over the flat of his tongue. Then I pull back and push forward, giving him just a little taste. It's hardly any friction at all, but his slack jaw, the wanton challenge in his eyes, has me clenching my toes in an effort to hold back the tingle in my groin that usually signals an imminent release. *Not yet.*

Mouth open, lust glazing his blue eyes, Niko holds still while I leisurely pump my swollen tip past his full lips, the visual is just as erotic as the act itself. Then those eyes fall closed as his mouth seals over me, and a gentle suction pulses rhythmically around my tip.

My hand reaches for the arm of the couch to help support my weight, which my legs feel too weak to bear. This man, this big, strong, gorgeous man is flat out worshiping my body right now, and it looks like he's in absolute heaven. It makes me want to reach out and cup his face, run my thumb over his cheek, or replace my cock with my tongue so I can taste him and breathe his air.

Whoa, slow down! An hour ago, he seemed ready to throw in the towel so I wouldn't be forced to hide who I am. Who he is to me. It's entirely too soon to add intimacy to sex. Focus on how your body feels, nothing more. Not yet.

The silky pad of his tongue, the wet heat surrounding me, makes my stomach flutter in anticipation as my balls tighten. I have to fight back another overwhelming wave of bliss. Holding my breath until the moment passes, I find myself on the brink again when Niko grips my hips and jerks me forward, filling his throat with my swollen cock.

The strangled moan that claws its way out of my throat seems especially loud until I realize he uttered a similar one, both of us seemingly caught in a fog of lust that's temporarily sated by my dick resting in his mouth. Then he hollows his cheeks and pushes my hips back, creating a vacuum around my sensitive skin that makes my thighs tremble.

As Niko releases me with an audible pop, I realize he's lodged himself at my entrance, and with a relieved sigh I sink onto his thick shaft.

The fit is snug—tight—at first, despite the lubed condom helping to alleviate the resistance. But the slight pain from the stretch quickly gives way to the sweet ache that only comes from being filled so completely.

"Baby," Niko groans as his head falls to the back of the couch, that single word causing my hole to clench firmly around him.

I can't explain why, especially in light of the fact that "angel" had the opposite effect, but hearing Niko call me baby turns my insides to this gooey, mushy puddle that's completely foreign and somehow familiar at the same time. Like a memory trying to claw its way back to the space it used to occupy. Or a subconscious dream turned reality. Either way, the word evokes a mix of sweet and sinful energy that makes me want to melt into Niko's chest then fuck him into oblivion.

Circling my hips, both to loosen me up and pull him deeper, I grind on his dick, causing my own to rub over his abs. Niko's eyelids flutter as my hole flexes around him, his chest rising and falling with each ragged breath. It's an image that will be forever seared into my brain, not because he's so sexy—though he is—but because I can put this look on his face.

Though I'm not moving fast, or rough, Niko seems to have a tenuous grip on his control, his fingers curling tightly into my thighs as the rigid set of his jaw betrays how hard he's clenching his teeth. Sensing he's close, I start to rise up, only to have those strong hands hold me down.

"I thought you wanted me to bounce on your dick." I lean forward to place tiny kisses on his chest, expecting that will get him to relax his hold.

"That was before yours started rubbing all over my stomach." He lets go of my left leg and rests his big hand on my cock, pressing it against his abs. "Grind that pretty little hole on cock and slide yours under my hand. Do it until you come."

"You don't want to watch my cock slapping your skin?" I've noticed that sight seems to get him off, which is why I suggested this position.

"Not tonight. I want to see those sexy abs move. Just like this." He flexes his hand just enough to send a jolt of lust straight to my balls, though it's less the strength of his grip than the idea of him simply holding me close to him, waiting for me to spill all over, that gets me riled.

"Won't take long," I grit. "You're rubbing against my prostate."

"And you're choking my cock." He swipes his thumb over the tip of mine, spreading the precum over my crown.

Bracing my hands on his chest for support, I exaggerate the swivel of my hips, straining to take him further, feel him deeper. With each pass his cockhead brushes over the sensitive bundle of nerves inside my core, and my body contracts around him, pulling the most carnal gasps and grunts from his throat.

"You feel so good, baby. So tight. I—" He sucks in a breath of air as I clench down hard, my release imminent. "Oh, fuck...baby. Oh fuck." His hips start to piston upward, shallow little thrusts to tip me over the edge so he can follow. And when his thumb once again circles my slit just as he pegs my prostate, I fall.

My dick pulses violently under his palm, spurting burst after burst of cum all over his chiseled abs as my hole contracts, strangling the cock buried inside it. My own euphoria is so great I barely register the flutters of his release deep inside me, though I can tell by the way his hips buck that I've triggered it, and we're both caught in the throes of all-consuming pleasure. Together.

Minutes later, or seconds—time has no relevance right now—we're both sweaty, panting and speechless. I can't speak for Niko, but until this moment I had no idea my body was capable of an orgasm like that without a relentless, almost punishing fuck. To feel it like this, slow and...sensual... I don't know what it means. Hell, I can't even begin to process it. Instead, I melt against Niko's chest, burying my nose in the crook of his neck. His hands rub my back in long, gentle strokes.

It's the last thing I remember before waking in my bed sometime in the night, Niko flush against my back. And it feels so right, I can't even stay awake long enough to question how we got here.

**

Two days later, Niko opens the door and drops into the passenger seat with an elated grin, holding up a sheet of paper. "I passed! They have to mail the actual license in a few weeks, but this counts until I get the real thing." The paper makes a crinkling sound as he shakes it.

"Good for you. Now instead of chauffeuring your ass all over the place you can drive me."

"Okay." He holds his hand out.

I smack it like I'm giving him five, and he wiggles his fingers. "What?" I ask.

"Keys."

"Having your license doesn't mean we share my car."

"Well, since I don't have one of my own, how else do you expect me to drive you."

"I expect you to get a car." I turn the engine over and pull out of the parking lot, heading in the opposite direction of his place.

"What, like now?"

"Why not? You don't have to make a decision, but you can at least look at the options in person."

"Um, yeah. Wow, okay."

Chuckling at the way his blue eyes go from curious to excited, I steer us to a section of town that has half a dozen dealerships. "Are you still thinking about the Wagoneer?"

"I like the look of it, yeah."

"New or used?"

"Why would I get a used one?" A tiny crease materializes between his brows, making me realize how cute he is when he's confused.

"New cars lose their value the minute you drive them off the lot, so used can be a better buy if it seems to be in good working order with low miles."

"So new is a waste of money?"

"It depends. New comes with warranties that will make it cheaper to maintain, at least for the first few years. And new has better financing options so you'll pay less in interest, if you don't plan to buy it outright."

"What would you do?"

I love that he trusts me enough to ask, but this can't be my decision. "Oh no. I can't make this call for you."

"Please."

"No way. You have to factor in your needs, your wants, and your finances. I can't do that for you." He looks so panicked I can't stop myself from taking his hand and giving it a reassuring squeeze. "But I will speak up if I think you're overlooking anything."

He leans back into the seat, visibly relaxing. "Thank you." He squeezes my hand back.

When we get to the lot, I wave away the salesman so he can speak freely, and we wander around, looking mostly at SUVs since Niko's a big guy who may need extra room for his gear from time to time. However, it must be some unspoken rule for athletes or big guys in general, because he veers toward a sleek sports car right away.

"I've heard people refer to cars as sexy before, but it never made any sense. Now it does." He admires the cherry red Corvette from every angle. "We should look at this one."

"Of course. Because it's made specifically for giants."

He stops drooling long enough to give me a withering look. "If you say this car isn't sexy, I might have to break up with you."

"It's sexy. It's also so low to the ground I honestly don't think you could get out of it without assistance. Unless maybe you roll out of it sideways and crawl on all fours until you can get your feet underneath you."

His hand lingers at the hem of his shirt before he seems to change his mind, patting his stomach instead. "My abs aren't intimidated."

"Maybe not but the car should be. You probably weigh the same as it."

"Are you calling me fat?"

"I'm calling you delusional if you think that's a good buy."

He casts the car a longing look before turning to me with a dejected pout. "Fine. Show me the smart buys."

We make our way to the truck section, and he peeks at the Wagoneer first, which is roomier in the back row than the front, then Yukons which are roomier in front. He even checks out a Range Rover like mine, although a newer model.

"I like the size of this one in general." He points to the Rover. "But the backseat looks pretty small."

"Why are you concerned about the backseat? Are you planning to shuttle your teammates around?"

"Maybe, if they need rides. But my first thought is that if we want to have sex in the car, we won't fit in the back very well."

Blinking away my shock I try to keep my voice level. "Why would we be having sex in the car? We've both got perfectly good king-size beds. And couches. And showers."

"All my roommates in college lost their virginity in their cars, so..." He wiggles his brows with a suggestive smirk.

"Fortunately for you, your cherry's been popped already, so you don't have to suffer that awkward rite of passage."

"Where's your sense of adventure? Plus, isn't there some sort of ritual where you break in new things?" He leads us back to the Wagoneer, walking around it like he's recording measurements in his head.

"It's called christening, and it's usually done in all the rooms of a new house. Not cars."

He gives me a suspicious once over. "Have you christened your entire house?"

"Apartment, and no. I've only christened the rooms we've slept in." Until Niko, I'd never invited anyone to "sleep" at my place. When those smug dimples appear I know he's put that together, which doesn't even make me cringe. In fact, I *like* knowing that he knows there's never been anyone besides him in my place.

"So, we still have to do the kitchen and the spare bedroom. That's not a lot of rooms. What if I buy a house? Then we'll have lots of rooms to christen." He bites his lip playfully, and I have to trap mine between my teeth to keep an uncharacteristic burst of laughter from escaping. Not that I object to laughing at his eagerness, but we are in public so it's best if I don't act like some smitten teenage girl.

"We're shopping for cars, not houses. Let's focus on one big purchase at a time."

"Fine, but only if you agree to christen the car with me."

Sex in a car is never something I wanted to experience, but my gentle giant is clearly fascinated with the idea, and like pretty much everything else when it comes to him, I don't know how to say no.

"This is the one you want then?" I tip my head toward the brand new Wagoneer.

"Is it a good buy?"

I did my research before this little field trip, so while I know this model isn't predicted to be as reliable as its competitors, it is projected to hold its value pretty well since its priced a bit lower. Plus, it'll be nice for Niko to have something under warranty for his first car.

"Yeah. I'd say it's a good buy. Let's go tell the sales guy you're ready to talk." I spin towards the building before I can get distracted by the unrestrained gleam in Niko's eye, and the knowledge that I helped put it there.

Chapter 19
Niko

P ractice is especially brutal, probably because we lost our last preseason game and there's only five more days until the season opener. I get it, but *fuck*. My legs have never been so jittery, and as Xander likes to say, I drink nuclear coffee.

"Can I get Gatorade in an IV? Because I think I really need that."

"Gatorade is one of the least efficient way to replace electrolytes. You'd be better off with water." Justus sets his helmet inside his locker and starts removing his jersey.

"Seriously? How do you know that?"

"Science fair in eighth grade."

"So... Water?" I hold up the half-empty bottle I took with me after leaving the ice.

"Pickle juice." Noah's booming voice echoes around us as he strides past to get to his locker.

"We're talking about the best way to replenish electrolytes, not strange dietary practices."

"I know."

"Okay, I've lived here long enough that fuck with the foreign guy doesn't work anymore, so you two can drop it." I point an accusing finger between the two of them.

"Noah's actually right." Justus flashes a guilty smile. "Pickle juice is by far the most effective recovery drink."

"But... It's green."

"So are most smoothies," Luca chimes in from the locker next to Noah's. "The ones that are better for you anyway."

"I don't drink my veggies, I eat them. Like nature intended."

"It's like he thinks he'll never lose his edge." Luca nudges Noah's shoulder with his own. "Remember when we were twenty and just as naïve."

"You've got three, maybe four years to exist in the "my body is a temple" bubble before you actually have to start treating it like a temple." Noah's smirk has an almost wicked air to it. "Enjoy it while you can."

I turn an astonished glance to Justus. "We've got until at least thirty, right?" I'm not ignorant of what happens when you get older, especially in pro sports, but I did think, barring any injuries, I had more than just a few years. He gives me a wary shrug that's in no way reassuring.

"If that's your goal, I'd learn to love the taste of pickle juice," Luca snickers.

"Sven." I whip my head in the direction of the door when I hear my last name. "Coach wants you in his office," one of the assistant coaches says.

A brief glance at my teammates tells me they have no idea why I've been summoned. That's a little disconcerting, but I've been practicing really well and even played a great game in our last loss, so it's unlikely I've done anything to get on his bad side.

"Be right there." I make quick work of shedding the rest of my gear, take a quick rinse in the shower, and make my way to his office in my team issued warm-ups.

"You wanted to see me, Coach," I call out as I knock on the door.

"Niko, yes. Come in." He waves me forward, gesturing to the seat in front of his desk. I take it and cross my hands over my stomach, waiting for him to speak.

"How are you adjusting to the team? Any concerns?"

On the surface it's an innocent question, but the first thing that comes to mind is why he would even ask. Have I given him, or anyone, reason to think I don't like it here?

"The team is great. Noah and Luca have been really support-ive—they're helping with plans to get my sister here for the first game—and Justus and I have hit it off pretty well as the new guys."

His head bobs up and down as I talk, like he's cataloging every word.

"Yes, I think I have your sister's flight details here somewhere so we can send someone to pick her up. And the team condo? I know it probably doesn't feel like home yet, but you can stay there as long as you need, and if you want something different there's plenty of people on staff who can connect you with the resources to find what you want."

"Uh, thanks, but right now I'm fine. Once the road games start, I'll hardly be there anyway, so it's all I need at the moment."

"Good, good. And Denver? It's a bigger city than what you're used to, and any of the guys would be happy to show you around town."

That's the second time he's mentioned how willing people would be to help, which would be reassuring if I thought all the new guys were getting the same treatment. Since none of them have been called in for a meeting, I doubt that's the case. I suppose I could just be lucky number one, but my gut says otherwise, and I feel like testing whether I'm right.

"They've already done that, but thanks for checking. Should I send Justus in next?" I play the innocent rookie card.

"No need." He reaches for some papers on his desk, a subtle dismissal, and one I should take since it'll keep this from turning into anything other than a friendly check-in. But my curiosity gets the better of me.

"Am I missing something? Has the rest of the team suggested I'm not fitting in?"

"No, nothing like that."

"Okay, good. Have I done something to make you concerned," I press, "because I don't want to give the impression I'm not excited to be here."

He sets the papers down and meets my gaze, clearing his throat before he speaks. "I know you've been hanging out with my son."

It's impossible to keep my face blank, so I do the next best thing, hoping it will camouflage my visible shock. I give him the biggest smile I can muster. "Yeah, Xander's great. I'm so glad I bumped into him at the team cookout. He's been showing me around, so he's made it a lot easier to adjust to a new city. He even helped me buy a car the other day."

Since every single word of that is true, I'm hoping I don't come across like I'm trying to hide anything.

"Yes, my friend saw you two at the dealership." Coach's comment makes me especially glad I volunteered that information, but it does little to make me feel better about this conversation. "It got me curious since Xander's never actually purchased a car. He's still driving the one I bought him when he graduated high school."

"He mentioned that. I looked at a similar model, but I wanted something a bit bigger."

"Hmm." Coach's expression doesn't soften as much as I'd hoped. "You know, cars are another thing the organization can help you with. You don't have to rely on my son to figure things out."

"As long as Xander doesn't mind, I like getting his help. Besides, he's easy to talk to, and he's one of the few people who doesn't make fun of my taste in movies." I'm hoping that explanation is enough to make my exit, but when Coach reclines in his chair, I know that's a futile thought.

"You know, Xander doesn't usually hang around the team."

"Makes sense since he's not much of a sports guy." I stick to my plan of saying only things that are true so I can't get caught in a lie, and this particular truth came up during the cookout so it shouldn't surprise Coach that I know about it.

"I think he feels like he doesn't have much in common with them," Coach continues with what I'm suspecting are meant to be subtle hints, so I continue to play dumb.

"That's why I like hanging out with him. It's a nice change from talking hockey all the time."

I know we're playing a game of—chicken, I think is the term—and it might be incredibly stupid of me to do that when my position on the team is still pretty precarious. But if I'm right and Coach is hinting at Xander's sexuality as something I should distance myself from, he's going to have to come out and say it. And truth be told, this whole conversation is turning into motivation to perform so well that no one will question what I do off the ice, Coach included.

"Yes, well... Just remember the organization is here to help in any way you need."

I give myself a mental high-five when Coach folds. "Of course. Thank you." With a gracious nod I exit the office, pulling my phone out to text Xander as soon as I'm clear of the door.

***

"So, what's the big emergency?" Xander asks when he gets to my place that evening.

"You haven't talked to your dad, have you?"

"I haven't talked to anyone but Tripp since you texted me, just like you asked, and I came straight here from work. What's going on?"

Pulling him to me for a kiss, partly for bravery but mostly because his slightly annoyed, slightly skeptical expression makes him look edgy. I let the feel of his pillowy lips on mine remind me why we're going to such ridiculous lengths to see each other. Then I lead him to the couch and sit him down while I pace restlessly in front of it.

"Your dad pulled me aside after practice today. Some friend of his saw us at the car dealership, and now he's asking questions about us."

To his credit, Xander holds his neutral expression. "What did you tell him?"

"The truth. Everything but the sex, obviously, but he knows you've been showing me around town and helping me with the car."

"You're afraid he suspects something."

I pause my steps and turn to face him, trying to ignore the pinpricks of regret—not guilt—that spear my chest. "He did seem to be dropping subtle hints about you not having much in common with the guys on the team. I told him that's why I like hanging out with you, so I don't have to talk hockey all the time, but I'm pretty sure he decided to let things drop rather than come out and ask a question he didn't want to know the answer to."

"So, should I assume I'm here because you've changed your mind? You don't want to pursue this if my dad's already suspicious?"

"What? No." I shake my head, stunned he would jump to that conclusion. "You're here because I've probably put you in an awkward situation, and I wanted you to hear that from me before you got blindsided."

"His questions didn't give you second thoughts?"

"Hell no. I'm ready to kick ass so hard no one can bitch about what I do off the ice. I'm worried about you though. I get to play the dumb rookie card who's soaking up the whole experience, including making friends with the coach's son. You don't have that luxury. And while he wouldn't admit it, I got the impression he'd rather I not be friends with you."

"That pissed you off, huh?"

"Why do you say that?"

Xander gives me a little up-nod, pointing to my hand with his chin. "You're clenching your fists so hard they're white."

I look down to see my hands are indeed balled into fists at my side, and I make a deliberate effort to release them and get my circulation going again.

"You're his son. Wouldn't he *want* his players to be friends with you? Why have you go to that preseason cookout if he didn't."

"Having me at the cookout is part of an image. It's a compromise we came to a long time ago, so I didn't need to go to all the games. Or any of them."

"How can he think so little of you?" I start pacing again, needing an outlet for my restless energy.

"It's more about thinking so highly of his players than thinking so little of me. He doesn't want them getting caught up in any press that might have an air of scandal."

"You being the scandal?" I shoot him a pointed look. "That's bullshit. He could stop it before it starts by saying he's glad his actual family and his hockey family get along so well."

"I'm aware." He runs a frustrated hand through his hair with a heavy sigh. "Look, it took me a long time to see it, and I won't say I'm okay with it, but he does the best he can considering he doesn't know how to relate to me."

"You're hardly difficult to relate to," I snort.

"Not for you, but for a guy like my dad, who knows sports and only sports, I might as well be speaking a foreign language most of the time."

"What about your mom? How does he get along with her?"

"She's spent decades in his world. She knows it as well as he does by this point. Truthfully, I do too, I just try to avoid it."

"I'm gonna make that nearly impossible, aren't I?" I blow out a puff of air, fearing once again that Xander will eventually find me more trouble than he's comfortable with.

He holds a hand out in invitation, and I take it, collapsing into his side on the couch and closing my eyes as I rest my head on his shoulder, his fingers sifting tenderly through my hair. "It would never be possible for me to avoid hockey completely. I may fight it, but only out of spite, not because I hate it. Who knows, maybe you'll get me to love it again."

I laugh without any joy. "How would we explain that to your dad?"

"You've already taken the first step. You told him we're friends, and as long as we act that part in public, I don't think he'll find it weird that I keep up with how my friend is doing on the ice."

The gentle tug on my hair helps my muscles to relax. "So, you won't get any shit from him for being friends with me?"

"Oh, I'll get shit for it. But since you basically told him to deal with it then he has no other choice but to accept it."

"Do you think he'll ever accept us?"

"One obstacle at a time, Nikolas."

Another pang of guilt races up my spine, not only because I'm one more barrier to his relationship with his dad, but because a few weeks ago he wouldn't have considered being with me in secret, and now he's actively planning to keep his dad in the dark.

"Will you meet my sister?" I'd been meaning to ask, though not as a way to make up for the secrets he's keeping from his family on my behalf.

His fingers still on a deep inhale. "You don't think it's too soon?"

"No. She's the most important person in my life, and I want her to meet the other most important person. Plus, she already knows about you, and I've met Tripp, so..."

"Using Tripp's name to justify something is almost always a bad idea." I feel him fighting a smile above me.

"But in this case, it's a good one, right? We could even do something together, all four of us. Then it'll be less like meeting the family and more like an evening with friends."

"My friend is an attention whore with no filter, and his best behavior means he'll only wait about ten minutes, maybe fifteen, before bringing up dicks. Are you sure that's the first impression you want your sister to have of me?"

"Anna likes dicks too, so I'm sure it'll be fine."

"You've been warned," Xander mutters under his breath. "In that case, yes, I'd love to meet your sister."

I pick my head off his shoulder just long enough to see an actual gleam in his eye. Then I kiss the hell out of him and drag him to bed.

Chapter 20
Xander

I t's been days since my dad confronted Niko about the two of us being "friends" and he still hasn't called or demanded I come over to explain. Either he's too pissed to speak to me, or he's afraid of what I'll say.

Truthfully, I do feel a little bad that he didn't learn about our friendship from me. For years, we've had an unspoken agreement that I kept my distance from the players, except for certain instances where it'd be odd for me to be excluded, like the cookout. In exchange he didn't weigh in on my career choices or my dating life, both of which I think he envisioned looking different than they do.

I used to take offense to that way of thinking, but over the years I've learned that he doesn't object to my career or my lifestyle so much as he worries they're not in my best interest. He'd prefer me in a career that's more stable than "the arts," just as he'd prefer me to have an interest in women because that would eliminate the scrutiny gay people still suffer.

On some level, I know he gets that I am who I am, but that doesn't change the fact he'd choose an easier path for me if he could. Still, he mostly kept that to himself, and I mostly stayed away from his players. Until Niko.

Call it a technicality. Or a loophole. But since I met Niko *before* knowing he'd be playing for my dad, I figure I haven't broken our agreement outright. And since we formed a *friendship* when he was just visiting, it's only natural he'd want that to continue once he moved here. I can say that with a straight face because I believe every word of it, if only my dad would call. But he hasn't, and I'm not going to call him since that would validate his concern that we're too close.

Shoving the dilemma from my mind to stare at the screen in front of me, like I've been doing for days with no real success, I try to concentrate on the clip I'm editing for a movie promo. Tripp has other ideas.

"Do you know what they're saying about your man?" He rests his hip on the corner of my desk with what can only be described as an accusatory look.

Glancing around to make sure no one's close enough to hear, I lift my eyebrow. "Should I?"

"They say he could be rookie of the year. They've only played a few preseason games, and already they're predicting greatness."

Of course, I'd heard the chatter. I knew Niko was being touted as a phenom, but I was trying really hard not to dwell on it since I suspected the timing of his big reveal about us might have a direct correlation to his performance on the ice.

Trouble is, I still don't know how that correlation might work. If he kills it during the games will he want to keep the status quo and stay in the closet, or take that as a sign he's secure with his place on the team?

"Your point?" I ask Tripp.

"Did you know he was that good?"

"I had an idea." Though Niko plays defense, and has an uncanny ability to read the play as it's developing so he can stop it, he's also pretty good on offense. The pundits say his ability to wait for an opportunity to develop instead of forcing it gives him a better lane to drive toward the goal, which made him one of the highest scoring defensemen in college. It's probably what caught my dad's eye, and something they expect him to repeat in the NHL.

"Well, share with the class next time. Are we going to go to a game? Don't you want to see him play in person?"

"I wasn't planning on it. My dad found out we've been hanging out, and while we're both sticking to the story that we're just friends I'm not sure he's buying it. No better way to make my father even more suspicious about what I'm up to than to show up at the last place he expects me to be."

"What if you tell him I made you take me?"

"The only way he'd buy that is if I said you had a crush on one of the players, in which case he wouldn't let us into the building."

"Call it a work outing. We'll take the whole office." He sweeps his arm around the room, which is mercifully still empty since it's lunchtime. "I'm surprised they haven't goaded you into that already. A few of our cohorts are hockey nutballs."

"Fortunately, only you know my connection to the team so I can work here in peace. Mostly." I shoot him a pointed look.

"Remember how we talked about Mr. Hockey changing you for the better and making you shit rainbows? Now's your chance to prove it. Take your co-workers out and ogle your boyfriend in living color."

"Pretty sure that's the opposite of keeping our relationship under wraps."

"Pretty sure we also talked about you giving him the support he needs to come out. What better way to do that than to freeze your ass off with thousands of screaming idiots? Besides, no one would have to know out of all those people in the stands that you're the one he shuts up with his dick."

Only Tripp can make me choke on air.

"I'm really trying to respect his wishes and not draw unnecessary attention to us until he's ready. Showing up at a game would do the opposite." I'm also slightly afraid to come face to face with him at the arena and see firsthand how much he loves the game that could still come between us if he gets cold feet about coming out.

"Or—hear me out—showing up could make him realize how much you love him. I mean, you hate hockey, and knowing you'd suffer through a game for him might rev his engine."

"I don't hate hockey, I hate that my dad is so obsessed with it. And Niko doesn't know I love him because I'm still not sure I do." After our first, and so far, only conversation about my boyfriend, I've been trying not to over analyze things. The way I see it, my feelings won't change the fact that our relationship has to exist in this weird state of limbo, so there's no point in thinking beyond the moment we're in.

"Really? You're objecting that you're in love on the basis you're clueless?"

"Not clueless, undefined. Labeling how I feel won't change the circumstances, so why bother."

"So, that's a no to the hockey game?"

"Since when do you have an interest in hockey?"

"Two words. Thor lookalike." He raises a finger as he enunciates each word, then waves them in front of my face.

"Jesus, you've got a one-track mind. I told you, I..." My phone beeps in my pocket, and knowing there's only one person who would be texting me right now, I rush to read it. "Look at that," I tell Tripp as I type out a response. "I guess you're getting your wish after all."

"Thor's gay?" He claps his hands together with a wicked smirk.

"His name is Noah, and not that wish. The one about going to a game. The flight Niko's sister is on got delayed, and instead of going to the rink early with him he wants me to bring her after I pick her up at the airport."

"Ooh, that'll really get your dad freaking out."

"Maybe not, since I've got Niko's sister as cover. But just in case, that's why you're coming with me."

"I'm not going to object since I'm getting what I want, but doesn't my presence usually make things worse with your dad?"

"In this instance, since Niko knows you, I'm hoping it'll reinforce the idea that we're nothing more than a group of friends hanging out."

"You know what'll reinforce that even more?" He flutters his lashes like he's some sweet little girl asking an innocent favor.

"Getting Noah to come out with us." My shoulders slump as I exhale, knowing that however self-centered his request is, it's also a logical one. "I'll see what Niko can do."

Five hours later, I've successfully picked up Anna—who looks astonishingly like her brother and yet completely different, obviously, and who still sounds undeniably Swedish. Unfortunately, we don't make it off the airport premises before my forward friend opens his mouth.

"Are all Swedish men as hot as your brother?" He sticks his head between the two front seats, turning it so he's effectively blocking me out.

"Boundaries," I hiss.

"What? It's a valid question, and you can't ask it since you're dating her brother. It would just be rude."

Anna laughs throatily. "I'm partial to Spanish or Greek men since Scandinavian men are so white, but if you like your men tall you won't be disappointed."

"I love my men tall," Tripp says dreamily.

"You love men period." I snort as I merge onto the freeway.

"That's true, but I much prefer to tilt my head up for a kiss than to lower it. Looking down gives you the most annoying cramp—"

"You have to look down when you give a blow job, don't you?" Anna points out.

"Ooh, saucy. I love her." Tripp claps his hands together as I say, "Jesus, there are two of you."

"I know it's hard to tell since his face looks...like that," Tripp waves a hand in my direction, "but that's actually a compliment since I'm his best friend. The only time you need to worry is when he's *not* scowling. Now, where were we." He taps a finger on his lip for dramatic effect. "Oh! Blow jobs. I suppose in certain positions you do have to be looking down, but it's more like a hover than actually bending your neck, don't you think?"

"I do."

"Great we agree! Blow jobs are better than kisses."

"Yeah, that's what I was getting at." Anna rolls her eyes dramatically. "So, Xander, what's the plan to get my brother to come out of the closet?"

"I... Uh..."

"Oh, I *really* love her," Tripp gushes.

"No one but Niko gets to make that call." I find my voice.

"Bullshit," Anna retorts. "You have just as much say since you're dating him."

"I'm dating him because he trusts me not to take the decision out of his hands." The only thing I hate more than keeping our relationship a secret is the notion that someone could force Niko into the open before he's ready. It's *never* okay to take that decision away from someone, and even if we get to a point where I can't hide anymore and he's not ready to come out, I'd walk away before I violate his confidence like that.

She gives me an appraising once over. "Good answer."

"That was a test?" Tripp shrieks. "You're like my tenth-grade biology teacher, making me think you're my friend with your sweet and slightly mischievous smile then BAM... *Pop quiz*. I'd just like to point out you're the primary asshole here, not me. I was simply following your lead."

"The more you talk the worse it gets." I give him an eye roll in the rearview mirror. "Just admit you like to create drama."

"I like to push boundaries, and if you ask me, Niko needs a little nudge." He crosses his arms over his chest as he leans back against the seat.

"Not that I disagree with you," Anna eyes him cautiously, "but why do you think that?"

"Because I don't like to see my friend living a lie."

"I made a conscious decision to do that," I remind him.

"Yes, but for how long?"

"I don't have some arbitrary time limit in mind. We're taking each day as it comes, as you already know."

"Waiting to see what happens with hockey, right?" Anna interjects.

"It's a valid concern," I say. "He's in his first year in the league, and there's never been a gay rookie. Not that we know about."

"You don't need to convince me." Anna holds her hands up. "I'm well aware of the challenges, and I don't want to see anything ruin the dream he's worked so hard to achieve. That doesn't mean I want to see hockey stand in the way of my brother's happiness. Or yours."

"Mine? I appreciate the concern and all, but why are you worried about mine?"

"I know my brother, and I know he wouldn't do something as stupid as dating his coach's son unless feelings are involved." Glancing at her from the corner of my eye, I see the sincerity in hers. "He cares about you, and he won't want to see you get hurt. But there's no way staying in the closet won't eventually hurt you, which in turn will hurt him."

"It's a slippery circle, that ice rink. Pun intended," Tripp snorts.

"I'd rather see him out and happy," Anna continues, "but if he can't do that because of hockey, are you willing to live with that?"

That's the so-called million-dollar question, and in this case, it could actually be tens of millions considering the impact Niko's projected to have on the league. I'm not overly concerned with the money, and I don't think Niko is either. We'd both put our happiness before any amount of cash, but his happiness includes hockey, and while I'm still opposed to going an entire career's worth of secrecy, if that career lasts fifteen years or more, I'm starting to think five or so is a compromise I can make.

"I don't know what the future will hold, and I'm not going to make a promise I can't keep," I tell Anna. "What I can say is, I find myself more and more willing to accept the current conditions the longer we're together."

"That's fair," she says in a soft Swedish lilt.

"So, I assume since you're bringing up the elephant in the room, you have a solution?" Tripp asks.

"Unfortunately, no." She exhales heavily.

"Well, that was anticlimactic," Tripp huffs. "Why you'd get us all riled up then?"

"I had to be sure the guy Niko's willing to risk everything for is worthy of him."

"And?" Tripp presses.

"Thumbs up." She gives me a warm smile.

Chapter 21
Niko

Justus eyes me curiously as I go through my pregame ritual. Point and flex my toes, loosening up the muscles. A few knee bends before I shake out my left leg, then my right. Sit down and put on the left sock, then the right. Left skate, right skate. Stand and do a few more knee bends. Shake the legs out again, left then right.

"You're ambidextrous?" Justus scratches the bridge of his nose, clearly confused because he's seen me do most everything right-handed, from unpacking my gear to signing my name when we go out to eat, and starting left with my gear doesn't fit the pattern.

"Nope," I grin, enjoying his confusion. "I fooled my teammates once by going left instead of right to start my ritual, and I got a hat trick that day so..."

"So now you repeat it every time." He finishes my thought and I wink in affirmation. Getting a hat trick as a defenseman is rare, and hockey players are a superstitious bunch, so I'll gladly repeat everything I did that day if there's a chance it'll get me another one.

"Your folks make it for the game?" I ask as I double check my pads.

"Yep. They got here last night. Your sister?"

"Xander's picking her up now."

"Xander? As in coach's kid Xander?"

"Yeah. I was planning to until her flight got delayed, so he's doing it for me." I figure as long as Coach knows we're "friends" it doesn't hurt to keep the ruse up for my teammates. Besides, since Xander suggested it might look even better to include the guys when we all go out, telling them in advance that we're friends will let them have the surprised look Justus is wearing here instead of in front of a crowd.

"I thought the guys said he doesn't hang around the team much." Justus runs a hand through his hair as he ducks his head, hiding his confusion, I think.

"He doesn't, but remember how we ran into him and his friend at that concert? He was pretty drunk, so I helped him get home, and after that we kept in touch. He actually helped me get my license and taught me how to buy a car. We're all going out after the game if you want to join."

"Yeah, sure. My parents will probably crash afterward, and it'd be good to do something to unwind. I heard Luca mention something about a bar they usually go to. The Frosty Dog I think?"

"Works for me. Now, let's go kick some ass."

***

It's the third period and we're up by one, but I'd feel a lot more comfortable with another point on the board. And it's not just that I want the win—obviously—but the idea of losing to a team that's based out of a place where ice doesn't exist rubs me the wrong way. I mean, getting beat at your home opener is just wrong, but getting beat by Florida in Colorado... Not gonna happen.

Unfortunately, Florida has a beast for a goalie, and he's surprisingly fast for his size. Luca scored one goal on a fast break in the first, but he's shut us out since then. We're still in it thanks to our solid defense, and the few shots we've taken have been easily blocked by Noah. But their defense is equally good, and even though the puck has been at their end more often than not, we don't have a comfortable lead.

As my line takes the ice after a break, there's three minutes left in the game. We've got the puck, and we carefully work it around their side of the rink, looking for an opportunity. When the pass comes my way for a third time, I've conditioned the winger to think I want to go right since I've faked left and changed direction twice already. This time I start left and quickly shift my weight to make it look as if I'm going to go right again, but just as my opponent adjusts, I abandon the move and go back to the left.

All-in-all it burns about two seconds off the clock. Time seems to go in slow motion since I'm ready for the winger to react how I want, which gives me a slight edge. His weight is too far in the wrong direction for him to correct course in the half-second I need to capitalize on the window I created, which is more than enough time to get a shot off. I wind up, pulling my stick back and slapping it forward with a ferocious swing.

There's a lot of ice between me and the goal, but the winger isn't the only defender who bought my fake, creating just enough space that the only person who has a chance to stop the puck is the goalie. His reaction time is fast, but my shot is faster, slipping into the five hole before he can close the gap.

The flashing light above the goal starts to spin, registering the score, though my view is quickly blocked by a flood of guys skating around me in a circle, cheering, and slapping me on the back. It's not the game winning goal since we're now up by two, but it secures the win, and it feels pretty damn good to score in my first game.

I float to the bench, literally and figuratively, in somewhat of a daze. Though the NHL is faster than the NCAA, as expected, it seems like I've got the speed to compete at this level. That makes me giddy as a player, and gives me hope that I just might have what it takes to be valuable enough to silence any critics that may come out of the woodwork when I come out of the closet.

After the game, and a press conference where I get to play humble about my debut despite the fact I'm feeling anything but, I head over to the Frosty Dog with the rest of the team to meet Xander, Anna, and Tripp. Xander and Tripp give me one of those quasi hugs where you slap each other on the back, though Xander does at least get close enough to press his chest to mine and whisper that I was amazing. Then Anna launches herself at me.

"Careful," I laugh—more like warn—as I hug her back. "This body could be worth millions as long as you don't injure it."

"I didn't realize you were such a fragile snowflake." She rolls her eyes as I set her down.

"Have I mentioned that I love you?" Tripp gushes, "Because I most definitely do."

"Switching teams?" I cock my eyebrow at him.

"Tempting." He waggles his eyebrows in a way that should be ridiculous but coming from him seems oddly normal.

"They're like two halves of the same person," Xander sighs heavily. "I'm not sure whether to be amused or terrified."

"Terrified," Trip and Ana say in unison, then start cracking up.

"What is happening?" My gaze darts back and forth between them as I take a seat at the table they've claimed.

"They bonded over a game of kiss, marry, or fuck."

"What now?" I blink to hear him better.

"It's usually kiss, marry, or kill, but they decided your teammates are too hot to kill, so they amended it to kiss, marry, or fuck." He takes a seat next to me as the rest of our team trickles over to the area the bar helpfully reserves for us.

"What's this I hear?" Luca asks as he pushes another table next to ours and drops into a chair. "Who's fucking?"

"You, if you play your cards right." Tripp winks as Anna dissolves into laughter and Xander shakes his head.

"I'm always up for a good fuck." Luca doesn't miss a beat.

"Good, because you're her number one pick." Tripp tilts his chin toward Anna.

"Am I now?" Luca grins proudly, which fits knowing what Noah said about his penchant for an audience.

"No." I shake my head, intending to follow it up with a statement about no fraternizing between my sister and my teammates, but biting my tongue before I open that door. Anna wouldn't out me here, but I'd never hear the end of it considering my current circumstances. Instead, I say, "Luca, meet my sister, Anna."

"Ah, got it." He winks to let me know we have an understanding, but he doesn't switch topics, making me think he's playing along so I don't get shit about being the protective brother. Cool. "And how did I earn that honor?" He turns to Anna, whose face is a satisfying shade of red.

"Tripp asked who I'd kiss, marry, or kill."

"I thought I got picked for a fuck?"

"You did, after we changed the rules," Tripp volunteers. "We didn't want to kill anyone, so we re-named the game kiss, marry, fuck."

"You don't think I'm marriage material?" Luca grins mischievously.

"Well, um. I picked Noah for that." Anna presses her lips bashfully between her teeth.

"What am I picked for?" Noah sets down a pitcher and a handful of glasses as my sister turns even more red.

"She wants to marry you and fuck me," Luca says.

"I picked you to marry and Noah to fuck," Tripp tells Luca. "For the same reasons."

"What reasons are those?" Noah's brow draws together.

"You seem like the sweet cuddly type off the ice and Luca seems like he'd be fantastic in bed," Tripp says with no shame, leading me to pat Xander's leg under the table when he shakes his head again.

"You don't think sweet and cuddly are good qualities in a husband?" Noah cocks his head to the side.

"I think hot and dirty sex are good qualities in a husband, so I'd marry Luca since he's more or less known for that, and I'd fuck you because corrupting the sweet out of you would be so much fun."

Noah laughs good naturedly, though his face turns as pink as my sister's.

"Who'd you pick to kiss?" I try to take the spotlight off Noah.

"Justus," they say in unison, dissolving into another fit of giggles as if recalling some inside joke.

Fortunately, since he took his parents to their hotel he hasn't shown up yet, so he's spared what Noah just went through. "How much did they have to drink?" I mutter to Xander.

"Why? Do I lose points if I let your sister get hammered?"

"If that was her goal you wouldn't have been able to stop her." I smirk, thinking it's adorable that he's under the impression he could've. "So, how much?"

"Not as much as you'd expect."

"Better make this a short evening then." I glance up in time to see Tripp trying to fit his hands around Noah's arm, looking suitably impressed when he can barely get his fingers to touch.

Xander follows my gaze and rolls his eyes. "Tripp. What did I say about groping people?"

He blinks at Xander with exaggerated innocence before pointing to Anna. "It was her idea."

Anna smacks his chest with the back of her hand. "Liar."

"Fine, but in my defense, I'm measuring the size of their biceps, not their dicks, so there's no reason to get worked up."

I sense Xander getting ready to object so I bring my glass to my mouth to cover my lips. "These guys being friends with an openly gay man could take the pressure off us," I whisper before taking a sip.

Xander nods imperceptibly and looks at my teammates. "He will absolutely have you whipping them out if you keep playing his games. Consider yourselves warned."

"You say that like we don't see each other naked in the locker room all the time. No one here is afraid of someone getting an eye full." Luca grins slyly and sips his beer.

I stifle a laugh—because of course Luca says that—then remember I'm not supposed to know he's got an exhibitionist streak.

"I'm just saying if it comes out, he'll want to ride it." Xander jerks his chin toward Tripp, who's got a wicked gleam in his eye.

"That's actually true," Tripp agrees with a not-so-subtle glance at Noah, but before my brain can make sense of that Anna tilts her head to the side and blurts, "Huh, you're right I see it now."

"Who's right?" I ask.

"Tripp thinks Noah looks like Thor."

"Chris Hemsworth?" Luca asks.

"No, the cartoon version," she says.

"What the difference?" Luka gives Noah a critical once over.

"Chris Hemsworth has dirty blond hair while the cartoon Thor has more golden hair," Xander says.

"No way," I interrupt. "Chris Hemsworth has more of an oval jaw and the cartoon version is square. "Plus, there's no beard in the comic version."

"That's very...specific." Luca squints at me.

"I'm from Sweden." I shrug away the comment.

"Thor settles in Norway after Asgard is destroyed." Xander points out.

"Which is right next door to Sweden."

"How does that have anything to do with what Thor looks like?" Xander asks.

"It means I grew up with that character and I know exactly what he's supposed to look like. Hemsworth is close but his jaw is oval. Noah's is a little more square."

"That's what it is." Anna nods her head as she observes Noah. "It's in the jaw."

"Wow, you guys are..."

"Superhero nerds, we know." I finish Luca's thought, which, conveniently I think, answers the unasked question of why Xander and I are friends.

This night is going better than expected, minus my sister talking about my teammates' dicks of course, but I'm feeling pretty comfortable with the two different facets of my life being in the same place. Not comfortable enough that I'll put my arm around Xander or kiss him or anything, but I also don't feel like I need to hide the fact that we're close. And as long as we can keep things like this, casual banter and teasing, it seems like it'd be almost natural for him to hang out with us. Tripp too, considering the guys don't seem to be offended by his attempts to shock them. In fact, Luca seems amused, since it's apparently his turn to have his bicep measured.

"Sorry I'm late. What's going on?" Justus drops into the seat across from me with a confused glance at Luca and Tripp. I make introductions and explain the arm contest, and though he seems slightly embarrassed Justus lets Tripp do his thing.

"What's the verdict?" Luca asks. "I've got the biggest arms, don't I?"

"Oh, I don't know. I just wanted to feel everyone's muscles. I can do it again and actually measure this time if you want," Tripp says with a straight face, causing Xander to reiterate his previous warning about how far he'll go if they let him. Meanwhile Anna and I are both trying not to crack up, because now the guys really do want to know who's got the bigger arms, and they're flexing and trying to measure themselves while Tripp is leaned back in his chair enjoying the show.

Once Noah has been declared the winner, thanks to a hair ribbon Anna had in her purse that served as a tape measure, Justus turns to Xander. "Did you enjoy the game?" he asks politely.

"I did. It was the first one I've been to in several years and it was nice to be back at the rink."

"How'd we do?" Luca asks.

"Pretty good. You guys are faster but sometimes you need to be patient instead of relying on speed to help you score."

"Coach said the same thing," Luca chuckles. "You should be an analyst."

"Hard pass." He shakes his head with what looks like the hint of a smile. While I appreciate that he's trying not to be a jerk, I kind of hate that he almost smiled for someone who's not me.

"Why is that the first one you've been to in years?" Anna asks him.

For a brief moment I panic that she's put Xander on the spot, but he doesn't seem uncomfortable. "Growing up in a house that revolves around hockey and not playing myself was overwhelming. I sort of rebelled against it for a while because I could."

"What made you come back?" Justus asks.

"Anna's plane was late, and Niko needed someone to get her there. Plus, Tripp has been begging me to take him so, two birds and all that."

"You're a hockey fan?" Justus asks Tripp conversationally.

"I'm a hockey *player* fan." Tripp winks, and innocent little Justus blushes.

"I think that's my cue to get him out of here." Xander shoots a pointed look at Tripp.

"What? I'm behaving."

"Which means any minute now you'll stop behaving, and no one needs to see that," Xander deadpans as he pushes his chair back and drops a few bills on the table.

"We should maybe call it a night too." I look to Anna. "I bet you're pretty tired after your flight."

The four of us say our goodbyes and make our way to the parking lot, and while I'd like nothing better than to kiss Xander goodbye, we settle for a quick hug, and I whisper in his ear that I'll call him later. Then Anna and I head to my car so I can drive us home.

"He's quiet," she observes.

"In that setting, yeah. When it's just the two of us it feels like there's always something to talk about."

"Like?"

I lift my shoulder and back out of the space. "Family. Cars. Careers. Feelings."

"You? Feelings?" She couldn't sound any less skeptical if she tried, though I can't blame her. I spent years trying not to have feelings because I knew they could jeopardize my goals. Even if that may still be true, I've long since passed the point where I can deny them.

I feel heat rushing into my face and hope it's too dark for her to see it. "Yeah, you know. Whether we think what's between us is worth the secrecy."

"Is my brother in love?" Anna claps her hands together.

"I'm starting to think I might be." That statement doesn't cause the ground to open up beneath us, or my stomach to feel queasy, or any other sign that might suggest I'm getting ahead of myself. Instead, I actually feel kind of light. Weightless. Like something just fell into place.

"You picked a good one, Nik," Anna says softly.

"Thanks." I smile. "I think so too."

Chapter 22
Xander

Hanging out with Niko and his teammates felt good. *Too good*. Not because I was totally at ease—I wasn't. Nor was it due to me softening my brooding personality to act like one of the guys. It felt good because his teammates know Tripp and I are gay, and they didn't seem to have any issue with it at all.

It's worth noting that they've never given me any indication to think they'd take offense to my sexuality, but for the most part I've only ever seen them at the yearly team cookout, and it's not like they'd reveal any prejudices in front of my dad. Tonight, they weren't forced to sit at the same table, yet they did, and they made no attempts to exclude Tripp or me from the conversation. The opposite in fact. That doesn't mean they'd be okay with me dating their new star defenseman, but it gives me hope.

Unfortunately, I can't decide if hope is good or bad. Having his teammates' approval, or at the very least acceptance, would be an argument in favor of telling people we're together. Yet his teammates are only part of the equation. Fans, players around the league, even some sponsors, might not be so receptive. And then there's my dad to consider.

I know Niko still questions whether my dad is really okay with my sexuality, which is probably because I didn't explain our history very well. While things are often strained between me and my dad, that's not due to me being gay. Our biggest roadblock is hockey, though I expertly ignore my resentment of the game by not watching, and he expertly ignores my resentment by pretending he doesn't notice.

Dysfunctional? Absolutely. But it works for us, and it'd probably keep working as long as we both stayed in our designated lanes. I've stepped out of my lane though, and once he learns that, well, I have no idea how he'll react when he learns I've crossed the unspoken boundary of fraternizing with his players.

I'm sure he'll be livid for being placed in an awkward situation, because having his son's boyfriend on the roster will bring extra scrutiny about shit like favoritism. But as far as how he can react to that anger... There's not much he can do to me. I have my own place, I have my own job, and even if he revokes the trust that's supposed to kick in when I turn twenty-five, I can support myself just fine. There's not much he could do to Niko either, considering he was a top draft pick, and as long as he's playing well, my dad wouldn't be able to justify a trade.

He might have some initial anger and resentment toward Niko, but my dad loves the game too much to let personal feelings get in the way of winning. And considering his own son is gay, he'd be taking on some heavy criticism if he came out in opposition of Niko.

I don't relish the idea of backing my dad into a corner, but the reality is his ability to react publicly will be limited. Privately it might cause our rift to widen beyond repair, and while it might make me sound callous, that's an outcome I'll live with if it means I have Niko.

Could *he* though? Could Niko still play for my dad if we're estranged, knowing he played a role in that estrangement? I'm not sure he could. He's such a genuinely good person, he wouldn't want to be a constant reminder of anything painful for his coach, not to mention I don't think he could play for someone he doesn't respect, and if my dad doesn't react favorably to us, Niko won't respect him.

Jesus, this is a cluster.

Thank God, I'm staying at my place while his sister is here, since the "what-ifs" are getting out of control. I think if I were with him, they'd have passed by now, since we both seem to have a knack for calming each other off the ledge. I still can't explain where that comes from, I just know it's true. We seem to balance each other out when one of us panics.

Normally, I'd say that's a good thing, but since the panic is usually over whether we're fooling ourselves into thinking we can make this work, I'm not sure it is. Or more accurately, if we didn't have anything to worry about then there'd be no reason for us to alternately play the voice of reason. Since I'm sitting here worrying, there's obviously still reason to question our sanity.

So, what would Niko say right now?

He'd say it's only been one night out with his teammates. It was promising, but still too early to predict whether they or my dad or the general public will be okay with the two of us dating. One day at a time is still the best plan.

A tiny voice in the back of my head tries to ask for how long, but I shut it down before it can play on a loop. If there's one thing I can be confident about, it's that there won't be a big reveal anytime soon. One game of seventy-two has been played, and if the Bulldogs make the playoffs that could turn into over ninety. Therefore, wondering if Niko might come out to his teammates sometime this season is realistic, while wondering if he'll come out to the league is not. No sense in dwelling on that particular what-if until much, much later.

Still, that doesn't stop me from replaying the evening over and over again in my mind as if we were publicly together. His arm slung over my shoulders instead of a hidden touch under the table. Lacing our fingers together as we weave through the crowd instead of him following several feet behind me.

Damn, I sound sappy.

A few weeks ago, I'd have snorted my objection to that sort of public affection, and now here I am, wishing for it. With him.

Don't you dare break my heart Nikolas Sven, because I'm pretty sure despite all my attempts to avoid it, it belongs to you now.

***

"Have you heard from Niko?" Tripp plops his ass on the corner of my desk.

"Why" I keep my eyes focused on my screen so he doesn't think I'm inviting him to stay and talk.

"I'm worried about his ego. His own boyfriend didn't even pick him to kiss last night."

Leaning back in my chair with a sigh, I bring my eyes up to Tripp's. "What are you fishing for?"

"Why would I be fishing for anything?"

"Because you don't give a shit about Niko's ego, or my feelings or anything that doesn't in some way relate back to you."

"Well, since you brought it up," he smiles mischievously, "I was curious if my Thor had said anything."

"*Your* Thor?"

"He held his breath when I gripped his arm yesterday."

"*Man holds breath while being groped*. Yeah, that's headline news for sure." I roll my eyes and lean forward to grab my mouse so I can get back to work.

"Make fun, but Anna saw it too, and she thinks the same thing I do."

"Which is?"

"Thor likes me. Or at the very least he's curious."

"Even if either of those things were true, what makes you think he'd tell Niko that?"

"He wouldn't. But he might ask Niko to get my number?" A devious gleam flashes across his eye.

"What did you do?" I grit through my locked jaw.

"Nothing...much. Just offered to help him with some stereo equipment since he's a fellow music fan. But I didn't give him my number. I said he could get it from Niko. So, see—I was good."

"You weren't as bad as you could've been, I'll give you that."

"Thank you." He gives a mocking bow. "Too bad we won't be able to do that again. It was actually fun."

"Why wouldn't we do that again?"

Tripp looks at me like I've just asked the world's dumbest question. "It's only because Anna and I are so entertaining that no one noticed the little looks you kept giving each other."

"What looks?"

"The *I want to touch you so bad right now* looks."

I snort like he's lost his mind. "We didn't do that."

"Was he or was he not touching your leg under the table? Don't answer that, I already know. When he did, your whole body relaxed. And when he moved it, your eyes drifted shut and you took a fortifying breath."

A sharp pang slices through my chest as his words register, and the bleakness of what he's implying sets in. But I swallow it down and pretend I'm unaffected. "Fortifying?"

"Bracing, reinforcing, pick your adjective. None of the grown-up words I use will change the fact that it took all your restraint to act like just friends, and if you keep putting that show on in front of others, sooner or later they'll notice. And leaving together..."

"We left at the same time, not together. And you and Anna were with us."

"Again, it worked this time. It won't repeatedly."

It has to work repeatedly. It has to. Otherwise, we'll never see each other.

As the new guy, he'll be expected to hang out with the team. Maybe not after every game or day off, but enough that it'll make a dent in the time we have together. What little we'll have outside of his away games. And while I never assumed I'd celebrate with him and the guys after every game, I thought the success of last night meant we could pull it off here and there. Several times a month maybe. If Tripp's right, and we're more obvious than we realize, that's now off the table. *Fuck!*

"Oh shit!" Tripp's eyebrows disappear behind his hairline. "You were thinking you guys could successfully do the friend thing in front of his teammates, weren't you?"

"It crossed my mind." I scrub a hand over my face to hide the disappointment I'm sure is written plainly on it.

"You know I'm game to hang with them and provide some cover, but unless you and Niko can lose the subtle glances and touches and stuff, even my drama won't hide your secret."

I open my mouth to respond before realizing there's nothing to say. While Tripp is the most observant person I know, and he sees things other people sometimes miss, he makes a good point about the sheer volume of times we'll have to pull of the friend act with total perfection if we want to keep our secret. Maybe we get away with it for a few get-togethers, but each time we hang out publicly represents an opportunity for exposure. Considering we're at the beginning of the season, that's probably not a wise move.

"Oh. My. God." Tripp lets his jaw hang comically open. "That's not reason enough for you to put your foot down. Is it?"

"What do you mean?"

"You're considering whether you can live with only ever seeing Niko in private like some forbidden mistress. Or mister. Is there a male version of mistress? Doesn't matter." He waves his hand dismissively. "The point is, the old Xander would've rejected that idea outright, but you're not just thinking about it, you're going to do it."

"And?" I prompt, because the way his eyes are bugging out tell me he's got more to say.

"And you're supposed to be the boyfriend who supports him coming out, not the one who enables him to keep hiding."

"I won't force him out before he's ready."

"That's noble and all, but we both know it's not the life you want." Tripp huffs with an exaggerated eye roll.

"Not permanently, no, but I can make some sacrifices in the meantime."

"Sacrifices? You've gone from a strict rule about dating closeted guys to thinking you could play buddies in public to living like hermits. You're not sacrificing, you're regressing." He crosses his arms over his chest. "And it's not supposed to work like that."

"What isn't supposed to work like this?" I narrow my eyes.

"Love."

"You're a romantic now?" It's a low blow, but I'm feeling a little vulnerable and putting the focus on him is the only way I can think of to take it off me.

"Hardly," he snorts. "But just because I don't think I'm capable of love doesn't mean I'm denying its existence. You obviously wouldn't be making all these concessions for Niko if you weren't in love with him, but unless I've completely misunderstood the concept, love is supposed enhance your life, not hinder it."

"Weren't you telling me not too long ago that I'm different since I started seeing him? Happier and shit. That's enhancing."

"Yeah, but for how long if you have to live in a bubble?" Tripp retorts, and once again, I don't have a good response to offer.

"What are you saying?" I ask.

"I don't know." He blows out an exasperated puff of air. "I guess just make sure you're looking out for yourself as much as you're looking out for his career. Even though happy Xander is still kind of weird, I don't hate him, and I'm afraid I'll get the old you back if Niko breaks your heart."

"If there was supposed to be a compliment in there somewhere it needs work."

"There wasn't," he deadpans, "just a friendly reminder that you deserve the same consideration you're giving him, especially if this is the guy your heart is set on."

Tripp's only trying to look out for me, which I appreciate, and like he's cautioning against, I have no plans to abandon what's important to me in favor of what's important to Niko. But just as Niko said he'd consider coming out for the right guy, I'm willing to temporarily adjust my lifestyle expectations for the right guy. And yeah, I think he's it.

Am I risking heartbreak if I've gambled wrong? Yes. Will I revert to my old ways if that happens? I'd like to say no, though the truth is I probably will. I don't like that idea any more than Tripp does. But what he doesn't get, what he can't get since he thinks he's not capable of love, is that when you feel it, sacrifices like this make sense.

I can say that because the last time I thought I was in love was nothing compared to how I feel now, I just didn't know any better then. My teenage self thought words carried as much weight as action, and when I learned they didn't, it took a long time—until Niko—before I let myself start to trust words again. And even then, I only trusted the words because they weren't intended to sugarcoat anything. They were just brutally honest, backed up by gestures that had never been made toward me before, like bringing me out with his friends. Even though that was designed to look platonic, it's more than my last boyfriend ever did.

So, yeah. I'm in love with Niko. I've fallen deeper than I thought was possible. I'm not going to tell him that though. Not now, when it might add to the pressure he's already feeling with his career and the secret we're trying to maintain. And even though all of this is a big reversal, in my gut it doesn't feel like I'm making a mistake. For now, that's enough.

"I get how it looks from the outside, and I don't blame you for being concerned." Tripp blinks in rapid succession, evidently surprised I'm not blowing off his warnings. "But if you think we're obvious even when we're trying not to be, and you heard what his sister said, then you know this is just as real for him as it is me."

Tripp purses his lips, studying me critically, before rolling his eyes on an exhale. "Okay, fine. I concede that you have a point. However, I reserve the right to castrate him if he breaks your heart."

"Fair enough," I smile wryly, grateful that because of Niko, I'm finally able to see what a good friend Tripp really is.

Chapter 23
Niko

"Are you going to tell him?" Anna asks as we drive to the airport after an all-too short visit, though with my departure for the first away game scheduled early tomorrow, it can't be helped.

"I'm not sure yet." I tap my fingers anxiously on the steering wheel.

"Let me rephrase that. Why wouldn't you tell him?"

"It wouldn't change anything for one. It might even make things harder for him to know that's how I feel when I can't admit it publicly. Plus, isn't it too soon?"

I catch her chewing on her lip from the corner of my eye, a telltale sign she's deep in thought. When she comes to her decision, she takes a deep breath and lets it out slowly. "I don't think time should be a factor. If that's how you feel, and the right moment comes up, you shouldn't avoid telling him because you haven't been together that long."

"You don't think it would make things harder?"

"We talked a little about that on the way to the game, the whole secrecy thing, and he seems prepared to accept that if it means being with you. In fact, if I had to guess, I'd say he loves you, too." She gives me a soft smile, and I feel my face mirror hers.

Though I know Xander's feelings are strong, I haven't really allowed myself to believe they reached the love stage. I'm not sure if that's to protect myself or him, since he's lived through heartbreak before, and I know how scared he is to go through that again. Not that I think I'll break his heart, but if he allows himself to love me in spite of his fears... That's both an honor and a heavy weight to bear. It makes my stomach drop and flutter, caught between giddiness and my own anxiety.

Shit, I sound like my sister when she had her first crush in middle school, not long before I left for the states. I remember teasing her mercilessly, and now I wish I hadn't, because I get it. Despite the fear and confusion that comes with feelings this big, there's a sense of euphoria unlike anything I've ever experienced. Well, except for getting drafted, but even that doesn't quite reach this level of intensity.

I think that's because I spent my life working towards a career in hockey, so I had some expectation that I might get here one day, and things with Xander took me totally by surprise. I was wholly unprepared for another person to have such a massive impact on my life, and I think the shock of that magnifies the emotion that comes with it.

I'm not complaining. What I feel for Xander surpasses everything I thought I knew about love. I think it even surpasses what I feel for hockey.

Though the NHL has been my lifelong dream, I always knew it would be just a phase. A blip on the timeline. A monumental blip, but something that I'd eventually have to move on from, at least as a player. Xander could be permanent, which means I can't risk losing him over my career.

That's a terrifying thought in the sense that I always envisioned my life going one way, and now that it is, I'm entertaining the idea of walking away. Not willingly. I've never known a life outside of hockey, so I'll fight like hell to keep the spot I've earned on this team, both because I love the sport and because I don't think I'm ready to face a life without it. At the same time, if I'm forced to choose, how can I choose the thing that was always going to be temporary? Especially if Anna's right and he loves me back.

"Okay, sis, you've convinced me. If the right moment comes up, I'll tell him."

***

Five days. Between my sister visiting and our first away game, it's been five days since I've spent the night with Xander, and since I had to share a room with Justus on the trip, I couldn't even openly talk to him. We did text back and forth a few times, mostly small talk like how was your day and shit, though I did send him a picture to show him how much I missed him when I woke up with him on my mind two days ago, and the one I got in return sent me straight to the shower for a little relief. Needless to say, I'm feeling pretty pent up, and when he opens the door all dark and sexy and *mine,* I don't even think about it, I step right to him and take his lips in a searing kiss.

He stumbles a bit when I bump into his chest, wrapping one arm around my waist for support while the other blindly pushes the door shut. As my hands grip his hips, I feel his fingers slide through my hair, pulling on it even as he pushes my head closer to his, deepening the kiss. There are things I want to say and do now that we're finally together, but they sort of fade into the background as I get lost in the feel of Xander's mouth on mine.

When you're in the closet and meeting a guy strictly to scratch an itch, there isn't a lot of kissing going on. While I think that's normal since touching lips is somehow more intimate than sucking dicks, I also think it left a void in my sex life. I didn't realize it at the time since I didn't know what I was missing, but now that I have Xander, and I can taste his breath and feel his needy whimpers vibrating against my lips... Damn. Just, damn.

I find the hand he has wrapped around my waist and guide it between my legs, pressing it into the rapidly growing bulge. "Feel what you do to me?" I nip at his bottom lips. "That's just from a kiss."

Xander rubs his palm over my dick, gently squeezing its girth as he travels its length. It's sexual, yeah, but also kind of soothing. It's so sweet I find myself leaning my forehead against his, eyes closed in contented bliss as he fondles me over my pants.

Even though I can't feel his skin on mine, Xander's touch is making me lightheaded. I suppose that's partly since he's coaxing all the blood to my cock right now, making it hard for my brain to form any thoughts. But I think it's also partly because the way he's cupping me in his hand is so reassuring, so *loving*, that one singular thought is abundantly clear. I need to come out. Publicly.

Telling him I love him isn't enough. It's a start, but it's incomplete. And while his gentle touch right now tells me he loves me and he'll support me and wait if I ask him to, it also says he deserves a man who respects him as much as he respects me. I can't be that man if I'm hiding him from the world.

An unexpectedly firm squeeze followed by a feather-light pass over my length sends pleasure rippling from my groin up my spine, and has my hips rocking forward in search of more. A wave of heat rolls over me as Xander seems to intuit what I need, giving me another firm yet somehow gentle caress.

"Alexander." I sigh as his hand softly kneads my rigid length. "I need—"

"You need my mouth on you? You need to be inside me?" He gives me a quick peck on the lips as he rubs my junk, pulling a strangled moan from my throat.

"I need you to fuck me."

Though I wanted to say *I love you*, it felt sort of disingenuous to declare that while he's holding my dick. I'm hoping since I don't usually bottom, he'll interpret the meaning behind my request until I can say it out loud.

"Come with me." Xander takes my hand and pulls me toward his bedroom, guiding me to the foot of the bed where he stops to face me and slides his hands under my shirt.

Taking my cue, I pull it over my head as his fingers glide over my torso, his lips chasing them once the fabric is out of the way. My skin erupts in little fireworks everywhere he nips and licks, my body shuddering on a pained sigh that both begs for more and demands he hurry up.

Fingers brush over the sensitive skin near my waist as they worry the clasp on my jeans, a tantalizing hint of the pleasure to come. All the while, Xander's mouth travels over my skin, tongue flicking a nipple before he takes it between his teeth with a gentle tug.

"Fuck," I breathe. My teeth are locked together. My jaw tense.

"Your cock just tried to jump out of your pants." He suctions his lips around my nipple, and I feel it twitch again. "I think we should give it room to move."

He opens my pants and shoves them down my hips, freeing my aching erection as he latches onto my nipple. Once again, my dick bobs of its own accord. The tip brushes against his t-shirt in a plea for his touch, but it doesn't come. Instead, the pads of Xander's fingers map the ridges on my stomach, my pecs, ghosting over my hips as his lips and teeth and tongue worry the firm bud on my chest.

I reach for his head, needing his soft hair to grip onto, but he takes my hand and guides it behind my back. "Don't touch."

Though I hate that answer, commanding Xander is hot, so I obey, gripping the footboard so I'm not tempted to reach for him again.

As he peppers me with soft kisses, my whole body strains with the need for more. More suction, more friction, just...*more*, especially between my legs where my angry pink cock is flat out dripping with want. It's a battle to stay still when my skin feels so electric, my dick ready to shoot off from the mere thought of being touched. Then, mercifully, Xander's mouth starts to travel lower, down to my abs, the hair framing my package, and finally my crown.

I have to lean against the footboard for support as his tongue flicks over my slit, swirling seductively over the head before he takes it deep within his mouth and sucks softly.

"Holy..." I rasp, unable to finish my thought as the wet heat of his mouth engulfs me, the gentle suction so tantalizing my balls draw up as my eyes roll back into my head, and... "Fuck, baby. Why'd you stop?"

He squeezes my balls in his palm, rolling them around as his bottomless brown eyes rake over my body. "I've waited five days for this. I want it to last."

"We have all night," I pant.

"Still not rushing." He runs the flat of his tongue along my length, wrapping his mouth around my tip for one firm suck before it pops out.

"Have you ever seen my cock this hard? I don't think you can tease it like this and expect it to cooperate."

"It'll have to if you want me to fuck you." He sucks a nut into his mouth and hums around it, the vibration causing my dick to lurch upward on its own accord. Then he lets it go as his finger grazes my hole, shooting me a sly grin when his touch makes my thighs quake.

"Baby, please," I plead.

"Patience." He flicks the head of my cock, sending a tiny jolt of pain over my crown that he quickly licks away. "I've only had a picture of your dick to get me through the past five days, and now that I have the real thing I plan to enjoy it."

Once again, he takes me in his mouth, this time swallowing me all the way to the back of his throat with another of those hums that causes my balls to tingle. Then he pulls back and teases my balls until enough precum has gathered on my slit he has to lick it away. With him fully clothed and me mostly naked, it'd be one of the hottest experiences of my life if I were coherent enough to process it. Instead, all I can do is plead with my body to hold on.

Over and over again he mouths my cock and balls, occasionally pushing his finger into my hole, though whether that's to get me ready or add to the torture I'm not sure. When my cock has morphed from pink to red and my balls are so heavy I'm surprised they're still attached, he finally instructs me to lay on the bed.

Xander sheds his clothes and rolls on the condom I don't even remember him getting. Then he crawls to me like a tiger stalking its prey, dark and sexy and ready to pounce. Straddling me with his thighs resting on mine, our cocks brushing together, he hands me the lube. "Get me ready."

I squirt a blob in my hand and rub it between my palms to warm it up. Then I wrap my fist around him and pull from root to tip, mimicking the motion with my second hand.

"Want to touch you, not this condom," I grumble as I spread the gel over his length.

"You're clean?" He arches a dark brow.

"Yes."

"Me, too. Take it off then." There's a daring gleam in his eye, but I don't need to be told twice. I pull the latex off, add more lube to my hands, and start running my palms over his length.

Chapter 24
Xander

S tradling Niko, my dick sliding through his hands as he preps me
to enter him, only one word runs through my mind: *yes*.

Not '*yes* I'm about to get laid' or '*yes* he asked me to top.' Just *yes*.
This is right. This is perfect. This is everything.

Despite the totally valid warnings from Tripp, and the fact I'm
breaking the rules intended to ensure my self-preservation, I have no
regrets about this. Niko. I'm exactly where I'm meant to be, and the
man I'm meant to be with. I've never been so sure.

Though his cock is straining—so is mine—he takes his time spreading the lube, swiping his thumb over my slit, teasing the sensitive
underside, returning the somewhat torturous pleasure I put him
through. It makes me feel slightly guilty for edging him so long—I am
desperately horny—yet I'm also oddly content to let his hands roam
over me, admiring.

"Have you ever gone bare before?" His beautiful blue eyes search
mine.

My throat seizes up before I can answer as the magnitude of what
we're doing hits me. But it's not panic I feel. It's more like the realization that this step indicates permanence.

Yeah, we've talked about the future in terms of how long we can
exist in our current bubble, and there's been a commitment of sorts
in that he plans to come out with me once his career is in a more stable

spot. But all that is speculation. Words that may or may not come to fruition. This—what he's offering right now—he's basically saying he wants this to be forever. And so I don't choke over the words like a teenage girl, I shake my head.

"Me, either." His swallow echoes in the otherwise silent room. "I'm ready."

Still unable to form words, I lean forward until my lips press against his, holding them there for the few breaths it takes me to compose myself. Then I pull back to line up to his hole, and push slowly forward.

Once again, the ability to speak eludes me, and I can do little more than groan as my cock is engulfed by his deliciously tight ass. It's so fucking hot, I have to hold perfectly still since the tiniest friction will send me over the edge.

"Alexander," Niko groans with a subtle shift of his hips.

"Stop... Don't..." I squeeze my eyes shut with the effort of holding still. "Don't move yet. I can't... Fuck, you feel incredible. I need a minute."

"Come here." Niko wraps his hand around the back of my head and pulls me to him, touching our lips together just as tenderly as I did before I entered him. But instead of holding still he tilts his head, swiping his tongue so gently over the seam of my lips I swear I imagined it, until he does it again.

Over and over again, he licks at my lips until he coaxes them apart and our tongues finally meet. With delicate strokes he calms my racing heart, redirecting my focus to his mouth instead of the throbbing need between my legs. Not that the pressure goes away, my control is still precarious, but at least now I can breathe without worrying I'll come apart.

"You okay, baby?" Niko's fingers sift through my hair as he plants another chaste kiss on my lips.

"I didn't know it would feel this good." The words are a shock only because I didn't intend to say them, not because they aren't true. "Can you feel it?"

"Not yet. I will though, when you come inside me." He smiles almost shyly, his dimples making a subtle appearance that damn near guts me. Then his hand starts clutching at my ass, reminding me that my cock is only pacified, not sated.

"Keep doing that and I'll have to move," I grunt.

"I hope so. I'm dying here."

I give him another soft, lingering kiss, then pull my hips back. My retreat leaves a trail of pleasure rippling over the surface of my dick that flares up as I push back in. It's a sensation rivaled only by the way Niko pegs my prostate when he fucks me, but this time the pleasure surrounds me.

Groaning, I thrust again. "I feel you everywhere. So tight. So good." I'm turning into a babbling mess, but fuck if I can stop the words. It just feels so incredible to be inside Niko without anything between us to blur the friction, and it's sort of making me a slave to my cock. I can't help but to move faster, even as I fight to savor this moment.

"Deeper baby. I need you deeper. I want to feel you tomorrow, and the next day, and…"

"Jesus, *fuck*," I grunt, Niko's filthy words going straight to my dick, leaving me helpless to resist.

The slippery heat of his hole, the chokehold it has on my cock, his words, it's all coming together in this tsunami of ecstasy that I can't resist. So I pump deeper. Faster. Harder. And though I wanted to prolong things, the role reversal is flooding me with sensations I'm not used to, and which I have very little ability to ignore without the latex barrier to dull them.

"Fuck, Niko." I snap my hips back and forth. "I'm so close."

"Not yet, baby. Not—" His eyes roll back in his head as I find the angle that hits his prostate.

"Jesus, you just got even tighter." Shifting my weight to my left arm I thread my right between us and cup his sac, squeezing it in my hand as I piston in and out, giving him a taste of his own dirty talk. "Your balls are so full. You're gonna come so hard for me, aren't you. Show me."

"Need more," he grunts. "Grab my dick."

"My hands are full." I squeeze his sac again. "You hold it for me. Jerk yourself and paint your chest. I want you to cover it."

Niko's hand shifts from where it was gripping the sheets and wraps around his length, pumping it furiously. I match my rhythm to his, so that with each tug on his cock I'm pulling back, and bottoming out each time his fist slaps against his pelvis.

"Xander," he moans breathlessly, and I snap my gaze to his just in time to see the look of awe in them. And as our eyes lock, our bodies come apart.

As his release takes control of his body his ass clamps down so tight I'm helpless to hold on. I come deep inside him as ropes land across his chest. Our combined shouts bounce off the walls as convulsions ripple through us, the pleasure so intense my arms can't support my weight, and I collapse onto Niko before the tremors have left my body.

His stomach heaves beneath me as he tries to catch his breath, and I'm sure my weight doesn't help, but I'm too boneless to move, and he seems to be equally stunned, capable only of resting his arms on my back in a loose hug. So we lay together, me buried inside him while his cum dries between us, and I can honestly say I've never been so comfortable.

When his breathing finally evens, his hands comb tenderly through my hair. "I felt it."

"Hmm?" My mind is still foggy with a mix of awe and ecstasy.

"You. Bare. I felt it. I still feel it. It's running down my crack."

I lift my head and give him an exasperated look, which turns into a tiny hint of a smile as he grins broadly.

"Yours is sticking to my chest."

"You asked for that." He winks.

"I asked for you to coat *your* chest, not mine."

"And I did. You didn't have to roll around in it." He gives me a playful grin, and rather than retort with something equally stupid, I pull my softening dick from his body and offer him a hand.

"Let's get cleaned up."

***

One shower and two hand jobs later, we're back in bed, my head tucked into Niko's side as his fingers trace a path up and down my arm. It's soothing, but not so much that it turns off the voices in my head. Voices that have been plaguing me for the past several days. Of course, he seems to sense that.

"What are you thinking?" he asks.

"Tripp said we're too obvious. He advises us to not hang out together in public because we give too many subtle looks, so we'll give ourselves away."

"I was thinking about that actually." His fingers still for a moment before continuing on their path. "I know how important it is to you that you not be my dirty little secret—"

"Dirty little secret is harsh. I said that out of fear. I know that's not really what I am."

"True, but as long as I'm in the closet you're still a secret. Even if you are dirty," his hand slides to my ass and pinches it playfully, "you deserve better than that."

I retaliate with a pinch to his nipple, which he rubs away with a goofy grin. "I appreciate the thought, Niko, but we've been through this. We'll deal with it for now. "

"That's just it. *For now.* I know it's supposed to be the secret that's temporary, but that's backward. The only thing temporary here is hockey."

Holy fuck! Did he just say what I think he did?

Propping myself on an elbow, I lift my head off his chest to meet his eyes. "What are you saying?"

"I can't play forever." His blue eyes aren't glassy, but they do seem sort of sad. Pensive almost, like he's accepted the inevitable end of his career before it's even begun. It breaks the heart I didn't think I had until he came into my life.

"You could play for a decade or more though."

"I could, but even if I did, we wouldn't make it ten years in the closet. If Tripp's right, we won't even make it one. We're too obvious."

My lungs feel like they're constricting, making the rapid beat of my heart echo in my ears. "What are you saying?"

"I'm saying of the two most important things in my life right now, only one of them has the potential to be permanent. So why would I put it in jeopardy by keeping it a secret?"

Wait, he's talking about us being permanent?

I lick my lips, buying time to force my voice to stay level. "Who said anything about putting it in jeopardy? I agreed to the secrecy."

"Because I asked you to, not because you wanted to." Now his gaze is remorseful, and I have the eerie sense that he's already chosen me over the career that hasn't even started yet.

"Let me rephrase, I know what I agreed to."

"Yes, but for how long? Not my entire career. Probably not even half of it. So, if it's going to come out, why not just get it out there? Rip off the Band-aid."

"And risk your career bleeding out?"

"Okay, didn't need that visual, but yeah."

No, this is not what I want. I mean one day, yes. But not today.

"Nikolas, you've spent your whole life working toward this. I can be patient while you chase the career you deserve."

"I know you can, baby." He gives me a smile that doesn't reach his eyes or reveal his dimples, and reaches for my hand, lacing our fingers together on his chest. "But again, for how long? It could take years to solidify my place. And remember, I've done the secrecy thing for a long time, so I'm kind of burned out on it. It takes so much fucking work to hide that part of myself, and the logistics of trying to meet up in secret—I mean at least now I can come here instead of meeting for a few hours at a shady motel—but what we have isn't a shady hotel situation. I don't want to have to sneak in and out of here so people can't connect me to you."

"I don't want that either, but I can do it to give your career time to take off."

"I'm not sure *I* can do it. I'm going to have to put so much energy into hockey, I don't think I'll have any left over to put on some bullshit mask all the time. Just the idea of it drains me, and if I feel drained, I'll play like shit, which would end my career anyway."

Coming out in high school, it's been a long time since I felt this way, yet I remember it vividly. The constant stress of wondering if you've said or done something to give away the thing you're trying to hide, it's never ending.

"I get that. I really do. But I can't help worrying that you feel this way because you know my history with situations like this. And yeah, it's not a spot I wanted to be in again, but it's not the same situation because it's *you*. Don't make career altering decisions because of my hang ups."

"Your history may have made me more aware, but I promise it's not dictating this decision." He brings our hands to his mouth and kisses my knuckles.

"I still need you to be sure about that before you do anything. I don't want you to end up resenting me for giving up something you love."

"I love *you*, Alexander. I don't want to pretend like I don't."

The sincerity in his eyes tells me I heard right, but my brain has trouble processing. "You...you do?"

"Don't act so shocked. I mean, I wouldn't put my career on the line for just anyone." This time the smile does reach his eyes, giving me a glimpse of those sexy dimples.

Fuck, he's adorable. But this is too much.

"I don't want you to do that for me."

Niko rubs his thumb over the back of my hand. "I know you don't. That's why I love you." He leans forward to brush his lips over mine for a tender kiss before falling back against the headboard. "Besides, I'm not doing it for you. Well, not just you. I'm doing it for me. I've lived two different lives for too long. If that means hockey is done with me before I'm done with it... Then I guess it wasn't worth the amount of time I devoted to it, and I should be grateful to find that out before I put in even more."

Everything he's saying makes sense yet doesn't given how hard he's worked to get to the spot he's in right now. "You really believe that?"

"When I remind myself there's more to life than hockey, then yeah. Sometimes I get stuck on what else there is though, besides you." His brow furrows as he looks at our joined hands. "If I have to leave hockey behind... I don't really know anything else so it might take me a while to find my way. I can't promise that won't make me the brooding one until I figure shit out. Will you still love me if I turn into you?" Now the grin is out in full force, the dimples a sign he needs to lighten things up. So, I toy with him.

"Did I say I loved you?"

His eyes grow wide as they search my face. "Um, don't you?"

An uncharacteristic laugh makes its way up my throat. Panicked Niko is cute, but I can't torture him. "Yes, Nikolas. Despite trying my hardest to avoid it, I found it impossible not to fall in love with you."

"Thank God." He grips the back of my head, pulling me to him for a kiss that feels like a promise of forever, and I finally, *finally*, let myself believe it will be.

Chapter 25
Niko

"So, what's the plan?" I ask over breakfast the next morning, which consists of toast and some truly weak coffee. I make a mental note to start bringing my own, as well as something more substantial foods like eggs or oatmeal.

"What plan?"

"For me to come out. What's the plan?" I try not to grimace as I take a sip.

"Why are you asking me?"

"You've done it before."

"Ten years ago. And I only had to come out to my parents, not a team and a coach and, potentially, thousands of fans."

"Whoa." I sink into the closet chair, my mug hitting the table with a thunk. "I sorta forgot about the fans. Do I really have to say something to them?" At this point I'm still new enough to not have many, which I guess is why they weren't on my radar. And truthfully, since they're not people I know personally, I'm not sure how that translates into me having to address them specifically.

"Well, I guess you could just tell the team and not make any public declaration or anything. That way if, or when, it comes out you can shrug it off like it's old news, and for the team it would be." Xander gives a noncommittal shrug as he sips his coffee.

"I like that. I'd rather not turn myself into the poster boy for gay hockey players with some big announcement."

"The press might make you that anyway."

"They can try, but if I don't give them anything but hockey to talk about won't it eventually go away?"

"I have no idea." A stray lock of hair swings over his eyes as he shakes his head.

"Well, I figure the more I enable them the worse it'll be, for both of us. If I refuse to talk about it at some point they'll stop asking. I'm hoping that'll mean they leave you alone too." I force down another gulp of watery coffee.

"I guess that's as good a plan as any. So, you'll come out to the team only, and if or when it comes out, we just act like us dating is old news."

"Yep."

"So, are you going to tell everyone at once, or one at a time?"

That's actually a great question. I don't want to divide the team by telling them separately, but I feel like the guys I'm closest to deserve to know first. Plus, two of them are captains, which might pave the way to tell everyone else. "I think I'll do it in stages. Justus, Noah and Luca first, since they've hung out with us a bit and will hopefully have the best reaction. Then everyone else."

"And my dad?"

My stomach does a little flip as I think of facing coach. "Yeah, I haven't really worked that one out yet. On the one hand, it'd probably be more respectful to tell him first, but on the other, he's fucking scary. Am I making this up, or do you think if at least a few of the guys already know and are cool with it, he'll be more receptive?"

"That depends. Do you think the guys will be receptive?"

"I have a good feeling since they seemed to have a good time when we all hung out. What do you think your dad will say?"

"He won't be happy, but I think more of that will be directed at me than you. Plus, hockey comes first with him, so I don't think he'd do anything rash to you that might jeopardize the team."

"What about you though?" I wouldn't go so far as to say Xander and his dad don't get along, but there's obviously some tension there that makes their relationship a little touchy. There's no question news of us dating will make it worse, at least initially, which I'm conflicted about.

I don't want to be the thing that puts a permanent rift between Xander and his dad. But I'm also not willing to give Xander up. I mean, I'm prepared to let hockey go for him, so the disapproval of a parent doesn't even make the list of things that would make me stay away. That probably makes me a selfish bastard, but after years of denying who I am and what I want, I'm not going to let anything stand in my way. And unlike hockey, any rift our relationship causes with his family doesn't have to be permanent. That's my reasoning anyway.

"There's not much he can do to me without making it look like he doesn't support you. And before you blame yourself for whatever reaction he has toward me, I promise I've been prepared for this, and I don't have any regrets."

I really do hate that he has to prepare for backlash from his dad. I haven't told my parents about Xander yet since I don't want them to worry about my career, something they'd do in part because I conditioned them to think my sexuality could be an issue by hiding it for so long. But when I do tell them, there's no doubt in my mind they'll be happy for me. Which reminds me, as soon as we tell Xander's dad, Coach, I need to tell my parents.

"So tell Coach first, or..."

"I like your idea of telling a few of the guys first. When do you think you'll do it?"

"Today's as good a day as any." I shrug. "After practice. I'll take them out for a drink or something."

"There's no rush, you know." Xander drops into the chair next to me and takes my hand, his bottomless brown eyes rich with understanding. "And I'm not saying you don't have to do this, I know your mind is made up. I'm saying you can take more than a day to figure out what you want to say."

"I'm telling them I'm gay, babe. Whether I say it today or ten days from now there really aren't any other words to use."

"Yeah, I guess not. Come here after?"

I flash my dimples at him, coaxing a slight smile to his concerned face. "Obviously." Then I pull him in for a kiss that's entirely too indecent considering we both have to get out the door. Spoiler alert, we almost don't make it.

***

"So, what's up?" Noah asks as I set a pitcher and four glasses on the table at what's become our usual table at the Frosty Dog. "Are you missing home again?"

"No. Well, always if I'm being honest, but that's not why I asked you here." I pour everyone a glass and pass them out.

"Everything good?" Luca asks.

"I think so. But I have something I want to tell the team, and I wanted you guys to hear it from me first since you've been so helpful getting me situated and stuff." My heart is pounding so loud I feel like the entire bar can hear it above the bass from the music playing in the background, but if I dwell on that the words will get stuck. I take a quick, deep breath and just blurt it out. "I'm gay, and I've been dating Xander."

Three dumbfounded faces look back at me. Noah blinks rapidly, Justus cocks his head to the side curiously, and a slight crease forms between Luca's brows. I wouldn't say any of them look pissed, but I've definitely rendered them speechless. *Maybe I should've softened the blow a bit with a warmup statement like 'this might come as a shock.'*

Noah is the first to find his voice. "Coach's son, Xander?"

"Does Coach know?" Justus asks.

"Yes, Coach's son, and no he doesn't know. I'll tell him next."

"Think he'll be pissed?" Noah's eyes narrow, though more in contemplation than anger if I'm reading him right.

"Do you? You know him better."

"Hard to say." Noah rubs his jaw. "Coach doesn't talk about his family much, and Xander doesn't come around that often. I think I've only ever seen him at the cookout where no one outside the team is invited. I never knew why that was, but I have wondered if being gay was part of the reason."

"Xander told me his dad's cool with his sexuality," I tell him. "He doesn't come around much since he doesn't love hockey."

"He doesn't like hockey and he's dating *you?*" Justus's eyes are comically wide.

"I know right," I laugh, both because I still don't have a read on what they think, and that was just funny. "Guy has shit luck as far as that goes. Between me and his dad he's sort of surrounded."

"So, Xander wasn't just teaching you how to drive?" Justus starts connecting the dots.

"He was. He did. But we actually met when I came out here for my trial practice, totally by chance. I didn't even know who he was, so it was kind of a shock when I saw him at the cookout, but I was also pretty excited to see him again, so... what do you think?" I look at each of them in turn.

"About you being gay?" Noah asks. "Okay."

"Okay?" I prompt.

"Keep defending the goal the way you do, and I don't care who you fuck." Noah sips his beer like he always does, seemingly unaffected by my big reveal.

"Um, alright. Cool. Justus?"

"I'm good," Justus says.

"Luca?" I turn my head to our star forward, who I actually thought would be the most accepting given that I know he's got some kinks of his own. Not that being gay is a kink but... I sort of assumed being sexually adventurous would make a person more open-minded. "You haven't said anything. Does my being gay bother you?"

"Nooo." He shakes his head slowly back and forth as he drags out that one little word. "Dating Coach's kid though... How does that work exactly?"

"What do you mean?"

"Once you're involved with his kid, you're not *just* a hockey player anymore. Coach can't look at you impartially, not if he wants to keep his kid happy. Will that make him go harder or easier on you, and how will that affect your play?"

"Xander says hockey comes first for him. In my mind that means he won't treat me differently than the rest of the team."

"Will he even want you on the team? I mean, every move you make, good or bad, will start people talking about the fact you're dating Xander. *Niko cost the team a goal—he won't get benched since he's dating Coach's son. Niko made a brilliant shot—bet Coach is relieved he won't have to trade his son's boyfriend away this season.*"

Okay, mimicking an announcer's voice made that argument pretty effective.

"You're our top pick and there are some pretty high expectations," he continues. "Dating Xander will only magnify those, and you'll have to deliver if you don't want people to talk shit about your relationship."

"I have to deliver no matter what. If I want to stay on this team or in this league, I have to perform. Dating Xander doesn't change that, although I hear what you're saying about people talking shit. If I kill it on the ice, people are gonna be less likely to criticize what I do off it."

The three of them nod as they weigh my words, which is the sign I need to keep going.

"When I was weighing the pros and cons of coming out, I thought about the impact it would have. More so on the team than the press and the fans, because I don't have any plan to talk to them about my personal life. No one else has their dating life under a microscope, and even though they'll try to put mine under one, I won't take that bait. The reason I'm telling you is I want to focus all my energy on hockey, not living a double life. I think if you guys are okay with me, Coach will have to be, and if I play the way everyone expects me to, I'm hoping that'll keep the talk about hockey instead of Xander."

"So, you don't plan to make some big announcement, you're just telling the team and everyone else can say what they want but you won't address it?" Luca asks.

"That's the plan."

Luca's jaw tenses as he chews on his lip, making me wonder for a second if I was wrong to assume his own kinks would make him more likely to accept my lifestyle. Then he takes a deep breath and meets with his determined stare. "In that case I'm with these guys. I don't give a shit who you fuck as long as you keep kicking ass on the ice. And

I'm good with not making a big deal of it off the ice. I'd much rather the focus be on how we're playing than who you're dating."

"You just want them talking about your stats." Noah rolls his eyes at Luca.

"Obviously," Luca agrees.

The sense of relief that comes from their acceptance is indescribable, especially since I'm still an unproven rookie they don't have to feel any loyalty toward. The fact that they do, that they're prepared to support me through a personal decision that might very well drag them into a spotlight they never asked for... If I let myself think too hard about it my eyes might start leaking at this table.

They've got my back, and while I could sit here and resent the fact that I even need to ask, I'd rather just be grateful so I can get on with living the life I want to have. The one that includes both Xander and hockey. But I still have more hurdles to jump before I'm there.

"What about the rest of the team?" I ask.

"Off the top of my head I can't see anyone having a problem with you..." Luca trails off, chewing on his lip a second before continuing. "Dating Xander might be touchy until they feel comfortable it won't really change anything, but as long as Coach reacts like you say and puts the team first, I think it'll be fine."

"If anyone does have an issue, we'll make sure they know we won't tolerate that." Noah draws an imaginary line between the three of them, who all bob their heads in agreement.

"So, um. Cheers?" Justus lifts his glass. "You and Xander... It's good?"

"Really good." I feel a goofy smile spread across my face as I lift my glass and click it against all of theirs.

Three down, about a dozen more to go.

Fingers crossed, they all go as well as this. Somehow, I don't think that'll be true of Coach, but hopefully the support of Noah, Luca and Justus will help change his mind.

Chapter 26
Xander

Speaking with my father is never easy. Sure, I can talk hockey with him because I was conditioned to as a child, and it's stuck with me all these years later. But I don't enjoy those talks, which he's never bothered to acknowledge or accept. Yet right now, standing on his front step with Niko beside me, I'd give just about anything to be prepping myself for a conversation about hockey instead of the one we're about to have.

Though we aren't close, my dad and I aren't estranged either, and there's a very real chance we could be when he hears what Niko and I have to say. That's the worst-case scenario. Best case is he'll be extremely disappointed, which will hurt, but that won't exactly be anything new.

He didn't love that I quit hockey, he didn't love that I took up skateboarding, he doesn't love my choice of career—there are probably half a dozen things about me that disappoint him to this day, though none of them could be considered a deliberate slap in the face. More like, we're two very different people who have trouble relating to each other, and when I didn't turn out just like him, he didn't know what to think.

We're hardly unique in that regard—fathers and sons have this type of disconnect all the time. And even though it hurt, I understand why he's disappointed I didn't take after him. Yet even though being different made it harder for him to relate to me, I think deep down he knew I never intentionally set out to disappoint him. I still haven't, though I'm not sure he'll see it that way. Not when my actions could impact his career.

There's a very real chance he could come away from this conversation thinking I chose Niko over him, and while that's true in a way, what I hope he'll eventually understand is there was never a choice.

Call him my other half, my person, hell, even soulmate might fit given the way we seemed to instantly connect. Regardless of the label, the truth is Niko and I are meant to be, and the part of me that has repeatedly disappointed my dad *really* hopes he'll be able to see that. If not, this might be the end of whatever relationship we have left.

"Ready?" Niko gives my hand a reassuring squeeze.

I take a deep breath and hold it for about three seconds before returning the squeeze and taking my hand out of his in an effort to be a little less obvious. "Yes."

It takes a minute or two for the door to open, and once it does, my dad looks at us for about two seconds before the pink flush starts rising up his neck. "Fuck," he mutters as he spins away and walks inside, though at least he left the door open.

Niko offers an encouraging smile and puts his hand on my back, following me as we trail after him.

We find my dad standing at the wet bar in the living room, a glass of amber liquid in the tumbler he's holding. He slams it back, pours another, and tosses that back as well before turning to face us. "How long?"

"Officially, a few weeks. But it started four months ago." Though this could still go very wrong, it's a relief to finally admit it.

"So, you didn't just chat at the bar?" He snorts as he pours a third.

"We did, at first."

"And the whole friends line you both fed me?" His gaze darts between me and Niko, irises barely visible between his narrowed eyelids.

"It wasn't a lie, Coach. We tried the friend thing and it just," Niko pulls his eyes from my dad and gives me a warm smile, "wasn't enough."

"Wasn't enough?" My dad glares at me even though Niko was the one who was speaking. "You're putting the team on the line because you couldn't stay out of each other's beds?"

"I know my career is on the line, but how is the team's?" Niko puts my dad's focus back on him.

"Some of the guys will assume you're getting special treatment from me, and whether it's true or not, they only have to hint at that for management to start getting jittery about my ability to coach. Then there's the press. They'll hone in on your relationship, completely ignoring the team itself and focusing on your personal life. That would've happened with any guy you date, but my son? It won't be just you getting the questions but me too, and how do you think the rest of the team will feel if I have to talk about your personal life instead of their accomplishments?"

"That's a bit of an exaggeration, isn't it?" I try to take the heat off Niko. "I mean, sure there will be talk, but if you two steer things back to the game won't they eventually give up?"

"When have you ever known the press to give up something they're curious about? And if that curiosity has a negative impact on the team... The whole thing could implode. That's why this can't happen."

I expected my dad to freak out, but not to have the audacity to try to control my life, and if that's what he wants to do, he's going to have to spell it out. "What can't happen?" I challenge.

"The two of you." He points between me and Niko. "The ripple effect could be too big, it's just not possible."

I'm pretty sure my face is just as red as my father's, but before I can tell him exactly what he can do with his suggestion Niko's steady voice hits my ears. "I'm really sorry, Coach, but that's not an option."

"It's the only option." My dad's lips are pursed together so tightly they're losing color.

"Are you saying I can't be on the team if I'm with Xander?"

"I'm saying I'd keep your sexuality to yourself if you want a long future in this league."

"Isn't that hypocritical of you? Your son is gay, you know better than anyone what kind of struggle that presents for him to exist in this world, and you're going to hold my sexuality against me?"

"I'm not who you have to worry about. You've got teammates, sponsors, fans, all of whom will have an opinion, and not all of them will be favorable. In fact, some of it will be derogatory. Degrading. And it won't stop with you. People will blame Xander, accuse him of turning you gay as if that's a real thing. He'll take a beating in the press. Hell, he'll be lucky if that's where it ends instead of an actual beating since there are such high hopes for your performance, and if you don't live up, they'll point the finger at him."

I can tell by his suddenly pale complexion that Niko hadn't considered some fans might express themselves physically—I hadn't either—and it seems to have made us both speechless. But while he's thinking of my safety, I'm caught up in the fact that my dad's biggest objection seems to be based on that as well, not hockey. He's concerned for *me*.

When neither of us speak my dad continues. "My advice—keep this to yourself. Not just this, "he draws a line between the two of us, "which I know you aren't going to end even though you should, but your orientation."

"Why do you know we won't end it?" I ask at the same time Niko asks, "Why should we end it?"

My dad tosses back another drink and takes a deep breath before he looks at Niko. "You should end it because it's going to be tougher than either of you realize." Then he turns to face me. "And I know you won't because for the first time in your life you ignored my rule about dating my players, and you wouldn't do that unless he's really important to you. And I assume he wouldn't risk his career unless he feels the same." He tilts his head toward Niko. "But right now, you guys are thinking with your hearts, and that's not how hockey works. So, I'll say it again. This needs to stay between the three of us."

"Too late." Niko mutters.

"What?" My dad pales.

"Niko already told some of the guys."

"Tell me you didn't," my dad says.

"Sorry, Coach." Niko looks more tired than I've ever seen him, though his voice is steady. "I've lived this lie way too long. I could feel it sapping my energy. Energy I need for hockey. I couldn't do it anymore. The only way I perform as well as everyone hopes is if I live one life, not two. If hockey isn't a part of that life... Not gonna like that'll suck, but at least I'll have Xander."

"You're too much of a boy scout for your own good." My dad mumbles as he rubs his temples. "Alright," he blows out a puff of air. "Who'd you tell and how'd it go?"

Niko recounts the conversation he had with his teammates and their reactions, as well as our strategy to not make some big production over his coming out beyond the guys on the team. That way, if and when our relationship does become public, everyone associated with the team can honestly say they already know and it's not some big secret, effectively taking some wind out of the sails of anything thinking they've got some huge scoop to share.

"As far as plans go, it's not bad," my dad agrees, "but I don't have the final decision. Management has to be notified, as well as the PR team so they can have a statement ready if we get the green light."

"What if we don't get the green light?" I ask.

My dad exhales heavily. "They can't force you to break up, and they can't bench Niko for dating you without opening themselves up to legal challenges considering the official statement from the league is one of support. That said, they don't have to stand behind him and they don't have to keep him on the roster if they find a suitable trade. And—there's no other way to say it—your trade stock is probably diminished by being out. Gay players are still rare enough that most teams don't want the extra scrutiny they might bring. So, unless you really kick some ass this season, your career could be on the line."

Both of his dimples are absent as he nods. "I expected that."

"I'm still concerned about the fallout for Xander. The organization won't love the fact you two are dating while I'm the coach, but I think I can convince them it'll work. If that's the case, and they support you publicly, I think that could buy you some goodwill, but there will still be crazies who default to blaming Xander."

"I'll walk away if it means keeping him safe." Niko presses his lips together resolutely.

"No, you won't."

"But—"

"No," I repeat. "Crazies exist no matter what. Dating you doesn't change that."

"Dating me might make you a bigger target."

"If I can survive standing next to a guy like Tripp who loves to rile people up, I'm sure I can survive being next to you."

"Tripp isn't projected to be one of the best rookies of all time," my dad scoffs.

"You don't have to be a hockey fan to be crazy, or an asshole." I retort. "Fortunately, in my experience people tend to have bigger mouths than muscles. I can handle anything people say, and I doubt it would escalate past that, especially if I don't take their bait."

"Can you say the same, Niko? You'll have to be in control at all times, no matter what people are saying. Otherwise, you're not just gonna get labeled as the first gay rookie, but the first *unhinged* gay rookie. It's not fair, but one misstep and you'll make it even harder for the guys who come after you."

"Understood." Niko nods solemnly.

"Okay then," my dad gives him a curt head bob in return, then holds out his hand. "This isn't gonna be easy, son, and I still think you'd be better off not saying anything career-wise. But I respect a man who puts his partner first. I didn't do the same thing at your age, ever really. Xander's lucky to have you. I will be kicking your ass on the ice for making me coach my kid's boyfriend, though."

I'm not sure I've ever seen Niko's dimples as deep as they are as he pumps my dad's hand in return. "Thank you, Coach."

My dad just grunts in response. "Do me a favor and go find Xander's mom. Ask her to order some food for all of us. I don't know about you two, but I'm starved."

"You got it, Coach." Niko turns toward the kitchen but doesn't take a step before he turns back to face us, shooting an almost bashful look at my dad before he steps to me and traps me in the biggest bear hug I've ever received. "Love you," he whispers against my lips before giving them a soft peck and spinning away before he can watch my dad's reaction.

I make a mental note to get back at him later as I feel the blood rushing to my cheeks, but my revenge plans are cut short when I feel my dad's heavy stare.

"He makes you smile."

I do a quick inventory and realize the corner of my mouth is lifted the way it always seems to be around Niko.

"Annoying, right?" I press my lips together to keep them from spreading wider since happiness of any sort in front of my father still feels awkward.

"No, actually. It's been a while since I've seen it, is all." The voice I associate with authority is much softer than I'm used to.

"Did you mean that? About being worried for my safety?"

"I've always been worried about that. It's the primary reason I didn't want you dating my players."

"You really think fans will get violent?"

My dad's gaze turns distant as he seems to weigh his words. "Physically, not really. But the comments can be vicious. Remember there was that singer awhile back that dated a football player? Quarterback I think it was, and every time he played a rough game her name got brought up. They were a straight couple and still got dragged through the mud. Maybe it'll be different for you since you aren't famous yourself, but I never wanted you to find out."

"I'm sorry I broke your rule." Before this conversation I never thought I'd say those words, but now that I understand where the rule came from, I do feel a little remorse.

"I'm sorry I had to have it in the first place."

"It's not your fault the world isn't fair."

That gets a chuckle out of him. "I suppose not. You still always wish better for your kids than what the world is prepared to give them though."

Years of tiptoeing around each other makes it hard for me to respond, even knowing that at least some of our issues stem from his wanting to protect me. Part of me is flattered that he was looking out for me in his own way when I was convinced he was indifferent to my existence, but the other part of me vividly remembers feeling like a failure in his eyes, and retreating into myself as a result. So, I can just give him a hug and say everything's cool. Eventually, maybe I'll be able to say it's okay and I don't hold any resentment. For now, the best I can do is focus on the fact he accepts me and Niko, and he's in our corner.

"I don't have any complaints about what the world has given me."

My dad meets my eyes with his almost glassy ones and gives me a firm nod. "Come on, let's go have our first family dinner."

Chapter 27
Niko

"Get up. We have one more thing to do." Xander holds his hand out to pull me from the couch.

"Seriously? We just finished," I groan, taking his hand anyway since he's wearing this sexy smirk that has become sort of a staple over the past six weeks. I can't seem to say no to it, or maybe I'm just addicted to seeing it. Either way, he flashed me that look when he made the case for moving in with him instead of keeping the condo I rarely slept at, and long story short, everything I own is now in his apartment.

He pulls me to my feet with enough force to send me crashing into his chest, and the smirk turns to a full-blown smile. "I promise you'll thank me later," he says, his face a mere inch away from mine.

"We'll see," I taunt right back, nipping at his bottom lip.

As we bundle up—apparently, we're leaving the apartment—I realize my face actually hurts from smiling so hard. The past several weeks have been nothing short of perfect, everything from the support of my teammates and management to the privilege of having both hockey and Xander in my life falling into place as if the separate pieces were always meant to fit. I've never been so happy, and while I'm not shouting from the rooftops so I can guard what privacy I have, I also don't care who knows. That's why I've tried to live as normally as possible since we shared our secret with the Bulldogs.

Xander is a regular at our games, often joining me and the guys when we go out afterward. I'm not afraid to put my arm around his chair or give him a quick kiss, but we aren't over the top with the PDA, so we haven't drawn much attention on those outings. And more often than not we just go home together since my travel schedule means we get so little time with just the two of us. It's everything I could've dreamed of.

For the first time in my life, I'm not burdened with hiding who I am off the ice, and I think it's actually improved my play. I've got more goals than any defenseman in the league, and we've had the fewest goals scored on us. Obviously, I can't take all the credit for that, Noah is a beast in the cage and he's having a great season too, though the two of us together have an impressive record of keeping the puck out of the net.

Now, on top of a great season, I get to live with Xander. For now, that's in his apartment, but after this season... If things go well, I want to buy us a house. Something we can call our own instead of something that's just convenient.

Dressed for the cold air, we lace our fingers together and head toward the little town center area where we first met. Ten minutes later we're standing hand-in-hand in front of the little candy shoppe that caught my eye the first night I spent in Denver, minutes before I met Xander. I never did make it inside since I was hoping in vain to spot him again, and focused my attention on the restaurants in the area where he might be having dinner. I never mentioned it though.

"How did you know?"

"I saw you looking at it when we walked to your hotel that first night. Your face lit up when we passed by, and I remember thinking it was cute that something so simple could make you so happy. And since I don't have any chocolate to satisfy your nightly craving, I figure we should stock up."

Over the past six weeks I've been gone just as much as I've been here, so I wasn't aware Xander had picked up on my chocolate habit. The fact that he did, and brought me to a place he remembered from the night we met...

I give his hand a tug as I wrap another behind his neck, pulling him to me so our mouths are hovering just millimeters apart. "I fucking love you."

"I fucking love you, too." He closes the distance and brushes his lips softly over mine. "Now get in there and get your fix."

Sporting a grin so big I probably resemble a toddler instead of a grown man, I drag him behind me as I bound into the store, nodding hello to the stoic looking cashier before steering us to the wall lined with every kind of chocolate imaginable.

Light, dark, filled with a variety of flavors, there are so many choices I'm momentarily overwhelmed, not sure where to look first, which Xander watches with an amused smirk.

"You are so easy to please," he chuckles.

I give him a bashful little shrug before reaching for a box that indicates it should be paired with whiskey. I'm not much of a whiskey guy, but I'm intrigued. There's also one that goes with wine, and one for coffee. Then I spot one I've only seen a handful of times since moving to the U.S.

"Oh my God." I reach for the package, which contains dozens of bite-sized chocolates. "Daim."

"Is that your favorite?"

"As a kid, yeah. It's got caramel in it, so I don't eat it now, but before I had to pay attention to my diet I'd sneak these every chance I got. Have you ever had one?"

"I've never even heard of it."

Assuring myself I'll only indulge on special occasions, I open the bag and unwrap one of the dark candies, holding it up for him to see. "Matches your eyes. Open up."

He does as I ask, and I set the candy on his tongue, trailing my finger over his lip as he closes his mouth. And because that lip feels so plump and full against my skin, I bring mine to his in a tender kiss, licking softly along the seam to capture the sweet remnants. "Well?"

"You have to pay for that," a stern voice barks at us before Xander can answer.

I tear my gaze away from his and turn to the clerk, who strikes me as the epitome of a grumpy old man the way he's glaring at us. "Of course. We're still shopping but I'll buy this bag." I hold it up to signal my intent, then turn back to Xander, who's got a pensive look on his face. "You don't like it?"

"It's not bad."

Holding a hand over my heart I pretend to stagger. "You don't love my favorite childhood treat?"

"Caramel is hard to chew." He grimaces as he works his jaw, like he's trying to pry it off his teeth.

"Fair," I chuckle as I turn my attention back to the wall of heaven I get to choose from.

We spend the next fifteen minutes or so debating what to get—or rather I debate while Xander tells me to get it all—and take our selections to the register. As we're bickering about who should pay the bell over the door dings and two police officers step inside. I don't spare them a second glance as I slap several bills on the counter, feeling pretty sneaky about getting my money out while Xander was distracted. It's not until I feel his hand on my arm that I realize there's an unsettling tension in the room.

"Are these the two you called about?" One of the officers asks the clerk.

"Yes," the clerk replies. "They're stealing."

My eyes dart between the officer to the clerk and back, my pulse starting to race as I realize they're staring at me. "Stealing? I'm literally paying right now." I pick the stack of bills off the counter and hold them up for the officer to see.

"You ate before paying." The clerk scowls at me.

"This bag." I hold it up for everyone's inspection. "Which I'm paying for right now. I told you I planned to buy it."

"You can't eat it until after you pay," he sneers.

A strange tingle in my spine makes me think his issue is less about the candy than it is about me feeding Xander since his reaction to eating one tiny candy seems over the top. But calling him out on that will only create more issues, so I take the high road.

"My mistake. I didn't realize I was violating your policy. How much do I owe?" I gesture to the pile of candy on the counter.

"I don't sell to shoplifters. I'm pressing charges."

My jaw falls open as my eyes dart between Xander and the officers. "Is he... Can he do that?"

"Sir, we're talking about a few dollars' worth of chocolate, and this man is obviously trying to pay for it," one of the officers says.

"It's still stealing," the clerk insists. "It's my right to press charges."

"Is that accurate?" Xander asks.

"Yes," the officer replies before addressing the clerk. "I can't stop you from pressing charges, but I can tell you it won't go anywhere. Your customer is clearly stating his intent to pay, so this will get tossed."

"I can sue him for theft," the clerk insists.

"Which would cost you hundreds, if not thousands, of dollars to recoup the twenty he probably owes for that bag. Again, that's your right, but it'll put you in the hole financially when he's offering to pay now."

"I don't tolerate stealing," the clerk repeats.

"I'm the one who ate the candy, charge me," Xander faces the cop.

"He opened the bag and fed it to you." The clerk points at me.

"Since I planned to buy it, I didn't think it was a crime." I make my case to the room, noticing for the first time there's another couple in here watching. With a phone.

"Look, sir," the officer starts. "I'll take your statement if you want, but like I told you this won't amount to anything since he's trying to pay, and judges will toss this out before you make your case since we're talking a few dollars which can be paid right here if you take it."

The clerk seems to actually consider whether that's his best option before grumbling, "I don't want them back in my store."

"Not a problem. Keep the change," I bark with a nod toward the multiple bills on the counter, grabbing Xander's hand and storming toward the exit without a backward glance. Or my chocolate.

We're halfway down the block before I hear my name, and I pause, turning to see the officer jogging toward us. "Sorry about that," he huffs as he reaches us. "Legally, I couldn't stop him from making an issue out of that."

The adrenaline coursing through me makes me want to rage about the injustice we just suffered, but Coach's words about having to handle myself perfectly have me taking a deep breath before I respond. "It's not your fault. I appreciate you trying to diffuse things."

"I uh." He rubs the back of his neck awkwardly. "I also couldn't legally stop that other couple from recording the incident."

Xander's eyes grow wide—evidently he didn't notice that part—as he looks at me, a mix of panic and uncertainty clouding his gorgeous face.

"It's okay." I give his hand a squeeze. "We knew this day would come sooner or later. I'm almost glad we can get it over with." That's mostly true. The positive reception from the team and management give me faith, though this will likely shake it a little.

"I wish there was more I could do," the officer says, and with a quick glance over his shoulder he adds, "thank you."

"For what?" I ask.

"Hope." He gives a bashful little shrug as the tips of his ears turn pink, then he spins away and jogs back to his partner.

"Is he...?"

"Yeah," Xander says. "I think so."

"It's probably futile to think it'll always go that well."

"Probably," he agrees.

"Think it'll get worse before it gets better?"

"Doesn't matter if it does. We're in it together, right?" It kills me that he even has to ask.

"We are." I press my lips to his, letting them linger since I'm taking his strength as much as giving him my own. Then we head home to our safe little bubble for one last night before it bursts.

***

We won on our home turf, an astounding four to one. Yours truly scored two of those goals, hence why I'm sitting here with a microphone in my face. Yet, the first question I get is about "the incident" as we're calling it. Even though I knew it was coming since that damn cell phone video caught everything from the argument with the clerk to me grabbing Xander's hand and storming out, it still sucks.

The worst part is, that video only caught the discrimination, not the sweet moments Xander and I shared. If we're going to get filmed without our knowledge, I'd rather the video show the love we feel instead of the hate directed at us. Maybe then the narrative would be about how cute we are together or some shit like that instead of the bogus stealing accusation, which was made even worse by the fact the headline read *'Rookie Phenom and His Boyfriend Caught Stealing.'*

Fortunately, management took one look at the video and declared it bogus. They even congratulated me on keeping my cool and trying to diffuse things with an apology and the offer to pay. Then they drafted a formal statement saying they're aware of the bias we were subjected to and commend us both for rising above it. It didn't go so far as to say they're aware of our relationship and they support it, since the plan is to treat me and Xander like any other couple and not a *gay* couple. But the meaning was clear—they know and it's not an issue.

As anticipated, even that wasn't enough to prevent people from digging for more.

"Can you tell us what happened at the chocolate shoppe last night?" the first reporter asks.

"I'm not entirely sure, myself. I'm told there's a video, maybe you can make sense of it." I point to the next raised hand I see.

"It's been reported the man with you was your boyfriend."

"That's not a question." I point to someone else.

"The man has been identified as Xander Nydek, Coach Nydek's son."

"Yes, Coach has a son named Xander." I move to the next reporter.

"The clerk called the police. Were you two stealing?"

"Are the two of you dating?" The next question comes before I can answer the first.

"Look, guys." I scrub a hand over my face. "I'm here to talk about the game. If and when you ask all the other players about their personal lives during their pressers, I'll be happy to tell you about mine. Until then, let's stick to hockey."

"Your teammates aren't dating the coach's son. Isn't that a conflict of interest?"

I can't tell who asked that since I didn't call on anyone, but the way they're eagerly watching me suggests they all have the same question. *Fuck*.

I'm tempted to answer, if only to just get it out in the open so I can move on. But if I answer once it'll spiral, so I stick to the plan.

"The only conflict of interest I see is that you're all focused on things that happen off the ice, and I'm only here to talk about what happens on it. So, last call for any questions about the game." I point to a reporter I haven't called on yet.

"Is it serious?" the guy asks.

I know what he's asking, but I play politician and answer the question I pretend I heard. "Every game is serious. It's still early, but the wins and losses we have now can make or break a season when it comes time to make the playoffs. Thank you."

A flood of questions follow me as I leave the mic, but as far as I can tell none of them are about hockey so I don't respond. Instead, I make my way to the locker room to gather my things before heading home, stopping short when I realize the entire team is still here, staring at me. All except Noah, who had to sit with the press after I did.

"Do we have some sort of meeting I forgot about?" I look around the room nervously, unable to tell from the blank faces whether I've screwed up or not.

"I've gotta admit, I wasn't sure you could do it," Luca crosses his arms in front of his chest as he breaks the silence.

"Do what?"

"Sit there and take their bullshit questions without losing it, or caving and spilling your guts. You kept the focus on hockey."

"As it should be," I reply, making a beeline for my locker.

"You good?" Justus asks, which is a dumb question since I can feel myself scowling, but my issues aren't his doing, and I know he's only trying to help.

"Not really. But I guess I asked for this. Now, I have to live with it."

The room is mostly quiet as I gather my stuff, though the silence doesn't have any tension associated with it, like they're upset. It feels almost jittery, like no one knows what to say. I hate that, hate that I'm the reason for it, yet I appreciate that in my lowest moment no one seems to resent me for bringing this into the locker room.

They let me slip out with nothing more than a head nod, and I head straight for the family waiting area where I'm supposed to meet Xander.

Though we considered having him miss this game, and the media circus that was sure to come with it, in the end we thought it best not to hide. The only reason we debated it at all is because the news isn't that I have a boyfriend, but that my boyfriend and I were accused of shoplifting, simply because we're gay.

Even though the clerk was clearly out to get us for his own bias and not anything we did wrong, his actions imply gay people are criminals, and some people will see that video as proof that's true. I wanted to protect Xander from that, at least for now, by having him stay home, but he refused to let me face the critics on my own. He couldn't attend the press conference with me, but insisted on leaving the rink together, and right now I'm glad he's here.

"Baby," I whisper as I pull him in for a hug the second I enter the room.

"That looked rough." He returns the hug, fingers massaging my scalp as he holds me to him.

"It was." I let go and take his hand, leading him to the corner so we're out of earshot of the other family members who, while they've been really welcoming, I'm not in the mood to face right now.

"You did well." Xander leans his forehead against mine. "You diffused their questions without losing your temper, exactly how we planned."

I give a humorless laugh. "When we talked about it, I thought the questions would be about you and me, and in a weird way I was looking forward to that. Not that I was gonna answer them, but I've spent the last six weeks in this weird limbo, wondering when people would catch on, and when I saw that couple recording us last night, I was almost relieved, you know. Like, okay—here it is. No more speculating about when the questions will come. I'm ready. Only I wasn't ready—not for that level of hate. I didn't think it would be so explicit that people would make baseless accusations that would come up during a post-game press conference."

Thank God I didn't look online before the game today or I might've rattled myself. I owe Xander for that one, he ran interference with his dad, and management, to give them the heads up on what happened so I could focus on keeping a level head.

"No one's ever ready for that level of hate," Xander touches his lips briefly to mine.

"How do I handle that?"

"The same way you've always planned to—kicking ass on the ice. Like you did tonight"

Shaking my head, only slightly since it's still resting against Xander's, I huff out a deep breath. "I tried that, and all anyone wanted to talk about was you and that damn clerk."

"But you didn't let them. You kept steering things back to hockey. And if you keep playing like you did today, setting the team up for a playoff run, pretty soon that's what they'll be asking about."

I have my doubts, but before I can object, I hear someone calling our names from across the room. I break my head away from Xander's and we both turn to look at the TV several of the wives are pointing at.

As the volume is turned up for us to hear, I see Noah sitting in front of a bank of microphones, an uncharacteristic scowl on his face.

"Not one of you is going to ask who I'm dating?" His eyes scan what I know is a room full of reporters. "You ask me a million questions about hockey, and not a single one about my personal life."

"Why should we ask about that?" A voice echoes over the speaker. "You asked Niko."

"Because he's dating the coach's son," the voice says.

"Did he say that? I didn't hear him say that."

"So, he's not dating Xander Nydek?" the reporter presses.

"There you go again, asking about Niko's personal life and not mine," Noah leans back in the chair and crosses his arms in front of his broad chest. "Seems like a bit of a double standard, no?"

"Is he..." Xander trails off.

"Yeah, looks like he is." I stifle a laugh as a reporter gives in and asks who Noah is dating, only for Noah to say, *What does that have to do with hockey?*

"I wish we could see the reporters' faces." I laugh as I sling an arm around Xander's shoulder while we take in the show.

He wraps an arm around my waist in return. "How many times do you think Noah will have to put on this act before they stop asking you about me?"

"I mean, I wouldn't want that scowl directed at me on a regular basis."

Xander cocks his head to the side as he stares at the TV. "You know, if that was a smirk instead of a scowl, I'd almost think that was Tripp."

"Tripp?" I snort. "Those two don't look anything alike."

"I'm talking about attitude, not looks." I swivel my hips to dodge the pinch he tries to give me with his free hand. "Think about it. Who else would blatantly taunt the press like that just to fluster them."

Listening to Noah rattle on, I realize Xander has a point, which is odd because I never really pegged Noah as the type to deliberately push buttons. Either he's really defensive of his teammates—which could absolutely be the case—or Tripp's rubbing off on him. I didn't think Tripp had joined us often enough for that to be the case, but to be fair, whenever we all hang out my attention is usually on my boyfriend.

"The idea of two Tripp's sort of hurts my brain, but it's pretty cool Noah's going to bat for us."

"For you," Xander says.

"For us," I correct. "And everyone else who has to live with a double standard."

"I have to admit, I didn't expect that when you said you wanted to tell them. In my experience locker rooms aren't that supportive of gay guys. It's why I quit hockey as a kid."

Xander's never shared that part of his past, and it makes a few more puzzle pieces fall into place. Specifically, why he took up individual sports. Teammates are supposed to be like brothers, working together as one despite being separate minds and bodies. It's one of the things I love most about hockey, though if you don't feel like part of the brotherhood, you wouldn't feel the camaraderie. I hid who I was to fit in, and it sounds like Xander didn't, which they held against him. It makes me even more grateful that my team has supported me.

"I'm not sure it would've been like this when I was younger. Kids just... They're kids. They say and do shit they don't really understand, especially since no one wants to be different at that age. As for these guys... I don't know why they're so cool with us. Maybe it's your dad's influence since I doubt he'd tolerate discrimination. Or maybe they just don't give a shit as long as I play well."

"Maybe they just don't waste time with hate."

I think back to how Noah and Luca went out of their way to help Justus and I get settled. And yeah, you could say that's because if our heads are on straight, the team benefits. Though they could've passed us off to someone else to help with that and they didn't.

"You might be right about that." I watch Noah get up and leave the mics with a smirk. "So, what do you feel like doing? Head home to crash or go out and show people we don't give a shit what they say?"

"Definitely go out." He shoots me a coy little smile.

"Hell yeah." I give him one in return.

Chapter 28
Xander

The dimples I love are absent as we walk hand-in-hand to the bar, replaced with a cool demeanor that's both imposing and unapproachable. It's a look that screams *'don't fuck with me'* without coming off as hostile, yet sends a clear message that I am his and he intends to protect me. It's a stark contrast to the playful, flirtatious Niko I'm used to, and as much as I love that side of him, I could get used to this broodingly sexy version.

The crowd parts as we weave our way toward the section reserved for the hockey team, though I don't sense any anger or hate directed at us. More like curiosity, since this walk is usually punctuated with cheers and congratulatory back slaps—and sans the handholding on our part—and Niko's determined gait makes it clear he's not in the mood. I hate that for him, but I get it. The players' table is a safe space, and the faster we get to it, the less likely it is we'll hear any sneers or derogatory remarks.

Sure enough, when we reach our usual spot some of the tension seems to leave his shoulders, and we help ourselves to a beer from the pitcher on the table as we sit with his team.

"Nice game today." Justus clinks his glass against Niko's. "I'm not sure I would've been able to stay so focused after the shit you had to go through last night."

"Xander and Coach took care of working with the team to make statements so I wouldn't get caught up in it." He gives my hand a squeeze where it's resting on his leg. "I appreciate you guys not asking about it before gametime."

"Of course. How are you doing, Xander?" he asks me.

"I'm a little pissed that clerk ruined my surprise last night, but there are other chocolate shops." I shrug indifferently, pretending I'm not still hurt since losing our tempers will only draw more scrutiny for Niko. Despite the injustice of it all, we're both keenly aware that getting angry could get him labeled as difficult or worse, so for the sake of his career we have to keep our tempers in check.

"I still can't believe he tried to pin a shoplifting charge on you."

"That was unexpected. Usually, people just refuse to serve you." I sip my beer to keep from saying anything more.

"That happens a lot?" Justus asks.

"Not really, no. Sometimes people will give you a look while they serve you, like you disgust them or something, but I haven't seen it escalate the way it did last night."

"I'm sorry," Justus says.

"Why? You haven't done that," Niko points out.

"I know, just. It sucks, is all."

"It does," I agree.

"Anything we can do?" Justus asks.

"You already have." Niko pats him on the back. "All of you, just by standing by us. So, how 'bout that assist in the second?" He changes the subject to the big play Justus had to help clinch the win, and as Noah and Luca join us, they recount their favorite moments of the game. Occasionally, I add my thoughts, but for the most part I just sit back and relish Niko's excitement.

I know he'd be willing to give hockey up for me, and though I'm not a religious guy by any stretch, I pray it doesn't come to that. He comes alive talking about it, watching it, living it. And yeah, in the whole scheme of life his ability to play hockey is temporary, yet I want him to have that for as long as possible. So, even though we shouldn't have to sit silently when people discriminate or single us out for their own bias, I'll take the high road and tune them out if it means Niko can have moments like this, celebrating a big win on the ice. And hopefully, just by showing people it can be done, he won't be the first and last openly gay player.

By the time we get home, it's well past midnight, and the adrenaline from the past twenty-four hours is starting to wear off. We strip down and crawl under the covers. My back to Niko's chest has become our habit over all the nights we've spent together.

"That was exhausting," he sighs into my neck. "I knew it would be at first, but not to this extent. I think I was more on edge being in the open than I've ever been while hiding."

"I could tell. And while I hate that you weren't able to enjoy your celebration the way you would've before the press zeroed in on you, don't-fuck-with-me Niko is seriously hot."

"Don't-fuck-with-me Niko?" I feel the smile on his face as he kisses the back of my neck.

"Yeah. The one who's scowl cleared a path and who tugged me along behind him like he owned me... Got me hard."

His hand drifts lower, cupping the semi I usually have around him, which starts to grow the instant his warm skin surrounds mine.

"Did it now?" Niko lazily strokes my length as he nuzzles the back of my neck, his strong fingers surprisingly gentle as they travel from root to tip. "I thought my dimples were your favorite feature?"

"I still love the dimples." I suck in a sharp breath as his thumb skims over my slit. "But the glare that says you'll kill anyone who messes with me is so hot. I would've dropped to my knees and sucked you off right there if I could've."

"Jesus," he growls huskily as he pumps me, still slow, but with a firmer grip. It's like squeezing my dick helps him maintain control over his own, which is pressing firmly against my ass.

Closing my eyes, I let my body go limp so Niko can have his way with it, sighing contentedly when his hand drifts to my sac and rolls my balls in his palm before pressing them against the base of my cock. Despite being held snugly against his chest, I feel like I'm floating as the sweet burn of desire grows in my now fully-rigid length.

"This dick," Niko rasps, biting my earlobe before sucking it in his mouth to soothe the burn. "I love how hard it gets for me."

My eyelids flutter as his hand squeezes, plumps, and pulls on my cock. It drives me to the brink as he alternates his rhythm or his grip when my hips thrust forward in search of release. He denies me time and again, beginning anew until my crown leaks in desperation.

"More," I groan softly.

"Harder, baby?"

"More." I turn my head so my lips can meet his. "Fuck, I need to feel you inside me," I say against his mouth.

Cool air surrounds my cock as Niko lets it go to grab the lube. I hear the squelch of it before the slick gel hits my hole, and I feel his finger dipping inside to spread it around. Then it's gone, replaced by the round head of his cock.

Niko takes me in his fist again and he pushes his way into my body, the lube on his hand slicking my length so he can stroke it freely. My eyes drift shut as the dual pleasure of being penetrated and pumped sends wave after wave of bliss throughout my body.

"This tight ass..." He bites and licks at my collarbone as he buries himself fully. "I love how it chokes my dick, and quivers around it while you get used to me. God, I could stay buried in you all night."

My mind is too hazy to respond, lost to the absolute ecstasy of being possessed by Niko's body. Skin tingling everywhere, I'm pretty sure a strangled moan rumbles in my throat as his shallow thrusts peg my prostate, rubbing back and forth over that pleasure center and causing erratic jolts of nirvana to course through my limbs.

"Like that, baby?" Niko drives long and deep as he tugs on my dick, flooding my body with so much sensation I can't make sense of where the euphoria is coming from. The receptors in my brain churn in a frenzied stupor, not sure whether to chase his hand or his cock for more.

"Fuck yeah, you do. I can feel it. Feel your hole clenching around me. Bet your balls are high and tight, ready to unload. Aren't they?"

"Nikooo," I moan as he releases my dick, gasping when he cups my sac.

"So hard and full for me." He massages them in his warm palm as he nips the back of my neck, then wraps his fist around my length as he starts to piston with more force. "You're aching to come, aren't you, baby? It's okay. I'll go with you."

His hand yanks on my cock, hard and fast, as his hips pound into me, pushing me toward the precipice. My breath wheezes out of my lungs as my body seems to forget it needs air, its sole focus reaching the enlightenment that's just within reach.

I wrap my hand around Niko's, the two of us jerking me off together. And then time stops. Our bodies still, save for the tremors rippling through us. Not even our chests expand, our breath trapped in our throats as spasms wrack through us.

Warm liquid coats my length where it seeps between our fingers as spurt after spurt of cum jets from my tip. A garbled shout reaches my ears, though whether it's mine or his, or both, I can't tell. I'm too dazed to make sense of anything except the fact that I might've just found Eden.

I'm not sure how long we lay motionless, lost to the throes of our release. By the time I can move, I'm desperate for air. Niko too. Our chests heave, violently at first, as we try to recover, tapering to shaky inhales as our orgasms release their grip on us.

"Baby." Warm lips press against the spot where my neck meets my collarbone. "Are you with me?"

"Barely," I whisper.

"Did I hurt you? I think I might've blacked out for a minute there."

"I think I saw Heaven."

"It did feel that way." I feel him smile against the back of my neck before whispering. "It always does."

And right now, cradled in his arms as we bask in a post-sex haze of bliss, I'm thinking it always will.

Epilogue -Niko

It took longer than I would've expected for the press to stop asking about Xander. They're persistent little buggers, but after nearly a month, they finally clued in on the fact I wasn't going to answer. And since my teammates and coaches and everyone within the Bulldogs organization stuck with the *'we don't comment on our player's personal lives'* mantra, they had no choice but to give up.

Now, it's just sort of common knowledge that we're together, though it's not headline news. And while I am often referred to as the *gay* hockey player, my performance on the ice has earned me the label of both *Rookie of the Year* and *Defenseman of the Year*, so more and more *gay* is being left out. I'm not sure if that's because adding it makes an already big title more of a mouthful, or because I'm shutting the critics up. Either way, I think I'm on my way to being just a hockey player instead of a gay hockey player.

Though my untimely "coming out" caused the Bulldogs a bit of a headache, they stuck by me, and I'm coming back next season. Since I'm officially staying in Denver, and Xander's apartment is feeling a little small, I've decided it's time to find a place of our own. Actually, "find" isn't quite accurate, seeing as how I've already found it. I just have to convince him I'm right, which shouldn't be too hard to do. I think.

"Whose place are we going to again?" Xander asks as we pull into the driveway, which is long enough that the house isn't immediately available from the road, something I hoped would help with privacy.

"Uh, Noah's," I fib. Though since Noah lives down the street, I figure I'm only stretching the truth.

"If it's his house, why are he and Tripp standing on the porch with a 'Welcome Home' sign?" he asks as we round the bend and a mid-century modern house appears on the wooded lot.

"Dammit," I mutter. "They were supposed to be inside."

"Excuse me?" Xander blinks as I put the car in park.

"Um, surprise?"

"Surprise? What did you do, Nikolas?"

Not good. He only uses my full name when he's turned on or pissed, and he's definitely not turned on. Still, I cup him between the legs just to be sure.

"Nikolas," he hisses.

Nope, not turned on.

"Well, I'm still a Bulldog, and your apartment is kind of small. I thought we could use some more space." I flash my dimples, hoping to distract him.

"Don't distract me with your cute little smile. We've never even talked about what we want in a house. I didn't even know you were looking."

I rub the back of my neck, which is suddenly burning up. "True, but I was just killing time while you were at work, and I figure I know you well enough to guess."

"Really?" He cocks an eyebrow at me while Noah and Tripp exchange confused looks on the front porch.

"Yes. I think this style will appeal to your artistic side, and the big trees give us lots of privacy. It's been completely remodeled, and it's got enough room for an office for you, a workout room for both of us, and guest rooms for my family. What do you think?"

"I think your brain is as frozen as the ice you skate on."

He's probably not wrong about that, but I have another surprise I'm almost positive will have him changing his mind. It's why I bought the place as soon as I saw it instead of waiting to get his opinion. Normally, we make all our decisions together, but I didn't want to lose it.

"Just take a look, and if you don't like it, I'll sell it. Or rent it." I flash my dimples again.

"Fine." He sighs and climbs out of the car. *I knew the dimples would win him over.*

As we get to the porch, I give Tripp a playful smack on the back of the head. "Inside means *behind* the front door, not in front of it."

"Not my fault. Thor forgot the code." Tripp jerks his head toward Noah.

"Seriously?" I ask Noah, who has sort of a bewildered look on his face. I make a note to circle back to that later. Right now, I need to show my boyfriend why this is the perfect spot.

I plug in the code and let us all inside, with a special warning glance at Tripp so he doesn't get ahead of himself. He holds his hands up in mock surrender as we walk through the rooms and I point out all the cool stuff, like the chef's kitchen I *will* learn how to use, and the shower room that—well that's just obvious.

"Well?" I ask as we finish the tour.

"Okay, it's nice." I can't see any displeasure on his face, but my man is stubborn enough not to give up his frustration so easily. "I still might've wanted to see some other options though."

"I hear you, and I promise if we'd had more time we would've shopped around. I just couldn't risk losing this one."

"Why? What's so special about this place that you had to buy it right away?"

"This." I open the curtain that had been blocking the view of the backyard, and the empty pool in the middle of it.

Xander steps to the glass and goes still for a solid two minutes. When he finally turns to face me, he's got the dopiest smile on his face, which is a personal best for me. Though he smiles more than he used to, he still rocks the dark and brooding look, and while I find that incredibly sexy, I like putting cracks in the armor now and then.

"Is that...?" He points outside.

Tripp holds out the skateboard he helped me stash in the closet the other day. Though instead of taking it, Xander rushes me and throws his arms around my neck.

"You got me a skate park?" He laughs as I wrap my arms around his waist and hold him to me.

"I think it's more of a skate pool, but there's enough room to build more if that's what you want."

"I fucking love you," Xander growls in my ear.

"I fucking love you, too." I let him go with a playful slap on the ass. "Now, go try it out before Tripp takes the first run, if he hasn't already."

"Hey now, I pinky sweared I wouldn't," Tripp objects, though I'm not sure any of us believe him.

Xander and Tripp waste no time getting out to the pool, and since it's hot as fuck in July, it's not long before they're circling the bottom shirtless, sun glistening off their sweat-slicked bodies while Noah and I watch from the lounge chairs.

Yes, I may have had an ulterior motive for the skate pool.

"Are you really not gonna fill that thing with water?" Noah wipes sweat off his brow with the back of his wrist.

"And give up this view?" It doesn't occur to me until after I say it that Noah won't appreciate the scenery like I do, but like all my teammates, he doesn't judge. Nor does he get weirded out when I comment about my man. Hell, he doesn't even tell Tripp to stop coming onto him, which happens pretty much every time they see each other. Sometimes I think it flusters him—I bet that's why he forgot the house code—but he takes it in stride. I'm actually starting to wonder if it amuses him, seeing as he doesn't seem bothered that our entertainment is watching two shirtless men ride a board with wheels in an empty swimming pool... On the hottest day of the year.

"I may build him another one to cool off in though." I fan my face because damn, it really is sweltering.

Noah chuckles and taps his beer bottle to mine, nodding his head toward the pool where Xander is positively glowing, and not from the sun on his slick skin. "I think you won him over."

"I'm the winner here, Noah. I'm the winner."

Also By Michele Lenard

Colorado Bulldogs Romance (MM)

Bad Pucking Timing
Bad Pucking Influence
Bad Pucking Roommate

Love quirky small town romances with all the sweet and lots of spice? Try the Elevation Series, six books set in the fictional town of Katah Vista, Colorado, where life moves to a different beat and love happens when you least expect it.

The Elevation Series

Distraction

Validation

Revelation

Liberation

Absolution

Exception

You can also check out my contemporary romances in Mile High Romance, a collection of steamy stories about finding love when your career sometimes gets it the way. Set in Denver, Colorado, this series features sports, workplace and forbidden romances, with a flawed yet lovable "relationship whisperer" who is surprisingly good at offering advice that he doesn't know how to take, until its his turn to fall hard.

<u>Books in the Mile High Romance Series</u>

Not So Friendly Intent

Purely Novel Intent

Totally Inevitable Intent

Willfully Malicious Intent

Thoroughly Innocent Intent

Strictly Forbidden Intent

For the latest updates on other releases join my VIP reader group.

Acknowledgments: Thanks to my critique partner Amanda, without whom I wouldn't be whole. You have challenged me as a writer, and helped me improve my meager design skills. I'm on this journey because of you!

Printed in Great Britain
by Amazon

57784760R00179